GENESIS | THE FUTURE

First edition 2012

2nd Edition revised an expanded.

ISBN 9780645521429 (Ingram Spark 2022)

Cover design – The Albion Le Strange Family

Published Lothbroksigurd

GENESIS

THE FUTURE

LY DE ANGELES
(LORE)

To all the children frightened by talk of an end to this world. Life is stronger than anything religion professes to be a god.

SECTOR ONE

GHOST – TIME SORCERER

MY ORIGINAL HOME IS BENEATH the surface of any earth. I am the mycelium and I am a time sorcerer. I can be more than one person in more than one time, but the years I write of these events begins in 3030, a thousand years after that silly environmental catastrophe in the twenty-first century. I wore the skin of a human back then.

SHIT HAPPENS

The year was the eleventh hour of the twentieth century. Minds opened and empathy with earth surfaced, from where it had hidden deep in some crevasse-like cavern in the DNA of the human species, who'd seemed asleep, or lost, for at least a thousand years. Evolution quickened.

Problem was that the takers, and despoilers of the lands, and the critters of every species, were also aware that something strange was going on, and when the uprisings began and the earth responded with fury, they fought, like an threatened animal backed into a corner, and the backlash was terrible.

A kind of madness. Famine, brutality and unimaginable greed. Secrecy. Great plagues of untreatable virus and infection. The little-publicized ocean-dumping and landfilling of nuclear waste, and other toxins devastating to life, rising from where they'd been hidden, resulting in massive cell degeneration and deformities. Depression and despair unfolded like disturbed and warped wasps.

The seas were polluted, and the land was poisoned. The gaseous, vaporous shell protecting earth from the more vicious effects the sun began to perish. The race was on, by countries and governments united under the W.F.C. (World Federation of Corporations) to accumulate what they could without thought for the future, without compassion.

They declared war with those who protested against them. They didn't understand that this, too, was destiny. Faceless governments sent men in black armor, weaponed to the hilt, to eradicate opposition. Initially, resistance was fierce, and over decades the propaganda machine turned people against themselves. In the passage of that age it became clear that what was at the base of their greed was the fountain-of-youth of living only for today. The quarry was the chess of possession and corruption, lying and denial.

Populations were drugged into submission, shamed by categorization, or imprisoned. There was no choice. People had already been conditioned to accept their livelihood from plastic cards and were—consciously or otherwise—enslaved to debt and stuff.

Creativity, art, individuality, and self-sufficiency were frowned on if they went beyond the boundaries set by a standard paradigm. Recreational activity took the form of audio-visual virtual reality, much of which used the insidiousness of advertising and social media to manipulate and influence choice. That, of course, and vast quantities of pharmaceutical drugs. And addiction to self-medication.

What was not realized, was how aware of all this the descendants of the ancestral mycelium now were. Human, and telepathically linked. In every country and in every way. What networking through technology and worldwide communication began, developed into the recognition of a nature matrix.

The new wave of cutting edge techno-scientists created a device called, in the old days, a *prefrontal cortex integrative implant*, providing direct access and download, through the matrix, to the earth grid. The flower, the spider web, this dragonline, this songline, linking millions of species with each other, through thought and sensation.

THEN THE CHANGE. took a massive toll of life, much of it human because in those days most people, in both the southern and northern hemispheres, lived in sprawling concrete and steel cities. Much of this had come crashing down as the magnetic tilt had occurred. Tsunamis devastated coastlines over low lying coastal areas around, and south of the equator. Many vast pockets of the northern lands were hurled with ice and snow and even now, when it's not technically north like it was then, has not recovered. Damage rend enormous tracts of land as a result of seismic shifts.

The countries still controlled by the W.F.C. refused to close nuclear reactors and had fled for their lives as earthquakes ripped the land apart. Volcanoes blew their tops north and south and the earth heaved and screamed in the labor of her evolution.

Electrical storms zigzagged across the skies. The southern polar cap melted, land masses rose from the ocean bottom, and others dropped from sight beneath the turmoil of wild and raging seas. Over the coming decades desert became fecund, the southern pole became jungle and the ever-encroaching ocean took more and more land. Became quite deadly to travel within.

The country called Australia—the land of the people who took me in—has kept desert, mountains and forest to the coast and heartland, while much—but not all—of the coastal fringes were submerged and drowned. In the deserts underwater caches rose to the surface creating waterholes and lakes in abundance. Life was either very good or very bad. People changed, adapted and evolved. Remembered.

This particular story has survived.

ONE BY ONE SHE LIFTS THE BRIGHT BLUE cloths that cover all the items under her canopy, showing unique boxes of different woods beautifully painted or carved, unusual jewels in strange lace-like metal settings, strings of faceted beads, assorted hand-sewn leather garments. I admit it, I'm intrigued.

She removes a final smudge, the color of sky, to reveal a book, very thick and covered in red leather, tooled around the edges, an intricate, arcane design. Embossed on the front cover, in a delicate, unusual script was the word GENESIS.

'Why's it called that?' I ask, running my fingers over the indentation.

'You ever wonder whether if nobody answered all the questions, the destiny of a thing—and somebody's name—might never be what we suppose it to be?'

'I don't know what you are talking about. That some kinda philosophy?' I open the cover.

'Stupid little girl.'

PART ONE

CHAPTER ONE

LITTLE GHOST

I HATE MY FACE. MY SKIN'S the color of the moon and I have veins like creeks and rivers, pushed up against an organ that covers a naked body that almost glows in its whiteness. Like night-light worms.

I was ten, or maybe eleven when I was found. Not a clue where from or what I was doing there. Or who left me on the steps of the desert temple. A pouch around my neck like a dead thing. A roll of paper sticking out the top. Maybe an instruction manual on how to operate me. An explanation of what I am. I didn't read it. I felt like a piece of wind. I didn't remember who I was, how I got there or where I was from. Blank. I knew nothing about any of it then. But I knew things. Without knowing how. Every event that unfolded from when I woke up that day. I could recall every detail, every sentence, every unspoken gesture and what it meant.

The child that found me was young. Maybe five or six. She saw me and said nothing. Dark brown eyes and dark brown skin and buckets. She left me where I was and ran away.

The woman who returned, holding the child's hand, was named Insistence. Lean and long-muscled, strong and dark, tawny-skinned. Dusty black hair tied away from her face. Her head tilted like a hound, her forehead a question mark. Bare arms, except for a crazy number of narrow, colorful bangles, from her wrists to her elbows. Bare breasts, with dark amber areola. Gold-dipped bird bones through the long, stretched lobes of each ear. Riding-trousers of woven fabric, loose at her hips, held up by a bronze-bucked belt of some animal skin. A fat, lustrous blue-black bird on her shoulder, its talons dug somewhere in the folds of a dung-colored *brat*. Nothing else. Just presence.

She shooed the little person away and sat beside me. At first, she simply stared. Then she looked me all over, her face giving nothing away. Like she was calculating.

'What are you?'

I didn't have words. I was hot, I know that. And she smelled, but not in a bad way. No identification of it then. Later I'd recognize it as wood smoke.

She pulled the pouch from around my neck and unrolled the paper. Read it.

'Says your name's Ghost. Says we'll have a use for you.'

The raven made a noise in its throat a bit like a growl. 'What kind of name is that? Here, get up.' She pulled me to my feet and my knees creaked, I winced as she stretched out my arm. I must have made a face and a noise because she was gentler after that. She led me into the deep shade of bushes and trees smelling succulent and delicious. Fruit that I knew but couldn't name. Gardenias and jasmine.

She cupped water from a small stream that tonkled every few seconds, a deep and sweet sound. 'Here,' she said, offering me the ladle. I drank the whole thing down, immediately hoping for more. I pointed towards the water, my eyebrows lifted in a question, but she pushed me onto the ground instead. 'A ghost is the shadow of a person has died. Did you know that?'

I looked anywhere except at her gaze. Embarrassed because what she said made no sense.

'And you about as much a ghost as my raven friend here is a pigeon. As for having a need of you, that's as may be.' She pulled something smelly, brown and dry, like an old mushroom, from a pocket hidden within the folds of her clothing, chewed slowly, pulling me gently, slowly, towards buildings.

'My name's Insistence—' she replied. I was already so tired I just wanted to curl up and drown in the light. '—but you've already worked that out, haven't you?' she mumbled, without looking back.

I DIDN'T UNDERSTAND THAT I'd been forsaken in the fullness of the blazing, brutal sun until then. Didn't know I was a freak until I was walked inside the big building, to the clatter and chatter of hundreds of girls and women eating. Until they turned on me, and the silence of their stares caused my knees to go so weak I had to hold onto the back of a chair to save myself the humiliation of falling. While they were all clothed and bedecked in obscurely-marked gold amulets and strings if blue or amber-colored beads, their eyes brown or hazel were all similar, their exposed body parts ranging from honey-colored to ebony.

I was ragged, my feet bleeding. I stung in so many ways, from wherever I had been exposed to the daylight and whatever small creatures sucked blood, to the curiosity of the crowd. At first, I recollect that if I'd been one of them I'd have thought it wrong to be so bold. Then I wondered why I thought that way.

Insistence pulled me through the melee of the cafeteria, past rooms stinking faintly of rotting meat and formaldehyde, along a cool and empty hallway, into a room of eye-watering odor. Disinfectant. Polish. Bitter and astringent substances. Bright light reeking of ozone.

AN OLD WOMAN, HER SKIN AS face as a no moon night, scrutinized me, up and down, concerned, and something else. What's that look? A half-smile. Hooded, conspiratorial eyes that looked into mine, unflinching. Reading me.

'Hmm. I'm the most senior healer here, and I see juju, mysterious things, so you just keep that in mind if you think to muck about—,' she said, her hands on her hips to make herself look bigger. 'Insistence is my daughter and she's an educated alchemist so don't think she's your friend. She'll snap you, you not a proper person. My name's Desire.'

What about me? I need to defy something. Both women seem like enemies. Like the creatures that have been stinging me all day. I stand where I've been put and all I want to do is run to somewhere empty and alone. What am I to make of all this information? How am I supposed to process the inflections? The posturing? This place? It seems to sink into me as though I'm empty and need filling. Those girls outside. The smells and all this equipment. Trying to have it all make sense. I don't belong, so I'm agitated.

'What am I then?' my voice was crackly with disuse. Had I even used it before? I knew how. I knew lots and lots, but I didn't know *why* I knew, or what most of it meant. Words and images and certainties. Useless.

'I have to work that out. Might be that you're a mutant. Which case we don't have a use for you after all,' the enigmatic statement holding some kind of threat.

'I don't remember anything.'

'Doesn't matter yet. For the moment you're a small pale person-like creature, that's all.'

She turned me over to Desire, and the raven on her shoulder, its head to one side, ruffled its feathers and purred.

Desire sliced at my clothes with a scalpel, and Insistence chuckled briefly with her mouth closed.

'Am I funny?'

She went to sit on the high three-legged stool by the window. The thin wallet of screen that had been attached to her belt lit up as it fed on daylight. She pulled on the delicate gold-thread of the implant, called a *prefontlcortexl*, and it snaked like a reptilian thing from the implant behind her left ear, where the raven squatted all smug and sleepy, plugging into the device 'Get her out of the rest of that raggedy mess while I finish up.'

Desire's face gave nothing of what she thought as she opened a window, letting in a breeze that smelled of swamp, before examining the dirty red-brown of old rope burns around my wrists.

I felt like an experiment.

She busied herself at a bench of unguents and strange things, measured powders onto clay dishes, fine-tuned the titanium and glass alembics distilling goodness knew what magic. I watched her for a while, then Insistence, at her magic screen, the raven hanging from her hair like a barbed branch of fire-blackened leaves.

Desire blew out the flame under a beaker and poured the thin, clear fluid into a narrow vial. She stoppered it and set it spinning to the beep and whir of a centrifuge, keying a timer amidst dials and dimly lurid but meaningless numbers and moving lines.

I almost knew what she was doing. Something remembered, on the tip of my tongue like the taste of copper. Infuriated as I was by a mental murk I felt submerged in. The word *platelets* hinted at blood, but gave nothing else away.

Insistence threw my pathetic excuse for clothing into a big, yellow bag hanging behind the door then sat beside me on the gurney, swinging her legs and stroking the bird's chest with a feather.

She was unaffected, while I felt like a gutted and skun animal, waiting for the butchering. Desire lifted the little rolled up message around my neck, from where Insistence had left it.

She read the message, noises deep in her throat, her large white and tan rodent, Rupert, scuttling up her arm and nestling like a shawl around her neck, held in place by the thick long metal-grey braid. What was with these people and other species? Was I one?

'Daughter?' She handed Insistence the note.

'It's in the old tongue, Mama. You treat that skin o' hers before it blisters while I get this interpreted.' She left the room.

Desire pulled jars and clay pots from shelves and unlocked cabinets, placed each item beside me, each neatly labeled in hand-written gibberish, their smells making my nose itch, the clear liquid from the spun platelet vial being the first item in a salve to soothe my burning flesh.

Her hands were cool. How can a person's hands be cool in this heat? As though painting a newborn with life, she covered my neon-red body, the bite and sting gone within minutes. She fed me syrup from a spoon without telling me what it was. I should have asked. And I would have if I'd known how.

Turns out that, as well as a name, the message also read that I am a time sorcerer, and although I was devoid of the wherewithal of where I was from, my memory deliberately scrambled, the knowledge too dangerous to tell of, I knew. Stating that I'd be of use. The writer also assured the reader that I'd become accustomed to the sun the more I was exposed. That the nucleotide sequencing was all green light. And that I was a human, potentially dangerous, despite the aberration, or mistake, of me being so pale. Despite the darkly pigmented mottles.

NOW, THREE YEARS ON, I know all about life at Kata Tjuta, and the cultures of the country and the world. I'm apprenticed to Desire in the apothecary and, because of a hard-wired capacity to remember facts in eidetic detail, I also work with chroniclers, as one of them.

Miriam is my best friend as well as my boss. She is already sixteen years old and in charge of data security and administration. She wears a titanium key, the security access to the entrance to the library.

Around her neck like an amulet. Almost a challenge to those who perhaps think that they are more deserving. It's as old as the dome, which is ancient.

Naked or half-dressed girls and women attend each other. They preen, update the fashion of their dress, and adorn themselves in talismans for the festival. Like masks. Some are meant to attract a mate, others to announce the wearer's purpose to the pack. They work each other's hair, the helping hands slick with fat, and dripping with one color ochre or another. The concoction is worked into braids and sculpted to designs, the long, fine dreadlocks held high on each head with pins of gold or bone or thorn. Ink marks each face with rank and tribal lineage and new sky blue clay beads are hung, in chunky rows, down to their breasts—those ready for a mate or women delivered of living children already. Their fertility proven.

We heave and shove the enormous mirror into the dorm room, a feat that requires every bit of magic we possess, not to move it, as we're not weak, but to keep the crowd civil until we can get out of the way. And there's my moon-face, pale as fresh gardenias, annoying me with its oppressive and perennial lightness, against a backdrop of honey-skinned normalcy.

The message didn't lie. I'm immune to the savagery of the sun's ultraviolet savagery, but I haven't changed color, I just grown more rose-colored mottles to insult me. And I growl low in my throat at the irony of destiny. *Oh, she's so special. She's a time sorceress. She will be of use!*

So, I dress as splendidly as the others, despite everything I feel. It's not often we see our own likeness, other than in the lake on the stillest of days. I admit I sometimes forget that I may be a genetic mistake, and I hide the inner self-loathing despite Miriam's ability to read my every mood. I walk as casually as I can, with as much dignity as I can muster considering, to the trunk at the end of my sleeping pallet, lifting its stubborn, time-warped lid, rummage through the cloth and softly-tanned garments that I'm proud to say I've sewn and adorned myself, until I find the brown skin. The one with the bronze-and-button beads on the sleeves.

I've got a screen around my bed. To help me hide from curious looks. Desire made sure of when she decided I'd be her project. Protective of me, she is. A small, white, flaccid sorceress, with camouflage mottles and a mind of her own. A girl only. With an identity problem.

DESIRE IS ALSO SOMEWHAT WEIRD. Unbound to position or liege, and therefore thought low-born by what remained of the city cabals into which she'd been born. She's of the old ancestry, although she hid this information from most everyone, for safety's sake, and to keep from being processed. Until she'd accidentally conceived Insistence, an oops-factor illegality, and had sought asylum here, after who knows how long a journey? Her own mother had even denied Desire's existence. Can't have wild-born bloodline-women causing anarchy, disturbance, and asking questions. I know about that. Keep quiet. Don't draw attention to yourself. She never knew the identity of Insistence's sire—lot of rape back then—and she's an old woman now. Trying very hard to not be a hedgehog. To come across as sweet and harmless when she's not. Not really. She's got access to the subtlest of poisons and can tell a future in the cards set to reduce a grownup to tears.

From childhood, Insistence refused to hide her ability to read clouds and ensorcel a timid horse. To chat with ravens and other corvids. She'd always known her own destiny but that hadn't made the decision by the elders, to agree to her replacing the dead predecessor, any easier. No queen is supposed to be some rogue love-child get of a low-born healer seer, is she? Able to breed like any animal, with whomever she chooses, whenever she wants?

The screen lets me shimmy out of the head-to-toe garments I always otherwise wear, claiming they provide me with more breeze than clothing, when they actually stop the stares I inevitably once got if I had too much exposed skin. They always used to stare. There's an old word for the way I am, except it's not exactly correct: *albinism*. It's not quite right even though my eyes are violet, and I don't need dark glasses. I've read about it, trying to gain as much of a level of insight as necessary. Drawn to my own, what? Ailment? Disfigurement? Disease? The data, thus far, has revealed nothing. And even though my hair has pigment, it's also white. As long, and as darkless as fog on a winter morning.

Miriam pulls me onto the seat beneath the window to dress my dreadlocks. Blue ochre. That's her sense of humor. The color's supposed to mean I'm of an age to take a mate. Her idea of funny.

CHAPTER TWO

DUTY

EVERYBODY ABANDONS THE DORM. Going to breakfast before the journey to Redrock later today. Miriam sits impatiently by the window while I record this diary entry in my red book. She used to roll her eyes at the writing idea. Archaic that it is. But since I acquired the book, and learned to make the pens and ink, it's always been of a necessity. Something reminiscent of an ancestral skill working my fingers competently around the shaft of bird bone that holds the nib, second nature with practice, like a cormorant fisher or an eagle hunter. Like we were born for each other. Miriam's used to it now. She's even made a place in the library for it when and if I get around to filling all the pages.

'For the love of water,' Desire pokes her head around the doorframe, hair a cloud of stormy dark. 'Miriam, you just make her worse, you know.'

Miriam knows when to leave. Knows what Desire can be like when she loses her temper.

'Come find me,' she says, padding away, silent as an animal, Desire watching her go.

'Ghost?'

'Sorry,' I lie, 'I was just writing about you.'

'Well, save it, you're being precious.' And she's gone. Today's her day, as a mama, after all. I stash the book and straighten my garments.

DAWN IS COOL. THE LIGHT still all silver and pale blue. My skin responding to the chill with gooseflesh. A taste, of the coming months of what is loosely called winter is in the smell of smoke from the grass fires in the far distance. A cacophony of bird-chatter means no conversation; a body would have to yell to be heard over their yadayada. Besides, this is automatic work.

The first bucket slides over the edge of the well. It's so full some of the contents slop over the rim onto Desire's hand. A few unintentionally spilled drops of water can't be called wasteful, can they? I know she doesn't do it on purpose but it's also not the first time. She gives me her hoodoo version of the evil eye, but I just grin, immune. She knows it. I'm sure it's a lesson, and I'm sure I could conjure a curse back at here, if ever there was a need. She's a good teacher.

I heft my end of the pole onto my shoulder, as Desire sucks her fingers and licks the drips from the base of the bucket. Then she slides it along the beam to me, where I secure it in the notch. She hooks the second bucket to the rope and lets it drop into the bore. She listens for the glug as it sinks. Waits for all of a three count. Turns the windlass. Attaches the second bucket, still dripping, grinning as she runs her hand along the wet.

We cross the dust and onto the sand. The sound of her footfall now lost to the morning racket. Butcher birds fly down and land on the rim to drink their fill. It's a generational thing, taught by their parents from egg-break to first flight, just like last season. Dusty brown-fletched children, still with their stumpy tail feathers.

Desire leads, navigating the sandy ground, oblivious to our passengers, careful to keep to the narrow track that snakes between the bramble bushes. Just one of those barbs gets into the flesh it burrows straight into the bloodstream. Dead in a day.

I'd rather learn this now. With her. Not later with someone not up to the task. We get beyond the meadow and up the sand, and grass-tussocked dune. To safer ground. Then through the garden of delight, with all those gardenias, and on into the clay-baked clearing. We climb the massive age-worn sandstone slabs that serve as steps.

The birds fly off just before we enter through doors that can't close under any circumstances, they've been open so long. Into the dome. Into its dark.

It's immense structure, forgiving of any weather, any seasonal quake, lightning, since it was conceived and constructed untold ages past, by some unnamed architect in a civilization long forgotten. Built of massive panes of transparency, its arching height supported by granite pylons, each block curved, and carved with arcane symbols. The glass windows—we don't know what they really are—form vast diamond shapes, each gripped in a grid of an impossibly delicate, impossibly strong quartet of titanium alloy girders. The edges of every pane are beveled, to refract the light of sun, moon, star, storm cloud and mist, splashing the white stone floor with the only ichor of color to break the otherwise gloom.

At the center is a ten-foot length of carpentry. Could be called a receptacle as its doors are closed to hide the contents from those of us too young to be considered trustworthy with whatever lies within. Thigh-high, it is, to the tallest woman. Hardwood.

Highly polished. Mirroring our faces when we come here to learn, because the dome is a school of lore and story. The main one. The big one.

Desire and I deposit our buckets on the surface of the thing. They join the astrolabe and the telescopes, the sextants and the bundles of vellum.

I do nothing, just stand and watch as she lights the wicks of the oil lamps. She does it with her mind. I have no idea how. Calls it *wychlight* and says I'll learn. In fact, now I can hear the buzz of voices, like a whisper of distant bees, and I realize we've been slow. The elders—the heavies—are already coming.

Desire pulls a stem of a grass flower from her belt. Small but significant. She drops it, to float on the surface of the water in one of the buckets. The only rebellion she allowed herself today. She has been excluded. Shouldn't a mother be important? Not Desire. Despite everything she wasn't born here and her birthing of Insistence, however fortuitous that now is, was written about as taboo in the first years of the current era. When conception and population control became strictly enforced.

We exit by a side door, her head held high, a tight smile playing at the corners of her angry mouth. I know how pissed off she can really get.

THIS RITUAL CONFERS queen-ness. It had its inception here at the dome, at Kata Tjuta, when the ancestors settled here on their flight from certain death in the coastal cities to the east and south, and provided shelter by the First Nation people who, not long after the last, destructive shudder, made their instinctive way to the now-fecund and tropical southern pole where, as far as history tells, only ice once dwelt. Long melted. The continent beneath lived on once before.

When they left they'd threatened those left behind to take care of their country, or else…

RED DESERT COUNTRY. KATA TJUTA, and the dome that has remained a secret, from who knew when. With an underground library restructured from what had once been a travesty, drilled and gouged a thousand feet deep through the bedrock.

Once a uranium mine. Once yellowcake, the ingredient to create nuclear bombs that once proliferated the whole earth.

It's not a story anyone, other than the original queen daughters, know for sure. Only that her name was Molly. A story, in rhyme, passed along from initiation to initiation. Never changed. Exactly, in difference to the *china whisper syndrome* of the past. Those of us not trained in mnemonics don't know anything more than about the day of Molly's daughter was born. That she was named Baron and that all future names got to be consigned to remembering.

When Molly died, Baron became her own mother, as well as herself. She had access to the lives and wisdom of every other person in her matrilineal DNA. From those ancestors she learned the knowledge of substances, that would heal in this place, via neurons and cellular memory, extracted from the limbic brain. What we can eat. What to avoid if we want to stay alive.

Baron knew about the lands that remained above water in the northern hemisphere, and all about those who'd wrested power through heavily-weaponed, torture and *reeducation* camps, after the cataclysms. That they've kept an envious eye on the free southern lands ever since developing transport capable of maneuvering beneath the raging seas, called Our Lady of the Waters—an impossibility on the surface due to never-ending volatile, seismic and oceanic weather. Because they still live and kill as they've done since back in the twenty-first century. The people of the W.F.C. don't speak with the ancestors. They're stuck with an idea of an out-there-somewhere-deity and have rules to be obeyed or else. They only think of industry, use technology but... A form of soul blindness. Even today they are as sociopathic and apathetic as those who ignored the science of what was to come for their own reasons. As dangerous as ever.

The queens have never been wrong. We've a need of them. Need them now. We protect them as much as the queen in any hive. When we originally colonized our collective territories, people linked through the matrix and knew what Baron was. This one woman. Just the one. Called a queen for lack of a better title. With memory and knowledge that would become monumental as it became recognized. One woman with the accessible memory of history in her bones. Who can teach Ancestor knowledge to the people in the way of elder lore: through story. She also lives to make certain that the foolish desecration of earth never happens again. Not through neglect, not for any reason.

The current queen died over a week ago. Wizened and shriveled. In an opium-induced sleep.

Her born name, I have memorized, is Aurora. Now an ancestor.

SOMETIME IN THE NIGHT, A FUNERAL pyre was built in a tower of hard-cured dried hemp, on the highest Redrock plateau, for the ritual of Aurora's cremation, already decomposing in the late summer heat.

For the only time in our recorded history, there was no daughter of lineage, and everyone has been aware that this could herald something monumental, just not what that could be.

Aurora had a son. Named him Tabak. He'd remained with her away from the dome, in the city of Kata Tjuta, till he was seven—loved, and taught to listen to the voices inside his head, to trust he had a right to be alive, despite the whispers. By the time he was sent away he was a genius in some things—right brain things—and naïve in others. A loner because of his birthright, he had no friends, so wasn't bothered about leaving, other than that he'd loved his mother. He was sent to the west coast alchemeries to be trained in star lore, interdimensional access, mathematics and quantum philosophy. Stuff he was already good at. That and the warrior arts.

So Insistence was their only choice. The obvious choice. Other than Desire, and no one was that enlightened Though no older than twenty-nine years, and therefore just an adult, Insistence had been chosen by a corvid—a raven-familiar—for her person, a few years ago. A powerful thing known only in the legends.

DESIRE IS ANGRY—PISSED OFF. PICKING FLOWERS is against the rules. One less pollinator. When I give her a look of childish disapproval she just shrugs. I'm her conspirator so why would I tell anyone?

CHAPTER THREE

DESIRE

WEED OF A CHILD. HER SKIN might be the color of the old blooded northerners but her heart's as bloody as the rest of us, and she doesn't burn in the sun no more, so that baby-note was the truth. I like her, so. She's a punk. Possessed of a righteous, unforgiving attitude, and as shy as a bilby. And I think I know why. She's not the others, trained to talk the talk of the egalitarian and who believe, utterly, that to be the truth of things. But I have experience that knows otherwise, and Ghost knows it also.

I was pulled from my mother at the cutting of the cord. In the birthing wards of the hospital system in the ghetto. New York. The central control of the W.F.C. on what's left of the big continent in the northern lands. We were separated straight off. From the getgo, like everyone else.

And that is supposed to be that.

Except it wasn't.

I heard her voice in my head. Clear as starlight here in the desert. Every day until she died. She taught me of Guinea, about those earlier slaveries. I'd sit awake at night from oh… I don't know… maybe three?

Maybe four. And I knew it was her voice, and that she was angry. Because we're not supposed to remember anything, yet she does and it's my inheritance to do the same.

When I was little it was ditty songs. Plant names and what they did to a body. How they were put together, either a tincture or a poultice. How to bandage a limb that's been snake-bit. Sure as cloud I didn't know what a snake was, but I was taught anyway. So I'd know how to treat a body, so the venom doesn't kill. As I got older she taught me… other things. Contraband knowledge. Names. Things like tarot, and how to make condoms, lipstick. How to poison someone so forensics would never suspect. Things that could get me killed but would also pay me the creds I needed a meal if I was ever hungry. I never had a conscience because I never believed in the christian-enforced doctrine of meekness. Or that there was a god out there. Plain dumb, the way I figured it, from first I heard that rubbish.

I was always pretty, for a black-skinned girl, and I was ten when I got sent to the stables to train as a comfort woman for when the single men traveled long distances on their business. Called *exotics* we were. Treated well, I suppose, and allowed to wear color. Fed. Educated despite no man wanting us t'open our mouths unless it was to do them.

That was the same year my mother died. I thought my world was over. I intended to join her, and I tried hard enough. Out of sheer willpower. Because of the things I was forced to do just to pleasure a man. But I didn't, and the learning didn't stop with her death, neither. It just come from deeper. Raised itself from the length and breadth of my bones, guiding me even more strategically into healing, and seeing clear into tomorrow, so that I knew I'd get away one day, just never when.

But that's neither here nor there, and even though those women, in my ancientness, continued explaining and expanding on the things I'd need to be whole, it was the men-pleasuring what got me here. On a deep-sea raiding boat with five other exotics and a couple of dozen corporate men, their mercenaries and their human cargo hunters. Human resources. Destined as new breeding stock. Herded to the factories where the young dead were shoveled away and disposed of.

I was sick all the way.

You should be working, I was told, and I got a beating despite the vomit. Stabilizers, I heard tell.

Technology that meant we were not supposed to feel the roiling, pounding, ripping currents beyond the hull. Only I did.

It's the memories. And my mother's, mother's, mother and deeper still, told me the stories of the slave trade in *naqoyqatsi*. The one that was talked about anyway, because it never really stopped. They had the journey in them, as well. She was chained, back-to-belly, to the wooden shelves of the *Isabella*, bound for America in 1684. Bringing the lore in her mind, because that was the only thing not violated. So, suck it up, she warned me. And I did.

We made shore in heat like I'd never known except in theory. But lucky for all that because at least I was prepared. We was kept penned on the beach, with just a skeleton crew of three men. Drunk from the moment they was left alone. It was easy for me to dig beneath the wire. I tried to coax the other women to make the escape, but they was so afraid of the sun, having marched just half a mile in the stuff from the ship to the camp, and the religious propaganda about devils hereabouts, and cannibals. The unknown they'd never questioned.

It is not the land of my ancestors, so I had no knowledge of what I could or couldn't eat. I was eventually taken in by a tribe of brown people. They healed me and fed me but that was all.

They didn't want me. Human ration quotas. As soon as the annual traders traveled through I was sent packing. I was twelve when Kata Tjuta claimed me as a daughter.

Yes, I had the healing skill and learned at twice the pace as the other girls because my mothers were still talking, their spirits communicating with the dead of the Yankunytjatjara people and the Pitjantjatjara people, who'd been the land here. for forever, it seemed.

But I didn't speak of any of that. I'd waited to sense the way of things and had come to realize that I was a random thing. I learned about the queens but shut my mouth. I never stopped the lessons.

I was apprenticed to the apothecaries after two years. I felt the sting of what Ghost feels, even then, because everybody was beautiful, but everybody was brown. And I am black, as though no pale-skinned men made any of my mothers pregnant.

The lore understood, the seasonal cycles and festivals celebrated, the language second nature, a upbrought accent dissolved and a straight back claimed, I was accepted after several years. Traded for my first ever pack of tarot at a winter carnival. Samhain, the local people called the time of year. The days before the lightning and the rumbling earth. The warning times.

I kept them hidden till a year later. Another tribal confederacy. I was given a spot on the avenue of seers and risked nobody turning up.

Never did conceive, no matter how many men I laid with. I'd stopped even thinking about it. You can imagine how surprised I was, when I was all of maybe forty-two, or thereabouts, when I thought the menopause was on me, that I felt a baby quicken at sixteen weeks. We delivered Insistence when it was my time. And her inheriting the remembering also. I knew as soon as I looked into those brand new, squinty eyes, and saw Africa in them. Never knew which of them men I took up with was her father. Didn't seem to matter to these people, so I was fine with that.

Rufus-son-of-Rupert is my rat-familiar. Or, more likely, I'm his person. However, he has mites or something. He's chewing at his tail again. Must see to the diatomite for him. Last time he got infested was because he went foraging without me for a week. Only he knows what other species he predated and ate. Most like a bird as they still carry parasites to this day.

Yes, I'm proud of my daughter. From the getgo Insistence had more courage than me. Than most anybody. Showed that she was a rememberer. Refused the antagonism. She warrior-trained with the breastless two-spirit people, and took to the healing arts, in collaboration with the desert aunties. Trusted with the keys to the library even before she was twenty summers. Has, and has always had, the power of coercion, little smarty pants doing that to a mother, getting her own way, knowing she had a right to it. How's that old saying go? *Tough and tender, not bound by gender.*

She won't be mine after today. The queens are nobody's. I don't know what happens to her now. Truth be told I am relieved that she was seen. That she broke most every taboo known hereabouts.

And now? She's not my flesh and we're day and night, but Ghost has some destiny that is only whispered in my bones. So far off in the yesterday is the story of her that I can't hear it. I just hear her. Little white child, spoken of as this powerful sorceress.

This time-traveler. Poor young thing gets a staring like I used to. If she comes to be other than gutsy but shy? Yes, well. I'll eat my cards.

CHAPTER FOUR

INITIATION

MOST OF THE GIRLS HAVE GONE. EVEN Miriam has tired of me. I suppose. To someone outside my own brain, I must seem petulant. I'm not, though. What is it? Why do I look this way? I'm self-aware. I wish I wasn't. None of the others seem to be. They're all beautiful, no matter the hawk noses or flat faces, almond eyes, wild corkscrew hair, or acne, or genetic impediments, the bionic limbs of the mutant women, many of whom still need arms and hands to data input, garden or ride. Do any of them ever feel this *something*? This alienness? I don't fit in here. I pretend to, and my skills are good enough. It's not just my whiteness. That's on the outside. I'm lonely, and I'm homesick. For what? For where? How can I be those things when I'm loved, and this is the only home I've ever known?

Here.' Desire, proffers her arm and Rupert-son-of-Rufus uses it as a bridge from her to me. He wraps his long, soft-furred body around my neck and immediately sleeps, while I think for answers to my own questions.

It's in my eyes. In my eyes, reflected back at me from the mirror. I don't seem to be able to get my face out of it. If I look long enough at my appearance, will there be an answer? That's the hope. To stare down the beast. On such a day as this. But Desire is right. Her daughter is to take her place amongst the lineage of queens today and her mama hasn't been invited. And she's comforting me?

'Get up,' blunt-voiced, turning away. 'Stop moping and take Rufus to the fair. I've got a party to crash.'

'You reading tarot at the market?'

'For a while, Ghost. Then I'm up that cliff.'

'I'll come!'

'No, you won't. You'd be in more trouble than me, by far.'

'What? Cause I'm—?'

She snorts back a laugh, interrupting. 'Because you just a kid.'

She makes for the door to the garden, hitching up her robes, exposing old, black, heavily-muscled legs. 'Miriam's been waiting for you on the porch this whole time you been daydreaming of being brown, she says over her shoulder. 'She's a good friend, Ghost. This self-pity is good for nothing. Go buy something. Cheer up. You're off duty for three days.'

'I—'

'Not listening.'

I'm dismissed. Rufus nibbles my earlobe, and I'm then acutely aware of Miriam's thoughts across the matrix. *I'm coming*, I think loudly.

I also realize what's wrong with me. Why I differ from the others. I think about what I what I write in this here book, not input to SEVEN. I'm not supposed to be an individual. But I'm allowed to be, because I'm expected to be strange. I write everything, and I question everything.

MY WORK, THOUGH, IS AS A RECORD KEEPER. A chronicler. There are only thirty of us stationed here at Kata Tjuta. Our job is to input, exactly, what we see and what we hear. My own *prefontlcortexl* is implanted just beneath the skin below my left ear. Mine's body-modded with a gull in flight. I know what a gull is. There's a million of them down by the great lake. Something as pale as me. Something not indigenous to the desert.

I sat the exam for memory and input security clearance when I was thirteen. After a year of training. I scored high, a proud moment. I was accepted into the chroniclers' cabal the same year. They're okay. I'm not close to anyone, though, except Miriam, and she's head of the entire library complex, not just a chronicler. She has been my ally from the day I was released from the apothecary. Asked to be my mentor and show me the ropes (I love that expression. It's an ancient saying associated with sailing ships. Imagine ships sailing!).

Chronicling is exact. We record everything, every day, that we encounter. Nothing personal. No comment. What would that entail? Erroneous recording, that's what. We know. Everyone knows about the lies of the before time, *naqoyqatsi*. We are clean remembers.

My work has been singular. Hang with Insistence. Hang out at the library. See who is learning what. What the computer thinks of their study. What the computer learns today. No reference to my book writing.

ON THE OUTSKIRTS OF THE OF THE KATA TJUTA community, trainee initiates are housed apart, hanging about close to the dome and in the temple library. The general Kata Tjuta population inhabit the sandstone city. Beehive-shaped, sandstone houses and workshops, seemingly natural environmental structures. This's provided camouflage, from anything ever droning from above, for the last two thousand years, from potentially reinstated aeronautical spying. Abundant water is piped through engineered clay aquifers and piped from the great lake, only a mile distant, kept cold in underground reservoirs, the lifeblood of people, species and interspecies-sustained food.

On the day of the Redrock pilgrimage the people of Kata Tjuta are mostly awake before dawn, and the streets are bustling with activity as everyone prepares for the carnival-like gathering with others from far away.

Word spreads as word spreads. Almost everyone is implanted with a *prefronlecortexl* from childhood, linking them to the matrix and even with the people not genetically predisposed for the automatic download of communication, as clans from all over the inhabited parts of the country converge.

The women are dressed in their finest: light, adaptable garments spun and woven from the wool of free-ranging sheep, dyed with bark, and leaves or grass, or mosses ranging from green to scarlet to black, into the colors of earth. They're cloaked in finely woven cloth, draped around their torsos, arms and shoulders while leaving sun-bronzed breasts bare, as is tradition, on which are tattooed the lines and dots of their familial lineages.

Precious metal jewelry, passed down to them from their ancestors, has been recast and adapted into new shapes, now worn as talismans or amulets, and every one of them is adorned with at least one row, sometimes hundreds, of the blue clay beads, distinguishing the initiated adults from those still considered children.

Men, and all the women who display warrior markings—tattoos, body-mods or scarifications—wear soft, tanned leathers on their legs and shoulders. And animal rib breast-plates, also draped with strings of the blue clay beads.

Fish and eels, trapped and netted from within the great lake, are scaled, skun and gutted, and stuffed with herbs. Seabirds, swarms of flies and the begging eyes of the yellow camp dogs not making work any easier. People have brought tomato fruit, water gum and local fungi for mulled wine, nuts from goanna bushes down by the lake's edge, querned to flour. Sweetgrass and gourds are piled high with every local vegetable. Flat-bread, baked over the coals of fires, are stacked onto woven blankets.

Panniers are filled with food and loaded onto travois, or onto the saddles of camels.

Bole-wood casks, containing spiced and fermented fungi moonshine, potent enough to spin the inside of a person's head with strange visions if taken too liberally, are carried by the strong.

Meggie, hands on hips surveys the preparations from the within the shade of the longhouse. She's a chieftain of the Kata Tjuta desert clan, along with her life partner Farhan, an elder, having made it to forty years without dying.

CULTURAL INPUT: AN ELDER IS A SKILLED PERSON, OF twenty eight years old or older, who has been liberated from the anxieties that tend to dominate them when younger. At twenty-eight years old, the time of initiation into the mysteries, each person proclaims their independence from any and all prior learning. They don't throw it away, merely shelve it for later. This encourages self-determination.

Before that they study. From when they're little kids they're taught the correct use of the language for both culture and technology, the intelligences of numbers, the biological and esoteric laws of life, the arts, music, song and dance. All the known skills of building, maintenance and engineering, the seasons of the stars, for horticultural, astrological and navigational purposes.

At initiation, some enter the potteries where they train at designing and constructing kilns, vessels for storage and transportation, their decoration and glazing, making bricks, jewelry, aquifers, filtration and pipeline systems and repair, and the skills of extracting. molding and designing with the many-colored clays: red, yellow, purple and white, and the rare sky-blue for the coloring of clay rank beads.

Other people learn song and music, dij and drum, pipes and bells, and the ways of the harpers who carry intel, messages and stories from clan to clan. People train in the arts of entertainment and inspiration, or theatre and cooking and the wit and memory.

Stone-workers, builders, weavers, shearers, tattooists, and bodymod artists, and the makers of inks and needles for such. Horse and camel trainers, saddle and cloth makers, jugglers and carnies of all kinds. Horse and camel trainers and whisperers, aeronautical engineers and kite-makers, butchers and divers.

Others are healers, midwives to babies, and those who prepare the dead for cremation: those who light the fires and sing the songs of remembering, and when there is nothing but ashes, deliver that to the gardeners who feed the soil.

We've got cutters, stitchers and bone-setters in the doctoring arts, including the wizards who know how to insert, program and maintain the *prefontlcortexl* implants.

Most of the clan, at some time, work with lance and bow and staff and sword and knife and sling, for raiding and abductions still happen sometimes.

Some, specifically from around Kata Tjuta, work in the library under the direction of my friend Miriam, She-Who-Must-Be-Obeyed, SEVEN's intricacies mastered.

The body of this vast library, maintained by these initiates, houses clay tablets, papyri and vellum, documents from the most ancient, to works of modern thought and creative fantasy, housed in rows of time-lineage. Constantly being uploaded into SEVEN's virtual data banks.

The initiates of the alchemeries study the sciences. They work with both molecular and light-lasers technology and gain—over time—an unique understanding of atmospheric and dimensional interlay grids that form the matrix. They heal the worst wounds and form the highest art within the night skies. They keep and maintain, well-guarded, their knowledge of the use of stellar-fission and earth-core energy. They upkeep a continuous communication and connection with the ancestors—elders, past and present—and the many gates that lead to mythworld, where time ceases, and forests go on indefinitely.

Psychics, seers, geomancers and diviners. They've all come.

A few retain and work the knowledge of the deep-sea ships, that navigate the ocean to the south and sou'east. These craft hug the sea-floor fathoms beneath the raging surface of Our Lady of the Waters and are the only means of interaction with the stronghold of the many tribes of the First People living in the jungles of the southern pole, and with our brothers and sisters, both pale-skins and Maori, on what remains of the islands of the Long White Cloud, with whom we trade for their own specializations and exotica.

People-hunters who hunt slavers. Explanation? Body-snatchers working for the W.F.C., who are funded and have formed cabals, hitch rides to the southern hemisphere and back, on the deep sea craft that are capable of travel beneath Our Lady of the Waters specifically for the slave trade and to extort resources unavailable elsewhere. These men are paid to abduct girls and women of childbearing age—for breeding-stock—confined until they either escape, which is a rare thing or, told to us by the few who have made it out. Like Desire. Escapee, not born in these lands, upskilled from her arrival in both temple maintenance and the training of apprentices in suchlike. A woman born a seer and healer, like a rare few others. Touched by dreams and portents, inherited from untamed mothers, and boosted by mycelium medicines until she became spooky, and mother to a random factor, interspecies-chosen daughter.

They're all here. All setting up at Redrock for the cremation of the dead queen, and the coronation of Insistence, the new one.

CHAPTER FIVE

TABAK

EXAMS ARE SUPPOSED TO prove what? *Nothing*, is my current theory. I know what I've learned and none of that comes from the texts or the holos. What we're supposed to learn is smoke and mirrors. Is it the truth? Who can say? It's all dead authors' opinions trapped as fact and regurgitated like doctrine. Nothing unexplored currently on offer. I have my dreams. The patterns and the mathematics. Like I'm downloading directly from some skein of the matrix that causes the men to smirk and rumor that I'm *touched*.

'You in there?'

'Shut up, Jimmy.'

James-the-Maker. He taps my drawings. They have everything to do with this course except the exam. Which is ancient history.

Jimmy. I'm probably the only one of us game enough to call him that to his face. I don't have a come-back to his snide question, so I stop what I'm doing and think the test answers into our remote-view of SEVEN. Thank muck for prefrontal cortex implants!

James continues pacing the room. 'I can hear you, Tabak.' He doesn't look my way. Telepaths. The bane of existence.

'Can I go?'

'Can I stop you?' His hands join behind him. Some sort of self-satisfaction body language. 'And fuck the consequences, is it?'

Eyes in the back of his head. Mocking me through the cipher, tattooed on his neck, of *Euler's Identity*, $e^{\wedge}i$ π)-+1+= 0. He's not like the others. Doesn't treat me like I'm heavy water.

Done. Data input. Can I go now? It is not a question. All this takes less than here minutes to download.

THE MEN OF THE west are coming here now. Because of Tabak, Aurora's nineteen year old, unwanted and rejected boy child.

Study up, Desire tells me. For a psychic, she's hard on surprises but no one has seen or heard of him for the last twelve years. 'Cept, the computer—SEVEN—has. I punch in his code data and SEVEN bumps up both a holo and a screen of data she's compiled from all the records input to date. Both his and those of his mentor, an old *Wu-chi* master and telepath. With a mathematics background that caused me to forget to close my mouth. TABAK, no last name. Sole offspring of the late queen. I've never seen an analysis this complex. The computer has the fancies for him. I've wondered about her. How she deals with being semi-sentient. How she feels. Does she feel? What inspires certainly displays itself in such as this information? Layered and with so many intersecting tabs I'm nauseous. And, I admit, envious, even though the forensics she's got on me leaves me confused and walking away long ago.

Tabak. When he was little he'd been solitary.

Thought to be genius, surmised to be an Asperger person. Smells his food. Is able to communicate with most other species so was put with the horses very young. No friends. Avoids touch and all forms of affection. Intrinsic skills with geometric and computational mathematics and physics.

He was at Kata Tjuta until he was seven before being sent to the alchemery on the far west coast, to train in deeper sciences as well as physical disciplines. With the men. He hasn't come back here in Aurora's lifetime. Suspected animosity. So this will be interesting. Anticipation of his arrival is creating quite a stir. Unions ate arranged between sexually active people at every one of the tribal gatherings, and this will be no exception. But not Tabak. Not this time. And maybe never.

SEVEN advises no for partnering. No, for ordinary integration with anyone. His antisocial behavior has so far shown no signs of improving. He is potentially dangerous, although the data suggests this to be hearsay because, logically, potential has no relevance in reality. Tabak displays non-pathological obsessive behavior, is highly adapted to the most advanced *prefontlcortexl* and has upgraded his own according to wizardry that even SEVEN's analysis is seduced by, but that is not understood by any known human. He's a star lore guardian Has not been sexually oriented or initiated. Not even once. Considered likely undesirable, even forbidding, despite my own opinion of a fine-boned, lean, dark-eyed, dark-haired *something* of a man, slightly androgynous, with what I think is humor in the lift of his mouth. Why? Because he dislikes trivia or small talk? That's what this data suggests. I input the question to the mainframe, along with my findings. He is also encoded for a matrix opal.

YES rolls down the screen. SEVEN, can you expand? But her curser just flashes.

Tabak loves to learn. Has absorbed the teachings of both SEVEN and the elder males of the alchemery like a tick on a camel, from the martial arts to astronomy, but in no greater pursuit than art. Shy but, it seems, in recent years no longer withdrawn. Early opinion of spectrum disorder was withdrawn at the onset of puberty when he became what SEVEN designates as a smart arse. His best friend is his teacher James-the-Maker. Seeks no social outlet but rather opts to work extra time in the laboratories, or ranging further and further, on horseback or on foot, from his coastal home in the direction of the great desert lands.

He does, however, enjoy long debates with his tutor, whom he calls Jimmy and gets away with it.

The other initiates neither seek to evaluate nor change who he is. That's not their way. Most, however, avoid him because seeking camaraderie has long since been understood as pointless.

James-the-Maker, the alchemist responsible for Tabak's physical training, is at once thrilled by his protégé's skill at sword and bow, and at his fearless intensity at unarmed combat. But James sensed, also, a spark of danger, as every so often Tabak is debilitated by a mood of such bleak intensity that James forbids him from exercising with anyone else in practice sessions.

James is convinced that all the unusualness is the effect of immanence on a male (hitherto an unknown thing) that destabilizes Tabak so frequently.

As for causing anyone harm, well, Tabak would not. He knows himself well and recognized these periods of intense restlessness for what they are – intense restlessness; an overwhelming urge to visually capture something he couldn't name even if he'd had the information right in front of him.

When these moods strike he draws – star maps, buildings, architectural blueprints of places unlike any he has ever physically seen, topographical maps of landscapes in which he's never traveled, equations for the engineering of aircraft he's never flown.

He finally shows his datacore to James-the-Maker and a group of elder initiates at the alchemery.

They'd study it for ages, knowing it to be of importance but having no frame of reference for any of the data.

'We don't undervalue what you've done, Tabak,' said James at a council called for the final evaluation, 'but we don't have any idea what they mean. Are these everything you've drawn? Are there any reference sources?'

'These are the refined works, Jimmy' Tabak replies, hesitantly, looking over the shoulder of his teacher.

'Refined works?'

'Yes. These came in moments of little control despite all I've learned and everything I know.'

He gets restless, starts pacing, all the while smiling.

'Fuck, they excite me, Jimmy, and I d'you know why? Spontaneity. The ideas come and my hand draws them, and even while I'm in the middle of one I know that this bit's *right* or another is not. And then the feeling—whatever it is—deserts me for a while. Then it comes again. And I *flash*, and I know where I've made a mistake. I don't delete the discordant ones. They're in there somewhere if you want to see them. I think under *archive* maybe. From there I begin again.'

James scrolls through several of the diagrams.

'The places are uncharted,' he says. 'and some of the buildings seem to be sophisticated holding tanks. For what? The diagrams give dimension to the buildings. You draw vessels fueled by an unrecognizable mathematical equation. The astronomical maps are accurate in all details except you've added to them. Tabak? Is this some memory? Or is this something yet to be?'

Tabak is frustrated. He hadn't expected an inquisition, even a polite one.

'Not a fucking clue, Jimmy.'

James ignores the taunt and returns his attention to the work, scrolling from page to page.

'The drawings are very, ah, specific and realistic even though we don't understand a fucking thing you've done.' He smiles, an attempt to placate this rogue genius son of an otherwise sterile queen. 'But man, you sure can calculate the phases of mathematics with art, sweetheart.'

He paces. Thinks about the years he'd invested in Tabak. Sweats a little. Decides.

'Look, we're gonna take the whole lot to the library in the desert country, and get SEVEN to check it all out because to leave this hanging like it is, without resolution or reason, is to dishonor what is obviously of value.

'Great,' snarls Tabak, sorry he let anyone in on his secret.

'Think about it, Blossom. What harm do I wish you?'

Tabak squirms. 'Do you have to call me that, Jimmy?'

'While you call me Jimmy I'll call you whatever I want, darling. And doing nothing about this – not following it all up – could disrupt your pattern. Can we do this? Are you willing?'

'There's something even beyond all this data though, I tell you Jimmy, and if this is the ancestors doing the talking they're as oblique as they could possibly be. And the maps? Sometimes I think I have to leave here for always. But why? And where are the places? Except the one with the evil in it. That's here. I know it's on this country.'

He takes hold of the datacore and closes the diagram program, replacing the device into its antistatic titanium cylinder.

'What's this *evil*?' asks James.

'Somewhere there's a thing that's like an antithesis – the opposite – of the drawings and I need to understand what it is; because in that some-other-place where the thing dwells are any mistakes I've made within the process of each drawing. Whatever this thing is, it's power-dreadful and fucked up. It could be the death of everyone.'

The men with him shift nervously and Tabak is fully aware of their discomfort. He laughs softly. 'I guess that's a long way round to saying yes, we better go to SEVEN at the library.'

They wonder about him still, even to being wary of his grasp on sanity despite their magic. The variable – the potential threat—he poses, though, can't be tolerated, so they resolve to diffuse the dilemma by arranging the pilgrimage. They leave two days after that meeting.

CHAPTER SIX

KATA TJUTA

MEGGIE ARRIVES AT Kata Tjuta's sun temple, an intricately carved sandstone building at the center of the city near the fountain of the perpetual spring, with her long-time partner Farhan Ibrahim. He wears his raven-black hair tied back in a long braid that hangs half-way down his back, to his bum. His dark, hooded eyes glint with humor as do the wide gold earrings hanging talisman-like from both stretched earlobes.

Farhan is not a man to say much – he dislikes trivial conversation much like his brother Angus. He's also an elder and, as his intricate mechanistic tattooing proclaims to the world that he's the arch-chief in charge of all the petrol-fueled excavators, bulldozers, backhoes, graders, cranes, wheel-loaders, four and dual wheel automobiles, archaic but pristine, maintained for their svelte beauty and historic significance alone, kept hidden from the elements except for special events.

Together he and Meggie declare the pilgrimage, by sounding the great golden gong that hangs within the sun temple, the deep booming reverberating throughout the city.

Everything that is to be taken on the journey is brought to the compound and into the cool of shadows.

The brotherhood of the desert alchemery are dressed in feather capes and ride into the city on the big seventeen hand horses, with banners flying atop their lances.

Angus Ibrahim, Farhan's elder sibling, is a man with an unapologetic disdain for anything even slightly religious, an intelligent and lighthearted mystic and heretic, in charge of all the

44

alchemeries in the red desert. Their horses' hooves stir up dust goblins, as they circle to stop amidst the gathering clans.

Angus smiles, all innocence, as he slides from his multicolored and string-tasseled saddle. He saunters towards Meggie who is standing, leaning on her sheathed sword and observing the newcomers. He exudes an arrogant confidence that only slips a little when he trips on nothing and pretends he hasn't. He proceeds to flirt outrageously, ignoring Farhan who shrugs, used to this behavior.

'Morning, love of my brother,' he sighs, eyeing her up and down in mock-lust.

Meggie delights in his flirting (never certain what she'd do if and when she ever found that he truly desired her). She challenges back with a throaty chuckle and the swing of a hip revealing a muscled thigh over which she languidly rubs her hand.

'You got any news, for a change?'

'Nothing. At least, not this morning. But I could be wrong because I'm not somewhere else, so how am I to know what I don't?'

'Brat,' she sniffs, 'Fuck off with the word games. It's really tired.'

'What a crowd to see the queen away.' He breathes in the sweetness of the young morning, turning this way and that to take in the sheer numbers of people.

'Do you intend to give me this kind of party when my body dies?'

She snorts her strange laugh and he picks her up and swings her around.

'Put me down, ya puppy. People are watching and they always got to have something to stir me up about.'

FARHAN KNOWS, AS DOES MEGGIE, that Insistence is his match. He was never the same man once he'd met her.

He lips Meggie gently on the forehead and turns to take his brother's arm in the gesture of honor between warriors. Meggie knows their love for each other – the look between them familiar, and able to close out all others from their conversation.

'Take care, brother,' says Angus quietly.

He remounts and thunders off, white cape flying, his band of brothers whooping and galloping to catch up.

Farhan engulfs Meggie in his arms, nuzzling her neck, and she returns his caress with snarls of delight.

'Moving out? Everything ready?' she asks.

'Everything's ready,' he smiles, pulling on the strapping of his saddle.

Meggie turns her attention to the crowd. 'Moving out!' and several hundred people respond like a wave.

The journey to the Kata Tjuta gathering at Redrock is leisurely. Most of the people walk, seasoned in traveling many miles for hunting, or as runners when the games at the festivals brought several clans together.

CULTURAL INPUT AGAIN: THESE GATHERINGS are necessary for several reasons.

The women usually seek sperm partners from distant clans to mate with when they decide to procreate. Otherwise, those of any gender, choose lovers for pleasure, monogamous partnership not a prerequisite for conceiving or raising children, nor an assurance of happiness, as was presumed in the before time of *naqoyqatsi* (extant in the tainted northern lands) and demanded by religions.

Children, and adolescents not yet initiated are brought to the festivals to learn what they can't learn in their home clans, gaining an immeasurable cache of curiosity when in the company of strangers, like here.

The young gain their greatest understanding through the observation of the behavior of others. What will be available to them as adults. As is only appropriate.

THE CLANS—BOTH LOCAL and those visiting—congregate at the base of the Redcliffs, crags of rich red sandstone towering three hundred feet towards the sky. It's just like one of the seasonal festivals, a forest of multi-colored tents and splendor but without the usual barter stalls.

Pits are dug for cooking, and fires lit beside each hole. Wood is added over and over until beds of scarlet coals glow white-hot, onto which are laid stones that have baked right through.

Huge piles of wide fresh leaves are dumped in readiness beside each pit – these are sat or laid upon by the children, who wallow in their cool greenness and who tell each other wild and outlandish stories as the clans mingle and the meeting of old and new friends occur.

Ironwood poles, necessarily supported by two or more people, bring the lava-glass stones from the fires that are loaded into the pits for cooking.

The leaves are then heaped over the stones. Placed in some of these ovens are fish (all stuffed with pollen-maize and herbs and fruit) while in others kangaroo, deer, and boar is cooked. Wet leaves are piled onto the meat, the savory smoke giving the flavor of lemon to the whole, then sand is shoveled over the top to stop the heat from parching the camps.

I can almost taste the slow-cooked meat that will be ready for eating in a few hours.

The only usual festival thing here today are the foretelling tents: tarot, astrology, runes, dreams, bones, an long lines wait under the shadow of the Redcliffs for their turn.

Meggie waits in a queue along with more than a dozen others, to seek her future from Desire's tarot cards. She observes the people coming out of the old black woman's tent. Some smiling and some weeping, others with blank faces, confused and full of conflict.

She'll only sit with Desire because she's the only psychic she really trusts. She tells the truth without softening glances or simpering words, and courage is needed to take her cards in hand. She knows, she's sat with her before.

Meggie breathes slowly to calm her nerves, just before she enters the tent and lays the precious bangle on the table as barter.

Desire's now dressed for the occasion, in soft, yellow deer hide robes, decorated with beads and shells, feathers and the small holy stones passed down through the generations. Hand-painted designs tell of her role as seeress and healer, and her hair, that I personally braided with strings of many colors, is held back from her face by rows of little blue clay beads.

I'm allowed to be sitting in on the sessions this year. I have to shut up though. Be invisible. Learn.

'I know you,' says Desire, indicating to Meggie to sit opposite her, on the other cushion, at her little wooden table.

'What's with the kid?'

'She's not really a kid, are you Ghost?' She looks across at me where I blush through my albinism, my mottles, I swear, turning puce with embarrassment.

'Just pretend I'm not here,' I say, in a mumble.

'Three times,' says Meggie, returning her full attention to Desire. She remembers the prophecies of childlessness despite many intimate partners, then the meeting and love match with Farhan and the death of her blood-mother, by a king brown bite, that hadn't been treated in time, six years ago.

Desire hands Meggie the well-worn cards, Rufus-son-of-Rupert taking to her lap, cat-like, used to this.

'Mix 'em,' she says. 'You keep your eyes on what she does, Ghost. Rufus, you comfy?'

Meggie gives me a cursory glance, then shuffles, Rufus ignored in her lap, She hands the pack back.

I stand, as unobtrusively as I can, and look over Desire's shoulder as she lays the cards out in three rows of seven, with three at the bottom.

She sits back and sighs.

'Nothin' personal here, love...' Two deep furrows cut tracks between her eyebrows. 'I've laid out this same spread five times today already, haven't I, Ghost? Unless you're involved, Meggie...'

'What is it?' Meggie shifted uncomfortably.

'A monumental event is what it is. Environmental upheaval first, then… Somethin' just so hard to look at it freaks me blacker than I already am.'

Desire lifts the lid from a basket of food beside the table. She offers nuts to Meggie who shakes her head.

'Helps me think,' she says, popping a couple into her mouth and crunching, while Meggie and I wait.

'Okay—It isn't plague. I seen that before. And it isn't famine. But it *is* death. And for many. Here. And not once, but twice… Maybe even three times cause the outcome sure is weird.'

She fiddles. She pulls her hair into a ropey pile on top of her head. Initially, it seems like agitation but the more she lets herself dither the clearer the message becomes to her. She catches my eye and squints, doubt and certainty at war, then looks back at the cards, her eyes suddenly understanding.

'Ah, there you are! Ghost, look. See that?' It's been in the readings of a few people that morning already. So yes. 'Yes,' I say.

'The first time this is gonna happen is at the hands of others. Nasty bastards. Betcha it's a raid by the W.F.C. But the second event? From the *World* and the *Star* and the *Hanged Man* comes the *Magician*. From the *Magician* comes some kind of quest, and because of that the *Empress* and the *Fool* card follow.'

'What's all that about?' asks Meggie. 'You lost me at W.F.C.'

'Some huge event and not of our making. Can't control when the earth moves, Meggie.'

'Is it flood? Cyclone?'

'No. The *Moon* means water and it is not here. *Star* card? Maybe a meteor.'

Meggie could almost touch the concentration and the confusion. 'When?'

'The *Death* card and the *Ace of Wands* can be the turn of the seasons towards winter. Sometime around Samhain, I figure. Meggie, pass me my rat., we gotta go tell somebody important.'

She's so accurate in her prediction that, retrospectively, it's obvious. The second phase of the prophecy *is* to occur at Samhain. Just not that year.

CHAPTER EIGHT

PROPHECY

THE CLIMB IS LONG ENOUGH WITHOUT the knowledge that we carry.

The narrow stairs winds upwards through cavernous pinnacles of cave-pocked red sandstone, through narrow fissures where the sun never shines. We pass ta pool of deep transparent water that bubbles from far beneath the sands hundreds of feet below, and that has never been known to dry up. One after another we fill the little clay cup that hangs from a verdant patinaed chain of old bronze, and we all ceremoniously drink. The stone around this pool is carved with ancient designs, filled in with black and red and yellow ochre, done by some long-departed tribe of desert people who had once dreamed the person, or spirit, that is these towering cliffs.

We scramble up the last part of the climb and out across a finger of rock-bridge, spanning two pinnacles, to where the gathering of initiates sit in a wide circle.

DESIRE, MEGGIE, FARHAN AND I emerge onto the plateau, hundreds of feet above the desert floor and stop short before the grandeur of the gathering.

The initiates ear robes made from the skins of finely tanned animals, cured and softened by long-dead elders, and worn-in by wearers over many generations.

Each is adorned with the carved gold and silver talismans of their individual callings. These amulets were once other things, crude, gaudy baubles of *naqoyqatsi* that have been melted down and re-shaped. Cut and faceted gems and stones hang from woven strips around the women's foreheads, glittering in the sun, deep green and scarlet parrot feathers adorn the braids of everyone here, hair shining with grease in the brightness of the day.

Skin is exposed, in naked suggestions, from beneath half-open robes, amber skin glowing with health. All wear belts around their waists from which hang long, leaf-shaped daggers, sheathed in tooled leather, that were the gifts given at the completion of initiation. Us initiates all got 'em.

Only the men of the alchemies wear cockatoo feather capes. The matrix opals hanging around their necks hiding a microchip that gives each man the key to accessing both the matrix and translations from ancestral communications, each programed to create harmonic resonances, sufficient to enable the initiates to become as light as light itself. and therefore to be other than matter. Theoretically.

INSISTENCE SITS AT THE CENTER of the elders amongst them, naked but for a spotted leopard pelt, its razor-fanged head, her savage crown. The remainder of the skin trailing down her back to pool about her thighs, a plain, heavy-hide gauntlet on her left forearm.

A wide-winged raven is perched on her exposed shoulder, but Insistence is oblivious to the talons digging into her heavily scarred flesh. Named Lucifer for the morning and evening star, her white eyes watch us as though we might be enemies.

Insistence looks to be sleeping upright, the lids moving in REM, on an inward vision that only few can follow. She's somewhere in the night of mythworld, but without the need of a physical gate, and without anyone knowing for certain what she's learning. Queen things, I suppose.

The others are focused, silent, each of them telepathically linked to her, as much as is possible, through the matrix.

'We can't interrupt them now,' hisses Meggie.

Desire replies with a grumble in her throat, squatting on the rock, readying herself for what could be a long wait. But Insistence opens her eyes and stands. She stretches the kinks from her long limbs and lifts off the leopard skin, shaking the dust from her hair. The other initiates shift and relax.

She takes her time, still in contemplation as she walks to the smaller fire, kept burning at one side of the circle, and extracts a flaming brand. She goes to the bier on which the body of Aurora lies, bound from head to foot in cloth the color of the desert.

Insistence removes the delicate gold crown, and the ancient elm staff, that had been laid upon the body, and holds them in one hand while she thrusts the torch into the waiting pyre with the other. It erupts into high, wild blue, purple and green flame from the salt of the driftwood, brought from the distant sea by the ocean dwellers for just such a purpose.

Lucifer wings to the air, a blue-black arrow over the heads of the crowd below, *ark-aarking* the information of a new queen, plumes of white smoke filling the sky in the hot, pale day.

Insistence gestures for us to join her and the others. 'It's alright,' she begins, when everyone settles 'I've been seeing what you've seen. And more. Those of the people who'll stay behind are not brave, nor are they to be mourned or pitied. It'll simply be that theirs is a future, along a branch of the time none of us know about. You're all going. Betcha.'

Lucifer flies back with a bloody mess of some kill in her beak. She's busy bashing the carcass on the rocks, seeking admiration from Insistence who takes a moment to stroke her chest with a hackle feather before continuing with her take on the prophecy, effectively shutting her mother up. She's followed by the raven, curious about Desire.

W.F.C. REPRESENTATIVES ARE ALREADY gathering in the north, to fulfill their part in the prophecy, although they see it all so differently. I sense something pretty abhorrent. Some rubbish about a murdered god that supposedly speaks through their black-and-red-robed priesthood, who think that life is ugly and pointless. Seems the only way they know to control people is domination and subjugation. It's sad and silly but they believe it all the same… Oh, and yes, they are in league with the corporati boys.

'But. I digress. There's scheming going on in secret rooms that even I can't get to. They know how to block telepaths, bastards. There's talk up front of raiding, that's not true.'

Her eyes widen. 'Fuck me, if the W.F.C. are not already on their way here.' She laughs softly. 'And that's only the first bit.

'The second?' asks Desire.

'Second, my bird's gonna eat Rufus-son-of-Rupert, you don't put that fucker in your pocket, Mama.'

Desire isn't laughing but she knows her daughter's sense of humor. Rufus disappears beneath the elder woman's robes.

'Second's a journey to I dunno what. Though there's some weird twist. The ancestors will explain in due course. We just have to wait, I guess' She turns to the fire on which what's left of Aurora's body turns to ash.

'Thanks for trusting me,' she says softly.

A spirit splits like a lazy mist as the ashes cascade and the fire settles. It roiled and swirled until it envelopes Insistence, soaking into the new queen like rain after a dry week—all Aurora's lore, and that of all those who lived before her.

Angus observes with a little sadness. He, more than many of the others, understands just how much will be demanded of her in the times to come. He felt the prophecy through her journey, like a razor blade. Not as kindly as she professes to the others. He's a strong telepath, and all he experiences is a deep and biting fear for the woman he loves.

A HURRAH RISES up from the plain below as the people witness the billowing white cloud, clear as light along the matrix web.

Then they turn their attention to preparing the day for the carnival.

The adepts, me, Meggie, Farhan and Desire, descend the jaggedy steps and passageways, as carefully as we climbed, to join the party that awaits us on the plain of the earth below.

On the way down Insistence lifts her gauntleted arm and Lucifer alights onto it, back-winging, then ruffling her feathers into order.

CHAPTER NINE

MAMA NANEK

FRILL-NECKS COMING,' SHOUTS MAMA Nanek. 'Sea people riding in with my son.'

Farhan runs from the sparring field to wake Meggie who is still deeply asleep from the vision-induced ecstasy of the night's celebrations.

She'd danced with the other women until the windless, vague light of pre-dawn'd aroused other feelings, and she'd dragged Farhan from his conversation with his companions, to tumble, sweaty and wild, on the damp sand by the lake as the molten sun oranged the desert.

'Get up,' he yells. 'Oy, Meggie, wake up.'

She groans and rolls onto her back, one eye open. She drags her tongue over her teeth. 'Bleuch.' She moans, closing her eye again.

'I'll jump on you.' Farhan pulls some of the rugs from her body. Standing spread-legged above her.

'Go away.' She snarls from deep within what remains of her bedding.

'We got the sea people from the south riding towards us fast.

'Alright, I'm up then.' She rolls onto the floor.

She falls out of beds, rubs at her clay-encrusted hair and drinks an entire jug of water. When she finally exits their sandstone dome, into the heat of mid-morning, she has regained her dignity, gifting a few sidelong grins at those she romped with the night before. Mama Nanek is up and wide awake, sitting in the shade and *cooeeing* into the distance where her friends, waving and calling back, thunder across the sands on the giant reptiles that run like gangly children.

MAMA NANEK had been Nanek when she was found by the ocean dwellers. She'd escaped the W.F.C. mines forty years before she came to Kata Tjuta.

Her childhood had been lived in the mountains on the far north coast where the people were renowned for skill at building giant wind-kites that soar so high that those of her clan had difficulty breathing the denser oxygen of the flatlands. The kites were her craft since she had learned at ten years old.

The raiders came in their deep-sea long-boats. They attacked the village and abducted Nanek and several others. The men and boys of fighting age had been massacred by the raider mercenaries.

On that undersea journey to the northern lands rape and starvation were perpetrated on the manacled cargo and Nanek experienced the first of countless cruel and meaningless deaths.

When they'd arrived Nanek was processed and left, alone. in a tiny room, in a box of concrete and metal, with meager slit windows that bled discolored daylight onto the stained floor.

The buildings of the city were packed layer upon relentless and identical layer for miles in all directions.

In the still-dark hours every morning people were shuttled through the underground rail to their places of work and returned in a gloom of perpetual twilight.

The predominant jobs were the extraction of metals and oxides for smelting from enormous, cavernous mines that pocked the terrain in all directions.

Corporate giants continued to pollute the environment with the effluent from the factories and the burning of fossil fuels, while filth and oil fires sludged the horizon in every direction.

Untreated water was unthinkable; fresh food was unknown; self-sufficiency was impossible.

People were gray and pasty, and their bones broke easily. They died young.

HER BONDED CLAN, and others that she visited, loved to sit around the fire pits at night to hear about it—seems like everyone still likes a gruesome story, something unusual—and to have her tell of how she got away.

Over her years she'd secretly gathered contraband building materials. She made a huge, light-weight, collapsible sky kite.

She and a woman who had become her lover built it into the semblance of a covered cart.

They pulled it by hand, hiding from the curfew trucks that roamed the city after dark, onto a rarely traveled track that wound all the way up to the summit of Mount St George where they re-assembled it and flew to freedom.

They soared on the trade winds, side by side in the traces, all the way to Indonesia, before the buffeting of the perennial storms eventually brought them down.

The materials that survived were restructured into a raft. Then they hung on.

Currents finally beached them on the shore close to the clan of the ocean dwellers who found Nanek with her lover, dead in her arms. She lay amidst the storm-wreck of a two-day cyclone that had lashed the coastline with a fury that lasted as long as the moon was full. Nanek had a suppurating, gaping wound, taken when the brittle plas-poles had collapsed, splintering like glass. It opened the right side of her face from cheek to chin, down her throat to her breast, in a ragged, bloody tattoo.

She was left badly scarred, and in constant grief. She recovered, eventually, by taking aimless walks along the sand, as isolated from humans as she could get, but in the company of gulls and plovers. She said nothing to anyone for months and the people thought perhaps she was mute.

THE OCEAN DWELLERS evolved as a result of the Change. They became semi-aquatic, capable of living both on the shore and within the wild sea.

They were still human, but the lids of their eyes were so thin they could close them in underwater and retain perfect vision. Skin-flaps extended and retracted over nose and mouth, and the organ of the ear morphed, gill-like, that allow them to breathe. Skin, tightened and toughened by salt and sun, was dark and leathery.

The decimation of certain life-forms at the same time and within the same vicinity had created enormous feeding difficulties for the swift-running frill-necked lizards that had mutated over successive generations to the size of mythic dragons.

Huge but placid, they had been drawn to the settlements in search of food. When they'd first come to the people left their scraps and fish bits for them above the high tide line where they wouldn't be harmed by the sea but over time, and warily at first, the lizards had entered the village.

Finding nothing but tolerance they joined the sea clan camps, allowing firstly the children, then later the adults, to ride them, in twos and threes and, with the larger lizards, in fours and fives.

The reptiles ran on their hind legs, at incalculable speed, across dunes and desert sands alike and the people would cling to their back-ridges and holler with delight at the feel of the wind racing past them. In the natural order of things, collaboration became a pleasure for both species and so bound them together in an evolutionary triumph based on love.

The sea people bothered with few words. Telepathy and empathy and open emotional honesty were their ways of communication. The only lengthy dialogue they undertook was through song and story – songs and stories of survival, of memory, of passion, of death, of living with the sun and moon and wind and sea, and with each other and the giant, lovely lizards that would lie by the fires being stroked and scratched.

Nanek took months to heal, but eventually, she'd gone to them one night at their fires, and told them about what had happened—who she'd been, and what she'd known—before coming here.

In the morning she was brought to the ocean by the women where they washed her of the past. Then she learned their ways. She never returned to the mountains to find out what had happened there, all of those years ago. Instead, she became a speaking link with people living in places far from the sea.

Her time with them was over when she met Bill at one of the gatherings at Kata Tjuta. He was a blacksmith and a piper, the only man she would ever relax around. She moved into his camp in the caves at the base of Redrock, and when her people departed she stayed on. He ended up loving her till the day he'd caught the black lung, and died, a dozen years after they'd met. They had one child together, a boy they'd named Gallak who eventually went to live with the ocean dwellers to train as both a dreamer and an interpreter. She'd been *Mama* Nanek ever since he was born.

She became the Kata Tjuta instructor in both kite-making and aeronautical navigation.

Every now and again she'd go on a trek to the sea when there was enough news to entertain her clan there, and just so she could check up on Gallak without seeming to pry. He became their link with the outside world after her.

THE OCEAN DWELLERS THUNDER into the city on lizard-back, but only Gallak dismounts. He and Mama Nanek touch foreheads and take each other's breath, and he projects his thoughts, explaining his dreams of war and chaos.

We already know, she telepaths to him. He remounts and pulls her up behind him.

Meggie and Farhan are already on horseback and they lead the contingent to the Kata Tjuta temple.

CHAPTER TEN

ANCESTOR LORE

GALLAK, MAMA Nanek, Meggie and Farhan are all invited to come with Insistence, Angus, Miriam, Desire and me to the ancestral gate in the desert, accompanied by a handful of others, Lucifer flying ahead, scouting the terrain.

We depart in the early dark—the cool of evening—into the windless quiet of the red desert. Our camels and horses have to be held to a trot as the chill that rises after the sun sets make them frisky and uppity.

ANGUS AND INSISTENCE RIDE ahead of us, to a part of the country I've never been to. It's barren, unnerving and pocked with huge spherical boulders as far as the eye can make out.

The lunar hauntedness makes the little hairs on the back of my neck stand on end. No one speaks.

Several miles in and we come to a halt at the lip of a wide, inverted cone-like hole. We leave a couple of people behind to care for the spooked horses and camels while the others of us follow a spiral track down into the cone to the heart of a mythworld gate. A wide circular base is set at irregular intervals with single, massive stone menhirs that are were also placed around the perimeter at odd distances from each other.

Angus begins to sing his weird yoik, similar to the one I've heard him chant when he occasionally summons rain. He removes the microchip from his opal talisman and inserts it into his *prefontlcortexl*, where it glows white-violet, impossible to look upon without feeling dizzy and nauseous. It pulses with the rhythm of the song. (My *prefontlcortexl* is synced to the back of my neck right beside the atlas bone and it vibrated quite pleasantly because of its proximity to that vertebrae).

The atmosphere sharpens and wavers as the ancestors respond to his entreaty.

Insistence quietly explains to those of us who have never experienced this before that we are to stay calm and unfazed, no matter what happens.

'This is so weird though,' I say aloud, guileless.

Desire rolls her eyes and holds a finger to her lips to silence me, Miriam digging me in the side quite painfully, Angus stifling laughter.

THE SPACE BETWEEN the menhirs expands and vibrates and the ground beneath us trembles.

Apparitions form – not-quite material, not-quite-obvious-to-the-eye, like moon-shadow. An unnerving morphing and shifting of species-amalgams.

A rumble erupts, and my eyesight is affected, and when my vision clears several amorphous figures are seated in the circle around us, feathered, skin-covered, inked, furred, jeweled, horned and bright-eyed The air is zingy, ozone-laden and very cold.

Ancestors. Long-fingered hands reaching for ours, ebony black, bark-brown or pale as fog, reaching us from misty days and forests of nectar-laden flowers, or the memory of towering birch, ghost gums, redwoods or pines, touching each of us in turn. The closest to me seems like snow and ice and polar bear magic.

You are my relative! I think, ecstatic with excitement. I catch myself before I exclaimed *Wow* aloud.

Wow, the ancestor says, right into my mind. *You think?*

Little newbie to the old lore, whispers the one beside it, with humor. *Ghost reckons you're old, Fjörgyn.*

Shut it, said the first entity. *Hey, Ghost, you remember me?*

I didn't know if I was to talk to it, whether it was permitted for me to communicate with it.

I'm known as Fjörgyn, and I'm from sometime, and I'm a hunter of seal and walrus and the white gummy shark. Am I as pretty as I think?

I don't know what they are, but, hey... You female? I thought. It seemed to have a woman's soft voice.

It tipped its head to one side. *Gravel-in-a-graveyard, that's everso binary! I'll just ignore that, Ghost. Say me so you won't forget when you need to call me. Because you will… need to call me. Because you'll have need of me.*

'What am I supposed to do?' I whisper to Miriam from behind my hand. I'm all quivery.

'Answer… And. try to be normal.'

'I *am* normal,' I hiss at her.

'Sure you are,' Miriam smirks, here head tipping at Desire, who just raises her eyebrows.

Fjörgyn wavers like a heat haze. 'Course I can say it.' I'm huffy and excited in equal proportions. '*Fjörgyn.*' I say the name carefully, using the same inflection she does.

Clever sorcery, speaking using a mouth and not just mind-talking, Fjörgyn twitters, like some bird language.

We stay with Fjörgyn, and others who don't give names, in deep discussion, for what feels like a very long time. She reassures us, more than once, that what is to happen in the prophecy has happened times beyond counting. That it never really ceases to happen but that we are a small life force so history, for us, is easily forgotten or distorted.

She tells us that a process of disassembling and reassembling has already begun. Like turning the page of a book, one amongst shelves in a vast, unimaginable library that makes SEVEN look like a kid amongst a herd of grownups, impossible to count. She explains that this is natural, and whereas in the past the ancestors aided us to interpret and prepare for many predictable experiences, this time was different. She called it unprecedented. Events are inexplicable, using words, if they are outside known patterns in the forever-language of earth.

Be excited, she says. *An adventure, even. Later, Ghost.*

She then merges with the others, and like fog evaporating in the morning, they're gone.

We are left, bereft, with something comforting and safe, that's touched the yearning depths of person, abandoning us.

DAYS LATER OTHER clans, picking up on the events broadcast across the matrix, join us at Kata Tjuta's temple of the sun. When everyone arrives and settles, Insistence holds court.

'First thing's the fighting,' she says, over the heads of thousands.

'Everything we've deciphered from the prophecy indicates that a massive W.F.C. militia will come here for some unknown reason, and for war. One sure thing is known, however, and that is fear, based on their own interpretation of prophecy… So what do you all think we do?'

'Fight wind and stone and sand and sun, will they?' huffed Angus, angry but self-certain.

'Oh, yes. Fight thin air,' says Farhan, tense at the very thought of an invasion of the magnitude hinted at by the ancestors.

'So. We've much to figure out. You people are all please gonna stay till we got a plan,' says Insistence.

'As long as it takes,' Gallak adds darkly.

CHAPTER ELEVEN

OUSKA

CHANGE, ADAPT, SURVIVE. IT IS precisely events that shock, threaten or thrill us that prompt evolution. Ouska became an important ally in the stand against the invasion, and long after the events of the prophecy unfolded.

While still a baby, her mother had been banished. She'd betrayed her clan. Her exile was valid under the laws of survival, if not to the instinctive need of a mother to protect her child at any cost.

Raiders had come from the north and they had stumbled upon Ouska's mother while she was hunting.

Afraid for her life, and that of her baby daughter in the sling on her back, she had led them to the outskirts of her village where thick bush hid their approach.

They had said they would spare her life and that of her child, and that they wouldn't be hurt if she co-operated.

They'd lied.

The woman had been repeatedly raped by most of the seventeen raiders, and they had cut off her hair and both of her nipples. *To remind you, always, of our pleasure and gratitude,* they had said.

One of them, sympathetic, had cut strips of cloth and bound her to stop the bleeding but he was stabbed. They could not afford compassion.

Two had held her upright so that she could watch as they jeered, jabbing at her baby with the points of their daggers, drawing blood from a dozen small wounds.

One man even suggested that it would be sporting to do to the girl-child what they had done to her mother. Until that moment silence had been her tool to protect her child. But not then. She had screamed and screamed, outraged beyond control.

They beat her to unconsciousness, but they were too late. Someone in the village had heard. When she had recovered the warriors of the clan and the raiders were in a bloody sea of battle that engulfed both her and her wailing child.

The body snatchers had thought their work would be easy, but none survived. The women left behind—old or disabled—and many of the men of the village also died.

The wounds inflicted on both Ouska and her mother eventually healed. But then a council was convened to decide their fate.

Yes, great sorrow was felt for what had happened to her and for the atrocities inflicted upon her baby, but none condoned her actions in leading the raiders to her own people.

Her existence was eradicated from the records of the clan, her child's name being withheld, as she was innocent, and the event was told to the chroniclers of the desert temple for input into SEVEN's data mainframe.

Ouska heard the story from her mother when she was older: how she had taken what possessions she could carry on her travois. How she had wrapped her silent child onto her back, and when they had left, with nowhere to go.

The details of the events that had killed much of that village were relayed to other clans so that all would know not to take the woman in. They were also told that if the child was found abandoned or later came of her own accord, she was to be cared for or returned to her original home.

A HUNDRED OR SO YEARS before the cataclysm a great war had afflicted much of the world. It was called the Second World War.

Many nations fought and many millions of people died.

Huge ocean-traveling craft of *naqoyqatsi* that had sailed the great warm waters known as the Pacific in search of battle, had come to these southern lands for shore leave to rest and to play.

The military (almost all warriors of that era were male) had big predatory animals, called cougars, on board many ships, in a superstitious rite of protection, called them a mascot, believing they could prevent sinking or some such. Animist, it seems.

On arrival at the coastal ports, several of these giant cats escaped or had been set free.

Some survived.

Their descendants traveled north, or west to the red desert, and lived and multiplied in the rocky canyons and craggy caves, eating whatever. They hadn't remained in their evolved tawny colors but had reverted to black.

They hunted at night.

OUSKA WAS SIX WHEN her mother was mauled and killed by one of them. A she-cat, queen, giant and black as no-moon, took the woman down when she'd strayed too close to her lair. Ouska had squatted down where she was and put her hands over her eyes.

The queen sniffed her, prowled around her, raised a paw to bat at her. Ouska never moved. The she-cat, eventually bored, padded away towards the cave and Ouska followed.

Every now and then, aware of the strange creature's footfall behind her, the queen turned and snarled a warning. Ouska'd stop and wait until the cat moved on, but she followed.

IN ALL HER LIFE SINCE the attack Ouska hadn't said a human word. She could've if she had wanted to. Her mother'd chatted away, describing this or that, telling tales of her own past; sometimes yelling at her daughter in fits of rage.

Somewhere within Ouska's memory was the knowledge of what'd happened to her and that her mother had a part in it.

So Ouska didn't mourn the death. She tracked the she-cat for no other reason than the need for company.

She'd watched her mother kill animals and birds and fish for food, so recognizing her mother's corpse had basically the same effect on her.

She followed the cat to her cave and sat to one side of the entrance looking in. She heard the *rowl, rowl* of kittens before even her eyes adjusted to the gloomy interior.

'*!*' she thought, squirming her way through the entrance. The mother cat growled and snarled a warning at the intruder and swept at her with claws extended. She didn't kill the child as she felt no threat. Ouska snapped back against the wall. She stayed there and waited.

At nightfall, the queen left the cave, unconcerned with the child. Ouska crept from her cramped position against the wall and crawled over to the five spotted kittens laying curled and purring in a tangled heap. She joined them. She was hungry but tired. She slept.

When the night-black cougar returned dragging a kill between her legs she found her babies entangled with Ouska. Other than a slightly alien aroma that was not cat, the child smelled strongly of her own offspring.

The kittens woke at the smell of blood and fought and scrambled, as kittens do, to sink tooth and claw into the carcass as though they'd never been fed before in their lives. Ouska was with them, sucking the tender meat to, drinking from the mother when all were sated, and falling back to sleep in warm contentment with the other children.

She was not to know it was her mother that she had eaten.

NINE YEARS LATER OUSKA WAS living and hunting with sixth generation pumas with one enormous male, from that first litter, as her constant companion.

Hunting was for the night and the night was Ouska's time. She ranged with the cats through the vast network of cliffs and ravines that formed her world and she knew, intimately, every cave and fissure, every hole and den. The territory of the hunters was a ten square mile radius and they would cover this area over two nights.

Ouska had made a sling and a spear such as she had seen her mother use and her proficiency was deadly. Sometimes it was she who would bring down goanna red padymelon, at others it was Cat. They would stalk downwind of a herd of deer for many hours seeking the slower or younger animals at the edges of the herd until Cat would strike and drag down a kill.

They did the hunting for the queens that were confined in-kitten and they also hunted with the other cats, in a traditional formation, to strike while the animals and birds massed to drink at the waterholes.

ON ONE SUCH NIGHT Ouska and Cat stalked a small herd of deer. They had followed for hours from quite a distance, as the moon was full and the night was too light to come too close, too soon.

In one movement they saw the herd of deer stop and raise their heads from grazing. Ouska could sense that they had been startled and would have screamed out her frustration. She knew that would cause them to bolt, so she remained silent.

Then one of the runners hit the ground, dead, and the rest pounded away raising dust into the moonlit sky to blot out their passage. Cat licked himself pretending that he didn't care but Ouska was curious.

She snuck closer to the beast to see why it had died and she was almost to the animal when a man slid out from the bushes.

Ouska saw him watching her and adrenaline pounded a warning as fear clutched her throat.

Cat, still at a distance, picked up his companion's scent and roared. He charged towards the clearing in response to her fear-smell and stopped, absolutely still beside her, just as the man notched another arrow.

'Stop him!' yelled the man. 'Stop him or I shoot him!'

Ouska dropped to the ground, a sign to Cat of submission. Cat still stood, fur erect, and tail fluffed, ears laid back against his powerful head, teeth exposed in threat.

'I got that deer for my dinner, you! It's mine.' He waited to see what she'd do, but she was as still as stone. 'Share it?' And he moved a few steps closer. 'My name's Tabak,' he repeated. He waited. 'You?'

She didn't answer.

'Will you talk to me?' he continued, curious now, moving closer.

Cat readied himself to attack, but some unrecognized feeling stirred in Ouska. It was not one of danger – she would have known danger from the smell of the man, so she soothed the spirit of Cat with her own, willing her heart to stop pounding so that he would not pick up on her.

She had no doubt that the man could kill her friend, but he didn't. He just stood. Then he squatted down to wait.

CHAPTER TWELVE

SEVEN

DAYS of continuous riding are endured before Tabak, James-the-Maker and the other men reach the gardens of the Kata Tjuta initiates.

When Tabak first sees the desert temple from a distance he's awed.

'I forgot about this place, Jimmy' he says, his throat raspy from the dry air. 'My earliest drawings were of this architecture. I used to repeat the pattern of it over and over again. It wasn't until I'd perfected the dimensions of the dome that the rest of the images started coming.'

James-the-Maker rides high in the front of the double seat upon the camel's back, catching up with Tabak 'If we'd seen that we would have recognized it. Where are those drawings now?'

'That was before I worked out to back up my stuff. I was only about thirteen or so. Not long past my manhood rites. It was far too early for me to think that they were anything more important than scribbles. I didn't keep any of them. I figured they were only as an outlet for my moods. I thought they were rubbish.'

'Didn't you see the dome when you were a boy?

'Vaguely remember it. That was women's business. I mostly only got to Redrock for the festivals.'

An alchemist named Gabriel rides up to them, having overheard most of the conversation. 'We wait and see then, eh?'

They arrive at the empty temple, ascend the steps and enter under the enormous arching vault.

Then they wait.

INSISTENCE, MIRIAM AND I greet them formally then walk them around back to Insistence's quarters where Miriam make us all coffee. Insistence hears out the reason for the visit, and I take records for input to SEVEN later today.

James describes their conundrum while Tabak sits close by, clumsy, arranging his earlier drawings in linear order to conform with the newer ones, peeking looks in my direction time and again. Shy as an owl.

I'd done my research. I already know that he's never spent time in the company of women—hardly socialized at all—that he is a bit of a spook and is probably at a loss regarding any kind of social etiquette. But he watches me just the same. Of course, it could be my markings. He'd gone by the time I came, and he's probably never seen someone like me before but I'm a little embarrassed and concentrate all my willpower to avoid blushing.

'Come on,' says Insistence, taking Tabak by the arm, intuitively aware of his reticence, James-the-Maker and another alchemist from the west, trailing in their wake.

'We're going to the library before we do any other thing because if a connection's to be found anywhere then SEVEN will have it in her data banks. If it's not there, man, then it's gonna stay a mystery until it maybe shows itself sometime, of its own accord.'

Miriam leads the way over the sand to the entrance: a simple bronze door lying, seemingly dislocated in the sand, not far beyond the gardens.

Insistence hefts up the door and we take the several steps down into an empty crypt with a complex geometric pattern carved into the floor. Miriam takes a small, titanium rectangle from the pouch around her waist and inserts it into an almost imperceptible slot in the center of the pattern.

Tabak watches intently, his eyes examining the geometry, as well as the indented with dots and curves of the key, as they both hold the patterning of a matrix chip and this, indeed, is their marriage; there is no way into the library by any other means.

I'M DIMUTIVE, SO I LOOK LIKE A KID, and I got a body with no hips and almost no tits, so I don't look old enough to be mature and like the others. Despite what I know. I suppose that's the reason Tabak hangs as close to me as he does, as though hiding out with a nonthreatening buddy, who doesn't need to look him in the eye.

I can't help but watch him, though, out of the corner of my eye. I can see Aurora in him although his blue-black hair and skin coloring is darker than hers was, and I wonder at his father's bloodline. His hair is cropped short in the fashion of many of the warrior castes and it's blue-black – yet his eyes are soft brown, somewhat like images I have seen of the eyes of wolves, so I feel like I want to scratch behind his ears, although I don't, because that would be inappropriate, wouldn't it? He wears thick black metal rings in the lobes of each ear. He stands above me by about a head but then, I'm small so he's shorter than both Miriam and Insistence, but he's got presence, that's for sure. He looks tall even though he isn't. He hasn't an ounce of fat on him, his training making all cord and muscle, and with his stance, this gives him the appearance of someone taller. He's clean-shaven so that I can see his jaw clenched and unclench – he is extremely tense.

He turns to me and takes a deep, ragged breath, rolling his eyes in such a way as to make a mockery of his own apprehension. Then he smiles and I feel like the lights just came on.

Here it is. My first crush. And I use all my will power not to blush, or allow my mottles to roseate and so betray me.

I'm not about to show him how intensely he affects me, so I respond to his friendliness by reminding myself of the initiate's oath to always consider each situation for what it is without projecting my desire onto an event.

I dig my elbow into his ribs and grin at him when he gawps at his surroundings in awe. He's very loud, telepathically, and excited, and sponge-like with intrigue. Empathetic. He grins at me, and visibly relaxes.

It's all new to him for now.

We pass through the entrance-way into a foyer that leads onto an enormous communal room where many people sit talking and eating, or simply reading.

'This is the library's chill space Tabak, Brothers.' Miriam strides ahead, thinking they won't stay long enough for any of this to matter. Bored by them. 'Mosta these people have been working on projects for ages. We also have dormers for those who need to sleep with the access portals, or the written works, for the duration of their interaction with the library.'

'Which could be for how long?' asks Tabak.

'Sometimes years.'

WE REST FOR A BIT AT a wide landing at the top of one of a maze of stairs and Tabak leans so far over the railing I feel it in my groin, sure he's going to drop.

The stairwell looks as though it leads down forever. A structural Fibonacci masterpiece.

Beneath us is an intricate labyrinth of such immensity that he first grinds his teeth in concentration then shakes his head, laughing in recognition, looking from it to each of us, with questioning eyes.

The cavernous depths of data is lit entirely with solar actualizers that gain their energy from thousands and thousands of intense points of magnified light. Points that are holes drilled into the rock slab of the desert above. Each has an electromagnetic lens set into it that concentrates the sun into beams of brilliance that bring daylight to what would otherwise be pitch blackness. This can't be seen from the surface outside.

'How do you stop the sand from covering the lenses?' Tabak, the scientist-trained mind is so stimulated by this newly acquired technology he has to stop himself from laughing.

'The sand can't adhere to the chelodium magnets,' Miriam explains, 'and each aperture is lined with chelodium that works like the opposite of iron-filings to a magnet: a simple law of attraction and repulsion. The sand that builds up around the holes obscures them from observation anyway, so a dual purpose is achieved.'

'What's chelodium?' asks Tabak.

'And where's it come from?' asks James-the-Maker, silent until then, suddenly very aware of how distant from recent technological advances the western land's alchemery seems, and how lax the brothers have been, over the recent years, at keeping in contact with others. He and Tabak exchange looks of agreement and frustration.

'The entrances to mythworld. When an Ancestral gate activates, the rocks around it are coated in a fine yellow powder. When compressed under intense heat this dust liquefies, and when it subsequently cools it transmutes itself into the chelodium gel, in which phase it remains until it comes into contact with specifically conductive metals.'

'People used to power through wind generation,' continues Insistence, 'but mercenaries came here from beyond the ocean to the north several decades ago, and destroyed them. They didn't know there was a library – they couldn't glean their function at all – so all was well when the territory was defended but we were two years in darkness, our realm of words and information illuminated by torchlight while the techs did their work.'

'Chelodium had been in use for ages, deflecting the sand from the gardens,' Miriam continued. 'Then Angus discovered its practicality at solar-powered sights.'

Like uranium, from Kakadu. Legend! thinks Tabak, and he stores the information away for later experimentation in his own laboratories.

James determines, at that moment, to defer from his astronomical observational duties for long enough to become acquainted with other alchemeries; he isn't the only one of these men to feel so inclined.

'It then solidifies,' continues Insistence, not once losing her train of thought despite their mind-chatter, 'into a shiny coating that bonds with the metal at the molecular level, and thenceforth transforms itself into a repellent around which nothing that is not fixed can remain.'

'Hence, holding the lenses but distracting the sand.' James-the-Maker is thrilled.

'Exquisite, isn't it?' Insistence says, 'And it tests zero minus three on the toxicity graph analyzers. It's harmless.'

Tabak looks down the abyss of staircase below them.

Insistence likes him. We all do. He's quick. His mind processes information rapidly and his mental background circuitry begins dissecting and synergizing it, so clearly that it was beautiful to telepath with his field.

Insistence homes in on his thoughts and questions before he has a chance to verbalize them.

'The center of our labyrinth is as like the center of a spiral shell,' helping him, through empathy, to understand the layout of the whole place.

'Oh, like the *golden ratio*?'

'The same. The library tunnels for miles into the body of earth and is probably as wide as it is deep, although the exact size had never been fully mapped, for labyrinth it is, even though every nook, and the direction to it, has been mapped by SEVEN.

Tabak leans precariously over the railing, testing himself against the fear of falling.

'The rooms emulate the eons. At the lowest levels are clay tablets and papyrus rolls while closer to the surface range from elegant, hand-written Irish chronicles to paper books of unsophisticated construction, from the occasional modern paper tome to cellular storage and external *prefontlcortexl*.'

'Did you lot build all this?'

Miriam laughs. 'It was a top secret government security facility before the Change. There is a subterranean ship bay at the very bottom, with underground water channels giving out to places at the drowned lands many miles to the south. We have traveled them.'

Tabak's face doesn't even begin to express how eager he is to explore and experience what they've explained, but I pull on his sleeve, knowing that can't happen. Not now. Maybe never.

'C'mon,' says Insistence, 'this might take a while, Tabak. We'll scan the drawings into SEVEN's mainframe. It'll dissect and interface all components of your work and will compare it to all other information within the data recall function.

'What it'll do, when it discovers similarities within its neurals is to intersect it with all preexisting data. Work that transcends what it temporarily considers its own limitations. To do this it will fracture all the recognized variants into an infinitude of possibilities, mathematically, using software that it created for itself, and it will seek their images from within that infinite geometry.

'We'll find you meaning, my new friend, although a quantum rearrangement of purpose may need to be found that could be utterly challenging from the standpoint of the present diagrams.

'On the other hand,' she smiles wryly, 'the answers may be simple. Everything can mean nothing, ya know. We'll see, won't we?'

We bring them to one of the alcoves in which a virtual intelligence display bank surrounds a simple input/display holographic pad.

Insistence gathers Tabak's data tablet and plugs it them onto the laser imager that scans all the pages simultaneously. She hands him a headset and he plugs it into his digital implant.

The computer discerns, dissects, overlays, interfaces and compares. The visual display bank presents articulated reactions as it browses the entirety of its stored data. From works of Sumerian cuneiform, through the pictograms of the Maya, to advanced mathematics and physics; from aeronuclear dynamic radiation imaging to the most intricate compilations and strategies of chess it ranged, seeking all relevant comparison.

'This is gonna take longer than just a little while,' yawns Miriam.

'What say we introduce these people to the residents?

'Oh, yes,' exclaims James-the-Maker, who loves to meet new people, especially women.

Tabak pulls the off the headphones, grinning. 'Jimmy! Keep your dick in your pants, love.'

James-the-Maker is horrified and embarrassed. He leaves the cubicle without a word. Tabak, unabashed, says to the rest of us: "Is it offensive if I don't come?' I'd really like to stay and be part of this.'

Without waiting for an answer he dumps the headphones onto the bench and settles into his chair, snapping the probe from the umbilical filament of SEVEN's data access portal into his own *prefontlcortexl*, all the better to be a part of the proceedings.

I wonder if he's a brat, or just as weird as the data on him alludes to.

SEVEN IS ONE OF ONLY A FEW advanced sensate computer hybrids ever successfully born. These transformed computers are quasi-molecular, semi-sentient and completely self-sufficient. They are radially linked to both metaphysical, geomantic, electromagnetic self-centered geothermal sources of available energy both from beneath the desert substrate and the solar power actualizers above.

The reactor is capable of thought and empathy, independent of both its available data and that of any mind that links with it, having been programmed on knowledge gained from linking with the matrix itself. It absorbs the essence of anyone or anything that it encounters... it brings to sentience, for its own sake, any and all information – it experiences it as a kind of pleasure, perhaps similar to that of other sentient life. No one is quite sure. It 'falls in love' with all that it encounters.

Where the computers of *naqoyqatsi* had had no life-force, these current entities can emit emotion relative to knowledge to which they have access. They can argue their own logic transcending, at times, their own seeming limit of function. At such times all within their vicinity will experience an almost orgasmic facsimile of ecstasy vibrate through them as the computers energize their entire immediate atmosphere with their peculiar celebration of existence.

Each has its own personality, and the initiates charged with maintaining SEVEN in perfect working order are very fond of the library's system, as it was specifically set up to express itself in whatever language it desires, and with as much, or as little, enthusiasm as the data raised within its *mind* evokes.

Transcention of limitation-estimation function! Peculiar celebration of being. Interactively shared orgasmic ecstasy.

METAMORPHOSIS COMPLETE would flash onto every screen within the labyrinth, interrupting any work being input or accessed in the foreground, on the occasions it resolves encounters with its own intelligence.

The system shuts down while it experiences a three minute contemplation, of its own devising, thanking its own concept of a universal mind.

TABAK IS ENCHANTED AS the computer linked with his presence.

FASCINATING flashed intermittently.

Or LOOK OUT! LOOK OUT! INTERCODED DATA IRRELEVANT and Tabak watches and listens as the computer argues with itself over the illogic of its own assumptions:

WHAT?

INTERCODED DATA IRRELEVANT.

INACCURATE ASSUMPTION.

WHAT?

INACCURATE ASSUMPTION.

WHY?

NOTHING IS IRRELEVANT.

WELL?

DIVE! DIVE!

RE-EVALUATE PROBABILITY OVER-RIDE?

AESTHETICALLY BEGUN.

FASCINATING!

SEVEN's thought algorithms erupt onto the screen, and into his brain, every few minutes, and Tabak's first encounter with a non-organic, semi-sentient self-consciousness transforms him and gives him renewed faith in himself as it honors him with the occasional negative ion blasts. It is clearly enjoying itself as a result of his work.

It emits a sound either like white noise or a chuckle, as it reacts to Tabak's own changes to earlier mistakes.

Once it sends out a shocked emotion of awe as it passed over a miniscule, but correct, particle of its own being, mirrored in his mathematics.

HELLO ME flashes briefly onto the screen and into his mind. Then he senses regret as it passes itself by.

Finally, a holographic word fills the space of the cubical, turning like a strand of DNA: AHHHHHHH

The system shuts itself down for its required three minute's contemplation, and Tabak unhooked himself from the mainframe, smiling contentedly.

The entire complex reacts. Those of us associated with Tabak hurry, worried, to the room.

He's sitting with his chair tilted back, his hands clasped behind his head and his feet up on the desktop.

His eyes're closed, and a small, impish grin tilts the corners of his mouth as the computer's empathy strokes the air around him with conspiratorial communion.

PROTO-EARTH

THE COMPUTER HAS SUCCESSFULLY – by the highest of its own standards of logic, art, and empathy – transmuted Tabak's work into a quantum entirety that is seeded within itself with all the variables of a life-sustaining material existence.

The input stats mirror SEVEN's understanding of all its recent and archival data: scientific, artistic and philosophic, pertinent to the planet with which we co-exist, by way of the Law of Congruity: mutually interactive equations, all relative to each other in equally proportionate ratios. Anyway, that's the way it explains the principal.

The computer then bypasses its known function, for the first time we know of, by raising a hypothesis:

INPUT DATA UNIFIED.

INPUT DATA NOW HAS TEXTURE OF MATRIX BUT NOT MATRIX. EQUIVALENT OF MATRIX. FOURTH DIMENSIONAL REALITY NOW PRESENT IN SECOND DIMENSIONAL REALITY THROUGH MEDIUM OF TABAK. CAUSE UNRECOGNISABLE. EFFECT UNRECOGNISABLE. PROGRESSION OF FUTURE EQUIVALENT UNKNOWN. IF ONE KNOWS THEN ALL KNOW. IT IS A QUESTION OF WHEN IT WILL BE RECOGNISED.

Miriam goes to the console after firstly conferring with the others as to whether any of them know what SEVEN is talking about.

Tabak says he *sort of* does, but not really. Insistence jokingly implies that it sounds like the computer has become a prophet (I am slightly queasy when she says it, because it's true) and she suggests that Miriam question its hypothesis further.

The computer actually articulated, explicitly, the prophecy that was unfolding. It's just that no one knew that then.

'We don't understand what you are explaining,' Miriam said directly to the computer.

DO YOU UNDERSTAND THE WORDS.

'Yes.'

YOU UNDERSTAND WHAT IS HYPOTHESIZED?

'No. Explain.'

EXPLANATION INHERENT IN HYPOTHESIS.

'Are you implying that the hypothesis is a possible eventuality unknown to us experientially?'

NO.

'Help.'

WORDS ARE UNDERSTOOD YOU RECOGNISE WORDS. EXPERIENCE IS UNDERSTOOD, YOU RECOGNISE EXPERIENCE. ONE KNOWS – I KNOW. IF ONE KNOWS, ALL KNOW – IT IS SIMPLY A QUESTION OF WHEN IT WILL BE RECOGNISED. REFER *HUNDREDTH MONKEY* IN DATA RETRIEVAL ARCHIVES.

'If it's not a possible actuality then what is it?'

ACTUALITY.

'Now?'

NOW = CONTINUOUS FUNCTION MEASURED BY EXPERIENTIAL PARAMETERS.

'You hypothesize, then, on the actuality of a non-experienced event?'

NO.

'Explain.'

INEXPLICABLE. I CANNOT EXPLAIN WHAT IS UNRECOGNISABLE. YOU WILL KNOW. IF ONE KNOWS THEN ALL KNOW. IT IS THE LAW OF CONGRUITY. IT IS SIMPLY A MATTER OF WHEN.

Tabak sits upright in his chair, smiling to himself. 'I guess I haven't drawn what we need next, huh?'

The computer ends the function cryptically.
MAYBE NOT.

WHEN THEY RETURN TO THE ALCHEMERY in the west the adepts, including Tabak, carry on with their daily routines.

Tabak's mind, however, has been altered radically by the findings of the computer and the unanswered questions that it had evoked nag him ceaselessly.

The other thing, not put to the computer, is that feeling within Tabak that there is a *koyaanisqatsi* 'twin' theoretically in existence. Something that is the antithesis of life.

He's absolutely certain that somewhere within travelable distance there is an altogether lethal time-bomb ticking away.

Several weeks after coming home Tabak has a dream; an ancient dream that upon waking he recalls from his childhood years as a recurring nightmare:

Here I am running from a group of newspaper reporters. They are yelling at me, accusing me of manipulating the public mind; accusing me of possessing knowledge of undisclosed weapons of mass destruction; knowledge of undisclosed contact with an alien intelligence; knowledge of environmental damage resultant from weather-pattern interference.

They're taking photos of me which is a thing that I fear, for in the dream it is important that I remain anonymous.

I'm still running when I reach a double gate built into a tall, wire-mesh fence that has rolls of razor-wire at both top and bottom. A sign on the gate reads NO UNAUTHORISED ENTRY. MILITARY PERSONNEL ONLY.

I call out to the guards inside the gates and they trip the lock. I am obviously well known to them. I ask to see the president and they lead me to a tall, concrete building with massive steel doors.

We enter a chamber like an exalted and enormous bunker. A gaunt, emaciated figure sits at the head of a conference table. He looks like the hierophant in the tarot cards, with rosy skin and neat gray hair, a benevolent, blue-eyed smile that unnerves me utterly and a silly conical hat. I hurry to him and say, Mr. President, you lied to me. You told me that I was safe now – that they wouldn't ask me questions about my work.

Empty the vessels, then, as was ordained by god, he replies.

You told me they were destroyed, I say. I'm trying to stay calm, but I figure it's way too late for that. My skin tingles and I break into a sweat.

Empty the vessels, he continues, jollily. Take them to the sea and whee... And he and his companions, black-robed men with gold chains hanging from their necks, their bald heads glistening with oil, vomit all over the room, laughing in between retching.

What are they doing? I yell, disgusted.

Acts of penance, dear chappy, and also a rather spiffing way to stay lean don't you know? Fashion, dear boy. Clothes maketh the man!

Death is the way to prevent sin, says a tall, skeletal man in scarlet robes I hadn't seen until now. You see to the seas and we'll see to the skies, amen.

I'm to take two vials of toxic flora and drop them into the nearest storm-water outlet where they will make their own way to the oceans of the world, as long as I do this thing in a coastal city. The bacterium can survive and multiply in any water, whether sea-water, through evaporation into rain, river, puddle, dam or reservoir. The flora, having once begun its reproductive cycle, is virtually indestructible as long as it had an aquatic benefactor to act as host, including water-dominant life forms. I'm told to go to Adelaide.

Tabak wakes lathered in sweat, his heart pounding.

CHAPTER THIRTEEN

DREAMING REAL

TABAK HAD HIS ANSWER. OR PART of it. The other two sides – the other twin – were to come later, from the prophecy.

He departed the alchemery the following night with books, recording instruments, maps, food, a few clothes, his sword and bow and a blessing from James-the-Maker.

He was supplied with two of the very finest camels; one to transport him and one to transport his belongings and whatever he might find on his pilgrimage.

Tabak didn't know whether the defense installation in his dream was even real, let alone still standing. Even trusting in its existence he was unsure as to its exact location before the earth had shifted on its axis, but old maps from *naqoyqatsi* gave him a good indication of the general area in which to search. It took him months to find.

It was like in the dream with only minimal differences, one was that the installation itself was a long way from the fence.

The imposing security gate was so rusty that the hinges on one side gave way under his push and crashed into the dirt.

He walked for several miles along a dusty, weed-grown road. Barracks and shops showed window displays of the refuse of ancient, long-dead consumerism. And still, he walked.

Ahead of him was—to Tabak's mind—an extraordinarily tall

building. Light from a washed-out sunlight reflected off hundreds of mirrored surfaces.

The building was solid and intact. Inside the foyer was a counter, old seating, the machinery of one obsolete kind or another, and many metal panels framed one wall; that seemed to be doors, closed with the exception of two. He peered into one of these and was perplexed to see that it was a small, box-like room with nothing in it. On the wall was a system of buttons that displayed the numbers from one to fifteen and the letter U on a green background, and D on a red background. Tabak pushed buttons at random but nothing happened.

He walked back to the counter for perspective.

Behind it was another door. One with a handle. He pushed it open.

Stepping through Tabak was assaulted with light. Fluorescence was understood through his study of the power-systems of the era before the cataclysm, but he had never experienced it personally and its harsh whiteness was blinding.

Somewhere within the building, a back-up system was still active and that could only mean that sectors of the facility were still operational.

Stairs towered above him and disappeared into the depths below him. He proceeded to climb.

Hours passed as Tabak explored. Each door, atop each section of stair, led to a similar layout – desks, chairs, data-input facilities, brittle paper, photocopiers audio-visual equipment, dead laptops and cell phones, and electrical machinery of one kind or another.

He eventually emerged onto the roof of the building. His legs were like jelly from the strain of the climb and sweat dripped down his back and from his hair into his eyes. He turned in slow circles looking out over miles of barrenness. He sighed, sat down and pulled food and water from his pack.

Down, then, I got to go down, he thought. *At least, legs, you'll be happier going down.*

He sat on the roof until the light began to fade, then he rose, groaning at the unaccustomed cramps in his calves. He realized that the U must have meant up and, therefore, the D would mean down – fifteen down, then fifteen down again, still to be explored for the meaning of his dream.

Below ground level was floor after floor of computer power units, in white-tiled rooms all brilliantly lit.

By the ninth floor down he was fed up and thinking about sleep when he heard sound: humming, machinery humming.

On the tenth floor down was a vast link-up of multi-colored stars, all twinkling. He counted twenty-one monitors whose screens still flashed a cursor at the end of the displayed message: POWER-SYSTEM OVER-RIDE FUNCTION ACTIVE. MAINTAIN FUNCTION.

In the center of the vast room was a clear, crystal-like cabinet displaying the holographic image of a gyroscope; an interwoven dodecahedron in a pattern of purple, green, scarlet and electric-blue webs.

Tabak could find no way to open the cabinet. It was the source of the humming, and deep within himself was the understanding that this hermetically sealed box held the power source for the installation. He pushed at the cabinet and it moved gently away from him. On examination he discovered that it was not fixed to the floor but hovered on a self-generated cushion of air about four centimeters above ground level.

Tabak determined to take it with him when he left; this would go to the brothers. They would enjoy exploring its potential.

He went back through the door of this level and continued his descent to the lower floors where he found evidence of biological and scientific research.

The fifteenth level down was a fully self-contained residence with dining and kitchen cubicles, bathroom, bedrooms, and recreational facilities. There were two monitors: one displaying the same message as those on the tenth floor and the other showing the cryptic message: FULFIL REQUEST ON ENTER OR DEP ABORT FOR RETURN TO PROGRAM MENU.

None of the living arrangements of this sector allowed any privacy whatsoever. No doors. There was only the metal panel familiar to each level with the letters U and D displayed to their left, except that this one had U only, to the side. Tabak concluded hours before that somehow the small rooms in the foyer deployed the personnel of this building up or down.

There was one most peculiar thing, however. Set into the floor was a dull metal plate the size of the panel, but reminiscent of the bronze door of the desert library.

No matter how Tabak tried, he could not open it.

With nothing more to see and nothing else to find he sat at the console displaying the unknown request and thought very hard about whether or not to push the ENTER key.

The worst I can do is to blow everything up. He depressed the key.

The metal plate set into the floor slid open with a soft whoosh.

Steps led down into a crypt-like, dimly lit chamber. A jagged crack had formed on one of the walls and water was seeping into the place. When Tabak reached the bottom stair he was thigh-deep in its icy depths.

A badly rusted metal box floated near the corner of the crypt. He waded to it and carefully picked it up.

Nothing else was recognizable.

Tabak went back up the steps, carefully placed the box on one of the desks and levered the lid with the tip of his belt-knife.

Inside rested two glass vials carefully cushioned amidst the feather-light shavings of some solid, foam substance.

Tabak's dream flooded his mind: *You see to the seas and we'll see to the skies…* And he was afraid.

Each of the vials was about ten centimeters long, thin and elegant, and each had a stopper of some waxy substance sealing it shut.

Tabak wondered how long the stoppers would have remained preserved once the box had rusted through and the water did its eventual damage; for these were the vials, of that he was certain.

The people in charge in this facility had meant to create it only as a threat. Sure. Like no one would ever be Nero again.

How to get rid of it? He contemplated and raged through the corridors of his mind. Finally, he was too exhausted to think. The toxin was stable for the moment.

Tabak slept beside the box.

The next day, when he walked from the defense installation, he left behind the beautiful glass cabinet with the power-source so tantalizingly within.

He left with no other desire than to reach an ancestral gate and ask their help.

NINE DAYS LATER HE reached one, where one of his ancestors waited.

In the end, it was simple. It took the toxic material without judgment.

There are always places, it said, *where even poison is not poison. That's as life should be, Tabak; I'll take these to where they will be most productive. And thank you.*

Then Tabak began his return journey but along the route he crossed paths with Ouska and the legion of giant cats. This was destiny. The reason for the friendship not to be realized until what had been prophesied was well underway.

TABAK FORCED HIMSELF NOT TO STARE. HE'D never spent time in the company of any women, and here was one, beautiful and feral, silver-skinned by the moon's light with long, shaggy, fair hair and savagery in her eyes. No clothing covered the superbly muscled body as she stood in a posture of perplexed defiance; spear in hand and with the enormous cat at her feet snarling its warning.

He'd spoken to her, but she hadn't, or couldn't, answer. Between them, on the ground, was the dead deer that Tabak, very hungry, wasn't about to give over to the woman or her cat, although he'd share it if they chose to remain near him.

He walked slowly towards her, wary of making a move that could be interpreted as aggression, knowing that the big cat was more than ready to attack him. The woman emitted soft, throaty humming sounds to the animal, keeping him calm.

At a short, safe distance from her Tabak stopped and held both his hands out towards her in what he hoped would be understood as a gesture of benevolence. She was confused. Each of them held their ground for what felt like a very long time until Ouska moved slowly forward, the cat beside her on its belly, to touch his hands with her own outstretched fingers.

Ouska, having blocked out the memory of the appearance of a man, was momentarily out of her depths; the only human in her memory was her mother, but the power of natural attraction to one's own species when no smell of fear exists was sufficient to assist her in taking steps towards him.

The feel of his hands was unmistakably pleasant and once having touched them she was loath to let them go. She stroked them, turned them, smelled them, licked them and brought them gently to her cheeks.

TABAK STOOD STILL THROUGH this exploration, becoming slowly aware of her utter disconnectedness to other humans. The thought sent his mind into a confused jumble of possibilities while his face remained gently smiling and his body remained as relaxed as possible. When she touched the palms of his hands to her cheeks he tried very hard not to smile. He waited several seconds before taking her hands and placing them on his own face.

Then she smiled, or, at least, exposed her teeth.

Unaware that Ouska understood verbal communication, Tabak gestured that he wished her to come with him. She moved hesitantly forward as he backed towards his kill. He stopped and hefted the beast onto his shoulders and continued to indicate that she was welcome. Cat slunk warily beside her.

As they walked into Tabak's makeshift camp they became more at ease with each other's company and the puma stalked on all fours, unnerving Tabak with his size.

Tabak's pack, the camels and his few camping supplies were well camouflaged to his eyes, but the other two were aware of these things well before encountering them visually, and again they became wary. Until the camels began bellowing at the scent of predators.

IT WAS DIFFICULT AT THE best of times for Tabak to maintain patience, but this he now did with his new companions. With acute sensitivity, his every move was slow, calculated to instill trust.

He'd banked a fire prior to his hunting foray in anticipation of his meal and he bent to stir it into flame. When it ignited both Ouska and Cat seemed near to panic as it had been oh, so many years since she had encountered such. Tabak pretended not to notice as he skinned and gutted the deer to the accompaniment of much rowling and pacing from Cat who waited at the outer perimeter of his camp.

Tabak threw him the offal and he soon became so engrossed in exploring the discarded delicacies that he settled with elegance and arrogance to consume them without interruption or interest in the camels.

Tabak spitted the deer and suspended it from the Y-sticks at either end of the fire. Then he brewed a billy of tea.

He placed two drinking vessels side by side and waited, occasionally turning the spit. Ouska gathered her courage and joined him.

He chatted away, pleased, despite his hesitation around most people,

to have human company. He'd done so much thinking in the first parts
of his quest that he'd eventually virtually stopped intellectualizing
everything and just lived.

He had no idea of how clear of any and all complications of mind
this had on him, so that when he talked to the silent person beside him
it was of things he'd encountered during his wandering; things of
inspiration, things of beauty and challenge.

The whole time he continued to tend the fire and occasionally to turn
the spit.

It was when Ouska laughed that he responded without worry that
she'd leave.

'So you do understand me?'

She smiled with arrogant eyes, the wildness of her still dominant.
She nodded.

'You won't say anything?'

Ouska shrugged, then shook her head.

'You ever speak?' And again she shook her head, snorting.

'D'you make any other sounds besides laughing?' Tabak's curiosity
was now epic.

Ouska purred deep in her throat and then roared an authentic puma-
sound. Cat came running and skidded at her side. She laughed again,
then purred and stroked his huge head. Cat relaxed beside her,
communicating the same sound.

I can do that, Tabak thought. He tried unsuccessfully to mimic them,
the effort merely causing him embarrassment, and a coughing fit.

A SORT OF FRIENDSHIP FORMED, AN ACCEPTANCE. The ocean
dwellers, and the frill-necks, and certain of the initiates, such as
Insistence and Desire who were interspecies-bonded, had it.

Cat permitted Tabak firstly to stroke him and then, eventually, to
roll, play and hunt as a companion.

The three of them remained at Tabak's camp for many full cycles of
the moon.

One morning, before dawn, Ouska woke Tabak. She waited until he
sat up from his sleeping roll before gesturing that she and Cat were
walking.

'We hunting?' Tabak was sleepy and didn't register that this never
occurred in daylight. Ouska shook her head.

'Something to see?' he asked. Again she gestured no.

Ouska waved her hand at him with the *goodbye* gesture her mother had shown her when she was leaving their camp.

'You're going?' He felt despair at the thought of returning to a cloistered tame life. He'd become used to the wildness and the hunting.

He realized it was time. This was not his world.

'Will I see you again, d'you think?'

She nodded, and threw her arms around him. He pulled back as quickly as he could without frightening her, the touch alarming.

She took one of his rugs and smelled it.

She indicated whether she was allowed keep it.

'Of course,' Tabak said, arms tight to his body.

She smelled it again and gestured all around.

'You'll spread my smell?' He was hopeful that they wouldn't abandon him completely.

Ouska nodded and grinned. Slung the rug over her shoulder, and she and Cat walked away.

PART TWO

SECTOR FOUR

CHAPTER ONE

GHOST | TIME SORCERY

I'VE GOT THE SAME BURNING, GNAWING pain, from my gut.to my groin, as the before It's the darkest hour of the night.

Remember.

I didn't know, then, about the net of forgetting that had been thrown over me from my time training in the ancestral caves of my childhood. I didn't know it was time to wake up and remember; to work with my talent. But it was painful. And I hit a wall in my mind when I tried to work it out. And I couldn't get past it.

I'd lost the *how,* but I knew that my life depended on finding it.

This was the fifth consecutive night of this, and the confusion that followed was also a deep sense of loss.

I tried to get past the wall in my brain without anyone's help, but I reached the conclusion that either I didn't want to remember or that something from within those depths, beyond that barrier but connected to me like an umbilicus, was seeking escape; to teach me and that it *had* to get through to me. I could do nothing about it.

I experienced something between excitement and fear, but not really either. I didn't know whether to stir the others in the dorm, to continue to seek to remember what I was supposed to remember or to go find one of the adepts wise in the ways of weirdness.

I was disconnected, in self-imposed isolation, unnecessarily aggressive, sick. Disturbed. I felt alien to people around me. Angry even. Alone. Secretive.

It could be hormonal, my inner Rufus voice said. I laughed at that. It was not so simple.

I worried over my continued ability to function. I was so tired.

DAWN FINALLY LIT THE dormitory. *I need coffee,* I thought. I hadn't slept.

At breakfast, the other girls at the table looked at me strangely but said nothing.

'What?' I asked Miriam.

'You're looking *really* haggard and your camouflage pigment is ever-so pale.'

'Really?' I asked, reaching for my knife in which to view my reflection.

'You look almost like us,' added another.

'I feel pretty fuckin' peculiar.'

'Your skin is whiter than usual, if that's even possible, and your mottles are almost green,' said Miriam. 'You better tell me what's going on or go see somebody. You're sick, girl.'

'Give me time…' I gulped at the coffee and felt better for it. And I tried to formulate an answer through a thick brain fog.

'Something like a demand comes for me in the nights. I think I'm scared.' I attempted a rational explanation. 'Could I be going crazy or am I cursed, maybe?'

Miriam observed me, unblinking in a creepy kind of way, over her cup.

'You better go and see one of the healers in case you get out of control.'

I was already feeling quite ill again, my insides quivering. Nausea rumbled through me, and sparkles blinded my vision with zig-zags. Then the trembling became stronger.

'Shit,' I heard Miriam swear as I slid into darkness.

WHEN I RETURNED TO CONSCIOUSNESS I was lying on a pile of

cushions in a dimly-lit room feeling like I've broken the surface of deep water just in time to stop from drowning. Also that someone hit me over the head with a heavy object. I sucked in air, disoriented.

Julienne sat on the floor beside me, grinding some bitter-smelling compound with a mortar and pestle. Desire, idly shuffling her tarot cards, seemingly distracted. When I could see straight I asked them what had happened, but Desire shushed me and pushed me back down onto the bed. Then they both left the room.

Within moments person I'd never seen before opened the door softly and stood there simply observing me, her arms crossed over her chest.

She was a small and fine-boned woman, and like me, her moon-pale skin was interspersed with dapple patches of pigmentation that reflected the colors of the room as she moved. Her hair was pale grey and braided; wound around her head like a crown, but messy. Wisps escaping and annoying her. Her face was angular and would be harsh were her lips less full and her pale violet eyes not so alive with interest in everything around her. She looked old – maybe seventy – but obviously strong and she glowed with health and a 'something'.

Her wrinkles merged with her mottles like the bark of birch trees and, altogether, I suppose, despite it being old, her face was really very interesting.

She wore moss green leathers on her legs and upper body and an amulet of ancient red amber, fashioned into the shape of a hawk, from a collection of threaded, fire-blackened animal bones around her neck.

She was covered in a mass of faded tattoos. I had never seen another of my species, and I was enchanted.

She crossed the room and squatted beside me.

'Do I know you?' I asked.

'Stupid question, but I'll get to that later. You can call me Sabé. Right now though, I need to talk to you about you. This is not about me.'

'Ow.' I sat up too quickly and my head hurt. Sabé stuffed pillows behind me.

'Tell me what happens in the nights.'

I finally found my voice, but it was all scratchy, as though I'd been out of it for a month. 'What have you heard?'

She recited, word for word, what I said to Miriam at breakfast.

I was unnerved. She evoked emotions and sensations that were more overwhelming than any that the night's awakenings had, and I had a sensation not unlike insects crawling in my skin.

Sabé stopped speaking and examined me as though I was a specimen. 'What's happening?'

'I'm not sure…'

My heart was pounding so fast I couldn't do more than shallow breathe. I figure I'd probably pass out again if I didn't get control.

'You're strong, kiddo' she said enthusiastically. 'It's chrysalis time.'

'I don't understand.'

'Yeah, I know.' She settled herself onto the cushions at my bedside. 'Your mother should be slapped, I think. Not leaving you with a how-to manual You don't recall life when you were little, I suppose?'

'No. Well, snippets.'

'You're not from here, Ghost, nor are you from this era.'

Now I was really confused. 'Well, that's cryptic.'

'Oh, sense of humor have we? Good. Have you heard the legends of the time sorcerers?'

'Of course. They're written about in the histories kept in the library. And I know there are sorcerers in some of the clans.'

'Not the same. We changed—mutated—when our ancestors actualized *Lorentzian wormholes*.'

'You what?'

'They're everywhere. They collapse time as people think of it. They allow travel in both directions from one part of the universe to another part of that same universe very quickly or would allow travel from one universe to another. From yesterday to tomorrow, because neither truly exit. Some cultures taught time as being a rigid thing. Pretty funny, huh?'

'What's all this got to do with me?'

'You're a time sorcerer, Ghost. Your own ancestor. We all look like this. It's not an unfortunate aspect of your genes. It's camouflagic. Evolutionarily strategic. You never know when you'll need to blend in.'

'Haha,' I responded, deadpan.

'C'mon, though, really. I bet when you were young people thought you had a disease?'

'When I first came to here they did.'

'Where'd you come from?'

'I must've been really sick because my first memory is of waking up, parched, in this room. The sisters figured some tragedy happened. That I'd blocked it out. But like you say, no operational manual.'

'That's what happens when you land.'

'From where?'

'From wherever in time you've been before here.'

'This is mad. Am I dead? Is this another dream?'

She laughed and studied me again.

'Can you stop doing that?'

'You got to get up now. Do you need food? It can ease the feeling.'

'I'd throw up, and you're ignoring me. If you stop examining me I'll probably feel much better, you know. However, coffee seemed almost to work this morning, though.' Then I think. 'Was it this morning?'

She left me alone. Much later I smelled brewed coffee and she had a pot, and a cup, for each of us.

'So, you ready to listen?'

'You didn't answer my question again.'

'I know, so get with the agenda, Ghost.'

SABÉ SPOKE ABOUT AN in-earth brain network. Caverns and limestone vaults. That everything is not what it appears to be, that we can be in more than one place, and in more times than just the seeming one. That we can always access it all through dreaming because dreaming is not merely sleeping and having inner experiences but an actual leaving of the body to be someone else.

In times of extreme need, we're supposed to be able to move through time while awake. At will. She explained what's expected. That at some stage of my life, here and now, I'd be a link between the times thought of as past, present and future.

We age relative to our inter-relationships with people and things, and that the concept of being chronologically young or old alters depending on a web which is what she calls the interwoven ratios of spatiality: space and matter and energy. She told me she was much older than seventy.

'This web,' she said, 'is infinite in its dimensional and perceptual reality.'

Everything we talked about I already knew, but didn't know I knew, like a shadow having more substance than a body. Like finding things I'd hidden then forgotten about. Or thought I had but really hadn't.

I'd just forgotten where I'd put them like a dream I didn't remember until something triggered it.

It was also a little scary as she expounded on a purpose to existence other than the love and wonder of life. That we're born to carry seeds of knowledge and story, and to sprout them. To access legends, within whatever world we're living in, and give them to people so they don't end up lost in illusion and disillusionment. Mad. Or get cocky and destroy when they have no right or don't understand.

She told me about *simultaneity* and how the webs of existence move back and forth through these *Lorentzian wormholes*... Every ancestral gate, apparently.

'Simultaneity,' she explained, 'is like a kaleidoscope, where a certain set of little bits of color are experiences, ever-present but giving the appearance, to an observer, of infinite variation when moved about.'

'Like fractals! I get it.' I'm as alert as I've ever been.

'Time's just that, infinite fractals,' she grinned.

Of course, she told me, she's one of my ever-present kaleidoscopic pieces.

'So we've met before?'

'Um... I'm not ready to discuss that yet.'

I shrugged, helpless. As useless as a kitten trying to drag a dead kangaroo.

'Throughout any of your life experiences, you'll seem to meet one person after another. Not true. You watch. You'll revolve around one sort of people, or one kind of individual, for a time-sequence – with a passing collection and variety of others for spice and variety – and that then you're thrust into involvement with a *seemingly* new sequence of people, or individuals, through either some random element or through the conscious death of the previous connection.

'It'll be an illusion. You want more of that?'

She indicated the pot of coffee.

'It's cold.'

She poured it anyway and drank it in one gulp. 'Sorry. Need the high. Ready?'

I nodded and fluffed my pillows. I was wide awake and felt in peak health. 'Well, I don't care what you said earlier. I really do recognize you from somewhere. I don't want to be rude but are you actually my mother?'

'Oh, how funny. No, Ghost, far from it. Can I keep going?'

'Sorry.'

'You'll only ever connect with people in the kaleidoscope—this infinity of fractals—who've always been somewhere with you. Does that answer your question?'

'You know it doesn't.'

'Look, sometimes you meet one of us more than once in the same lifetime, but we're just moving from one image to another and so will look different have different characteristics and faces, but you get hit you know who's who. Like you and me, little Ghost. One day you'll know who I am, just like you'll figure out who you always are.'

'You're a nasty old lady, is what I think.'

'You're gonna love me, I promise.'

She stood and stretched and groaned and yawned. She flexes her shoulders and her leathers creak pleasantly. She resumes sitting on the edge of my bed, pulling on gloves.

'Ghost,' she said finally, 'Here it is. I'm here for two reasons. One is this conversation.'

'And the other?'

'To ask you to come with me.'

'To where?'

'We'll know that when we get there.'

'How did I figure you'd say something like that?'

'I'm not going to ask you more than the once, and I'm not going to coerce you.'

I thought about it for what seems like mere seconds. I cast a line into the future and when I pulled it back the word *same* was on the end.

'I'm coming.'

She took my hands in her own and was serious. 'Some things could happen that might crack you. I'll warn you beforehand. You'll know fear and you might even want to wish you were dead…'

'Can I change my mind?'

She ignored me. She'd already worked me out. 'Know only that when your thoughts tell you *I can't do it,* you actually probably can. But that you can sometimes say no because you can't really make a mistake.'

'That's cryptic, as well.'

'We do what we're born for no matter what we do.'

'What if that's just making babies and cooking?'

'I'll ignore that because it's like saying that's not important, Ghost. So… while we're on the move I won't be much of a conversationalist, I warn you.' She chuckles deep in her throat. 'It's one thing for me to say what I've said and quite another for it to be real for you.'

'I'm ready.'

'I know. Come on. We'll let the others know your decision and prepare. We're riding so cover well and pack for very cold and very hot.'

She slapped a kiss on my forehead and pulled me to my feet.

'Now get up.'

WE WENT TO INSISTENCE' study, its walls lined with shelves crammed with books and painted with maps and her own tropical forest art. Lucifer was perched, preening, on her roost and she ruffled her feathers in pleasure as Sabé stroked her underbelly lightly in passing, but the queen was elsewhere.

Julienne sat at a wide table engrossed in work, bent over brittle documents and dried plant samples, her *prefontlcortexl* pulsing as it recorded her thoughts directly into the mainframe.

Sabé tapped her on the shoulder and she nearly jumped out of her skin.

'*Great goblins*, you scared the crap outa me.' She laughed at her own discomfort. 'Ah… can I help you?'

'Can you tell me where I can find Insistence?'

'Hey,' called Insistence, coming through the outer door from the gardenia garden, the raven swooping to her shoulder where it preened Insistence' wildly tousled hair. 'What's happening?'

'Ghost knows what she is now. Do you know of what I speak?'

'We thought she was a weird mutant child when she was first found, you know. In the desert. At three. All splotchy and dried out and hard to see. But there it was, in the lore, so yes we knew. We treated her with the same respect as we give all the girls of course. And she took to her initiation without hitch.'

'It was theoretical,' I said, dry as a deer dead all through a hard summer.

'What was?' Immanence was confused.

'Till now. Everything, my lady. I have always felt so ugly.'

'Oh, Ghost.'

'I guess you know, huh? Not being born a queen and all. Desire being shut out of it and everything.'

'It never would've happened if not for Lucifer choosing me. Funny the things that make a difference. I don't think prejudice will ever get bred out of us as a species.'

'Give it time,' said Sabé, smiling.

THIS IS SOMETHIN' OTHER THAN telepathy, isn't it?' Immanence questioned us as we walked. 'Like foresight? Or folding space? Is this an art of time sorcery? I would that I could learn more about this when the season of learning's right—'

'I'm sorry, Insistence, but—'

'We communicate with mind through the matrix, of course, but not along the time-web and there're hardly any records of time sorcerers – we used to think that you were myth and legend only. Till Ghost and the chameleon-thing. And now you turn up.'

I could see that she was all set up for a lengthy conversation but Sabé wasn't.

'We gotta go, Insistence. The only way out of this place is around sunset. Will you help us with food and water-vessels, please?'

Insistence was unfazed, as we re-entered her study. 'Okay but you owe me a conversation, wizard. Rain check for the future?'

'That's funny but sure. Rain check,' Sabé laughed.

Insistence whispered to Lucifer, and the raven flew to the roost and ruffled. Then the queen was all action.

'Julienne, can you switch off now please?'

Julienne unplugged her prefontlcortexl, curious. 'What do you need.'

Insistence grinned at Sabé. 'A list?'

Julienne boxed her delicate work. 'I have to replace this in the library. I'll be quick as I can.' To Sabé she said, 'And yep, a list'd be handy.'

'You just do what you got to,' says Insistence 'We'll have you a voice memo in what?'

'I'm onto it now,' said Sabé, clicking on her borrowed holo. 'You'll have it in five, thank you, Julienne.'

'Meet us at the stables…' She looked out of the window, 'say one click of the lowering sun. Time enough?'

'Indeed,' Julienne agreed.

Insistence ushered us from the room to have the space she needed to prepare her records, and Sabé and I headed to the dorm to pack my gear. I was in the throes of an adrenaline-fueled sense of urgency and anticipation, so I ran ahead, laughing all the way, taunting Sabé who kept to a steady, old-woman pace. Or so I thought.

A TIGHTKNIT CONTINGENT WAITED at the stables when we arrived. My pack contained simple, durable clothing, washing things, eating and drinking utensils and my *prefontlcortexl*, pre-hooked up to a voice-actualized, solar-chargeable data retrieval chip, allocated to me for recording the trek, for input to the library when I came back.

The horse and camel grooms held the bridles of three of the strangest, most beautiful horses I'd ever seen.

The colors of sand under moonlight, with long, silky manes and tails, they were slender and muscular. Their tack was traditional to the desert tribes, with tassels and brightly woven saddle rugs of blue and scarlet, with hoods, like bonnets, to protect their eyes from the sand and sun.

We loaded the panniers, and other equipment, behind the saddles.

Sabé took the reins of one horse and passed them to me. I stroked the fine, long neck, wanting it to know my feel. I wrapped my hands around the leather straps, and it whinnied like it was laughing and turned its head to me. Its eyes were as violet as mine.

'She's figured you out already,' said Sabé, mounting, and the look from each of the horses told me they understood every word.

'This'll be interesting for you from the beginning, then, won't it?'

I stashed my kit into the panniers.

'Mount up.'

Desire stormed up to me, Rufus in her hand, an unreadable look on her face.

'Take him.' She held out the reluctant rat. I ignored the offering and took her in my arms. She pocketed Rufus and squeezed back, near breaking my ribs. 'Come back?'

'I intend to,' I assured her. Not really sure. Sabé shrugged and my guts roiled.

I put my foot in the stirrup, and heaved myself up into the saddle.

MOTHER FOREST

IT'S DUSK ON THE FIRST LEG OF the trip when Sabé reins her horse to a stop. I'm lagging behind and when I catch up to her, half asleep in the saddle, she reaches across and taps me with a forefinger, hard on the forehead.

'Ow! What—' but my outrage is cut short when we are suddenly plunged into a night of deep space. Sabé triggers a torch that flares all zappy with blue light indicating that I do the same.

'What just happened?' I ask, suddenly alert.

'Lose the complacency, Ghost.'

'Where are we?'

'This is the perimeter of everywhere. You're on the inside of a gate.'

'I don't understand.'

'Well, it will be imperative that you watch and learn. You're awake now. You can do this when you need to. And believe me, you're gonna need to. One day soon, and on into forever. You're going to have to remember this process to be able to jump the wormhole. Your destiny is to deliver messages to other ages.'

'Did you do this? How?'

'Willed it. Make sure you do it intentionally and without doubt or hesitation. They're toxic.'

'The thought terrifies me.'

'Get over it, little girl.'

'Hey!'

'Sorry, but you should hear yourself. Ready?'

'I thought I liked you.'

She laughs. 'You love me, Ghost.'

It's true.

Then I hold on for dear life as the horses lunge forward, their hooves thundering over the flat expanse at full gallop, fearlessly, into that dark night.

They know where they are going so for hour after hour I simply hang on, watching what I can. More alert than in my whole life, with my head on the sleek neck and my face brushed by tendrils of mane.

After what seems like an eternal night a sudden flare of light that could have been in the sky or could have been on the earth, illuminates the horizon. It flares for a split-second then is gone.

I gaze ahead in wonder. Star after star blazes, a delicately lit sky arching above us filled with an infinity of diamond points illuminating the barren landscape and rendering our torches superfluous.

Sabé slows the horses. 'Time to rest and we eat. Soon we'll pass beyond this place and you have to keep up your strength. The journey gets long after this.'

We dismount and sit upon the empty plain to eat a meal of fruit and cheese.

'How long will it take for us to get where we're going. And where are we going?' I ask through a mouthful.

'We've left all those worn out concepts behind now.'

'Then where are we?'

'Nowhere,' she replies taking a swig from the waterskin. 'Everywhere.'

When we're fed and well rested we repack the panniers, saddle the horses, remount. We ride only as fast as the horses choose, which was like flight even though we are on what seems like solid ground. The light from the horizon of stars becomes brighter and brighter, and we speed towards the very brink of the place of their rising because that is what it is. The lip of an abyss.

The horses slow, then stop, just before we enter the veil of starlight. 'This is it, Ghost.'

'This is what? What happens now?'

'Whatever you intend. It's intention sets the bridge that folds space, and that'll take you to a destination.'

'Oh, okay. Not a clue.'

She laughs at my naiveté. "Then I'll decide.'

WE PASS THROUGH THE VEIL OF starlight and out onto the edge of a precipice to which is attached one end of an infinite number of extension bridges spanning a bottomless void.

'I set this bridge up just for you. It's a branch of many lands and times. Like ancestry and genealogy.'

The bridge is alive. Its roots were enormous and gnarled and buried deep within the rock upon this side of the chasm. It is like vine and serpent simultaneously. Roses of every conceivable color, in full bloom, grow from the vine, and ivy interweaves itself between.

'You ready?' Sabé shouts, for a great updraft roars from the depths of the abyss below blowing away any idea of conversation.

'No,' I whisper. She pretends she hasn't heard, of course.

I'm terrified but the horses move onto the bridge prancing, pausing every so often to smell the flowers.

At the other end the roots of the vines pass into the solid rock around an entrance. There's no edge of cliff. Towering infinitely above, below, to the left and to the right is a wall, black and shiny, covered with fissures, each with a ghost bridge extending from each, and disappearing into the mist of distance.

We enter a cave. The walls form a tunnel: constricting, fleshy, moist to the touch. There is no deviation. The only way to go is straight ahead.

WE FINALLY EMERGE AND the journey starts that takes us through many lands that represent planetary associations, and into encounters with countless diverse situations and spectacles that'll require deep reflection when and if I get the chance.

I intend the specifics to be available, in full, if you type *Diaries of Beyond the Gates of Time* into SEVEN'S search function.

I'll brief the data:

THE FIRST COUNTRY's *Jupiter*. We ride through towns where merchants yell the prices of their wares; where commerce seems the only source of conversation other than matters of religion and government. Everyone with whom we speak in the taverns and in market-places, is deeply concerned with ideals or the lack of them. A lot of fat people live there.

IN *MARS* WE BEHAVE LIKE CROWS, spirits on a battlefield where warriors challenge themselves and others for glory and honor; where people dressed in all their finery are now just dead, and are covered with the blood of others.

We drop through the ages of conquest, from why it began, with greed and grain being locked away from the starving, with the conniving mind of the first banker, to the era of *naqoyqatsi* when explosives of almost unimaginable magnitude and the proliferation of tortures and degradations were enforced to suppress challenge, and creativity. For the gaining of the artifice of earthly possessions. To keep other species trapped in one place for reasons of mass consumption.

ASTROLOGICAL SUN IS A THEORYSCAPE IN WHICH all things are considered as absolutes – all predominating paradigms never questioned; a place where those who question the so-called rules of *Mars* are prepared to die for the right to challenging those who consider themselves in authority. We attend harvest festivals, doing our share of working with the people in the fields scything grain, querning the kernels and singing of the glory of death as life.

WE STAY YEARS IN THE garden landscapes of *Venus* where sensual delights are enjoyed as passionately as anything erotic or artistic. I've attended at the births of both human and animal, gazed on great works of art, feasted at the tables of sumptuous banquets and danced around the fires at the turning of the seasons and the rites of fertility.

MERCURY IS CITY AFTER CITY OF learning: libraries and halls of study accompany the quest for rational outcomes to inspirations; logic and philosophy are discussed and debated. Alchemy is researched and practiced, the process of transformation that is at its root, thought the greatest of all quests.

Delightful conversation, wit and humor are currency, and intelligence considered the greatest human attribute.

THEN THE ISLANDS OF THE *MOON*. We ride through mist and moonlight that shapeshifts and changes, and disorients the senses until I feel I'll go stir crazy with uncertainty. I'm unable to tell the difference between earth and water after a while as the land is marshy and seemingly shallow. The absolute timelessness of the moon and the landscape ends as we step onto dry land that slopes gently upwards through boundless stands of willows.

All that, in what SEEMS like a day.

We ride uphill that slopes at an unvarying forty-five degree angle. As we crest the summit we halt abruptly. At the very lip of an abyss. I look over the edge, squeamish, and step back quickly, my stomach doing flipflops because I can't see a bottom.
Sabé dismounts. 'Help me unload the horses, will you?.'
Confused, I do. As soon as they are liberated from our gear they gallop back into the mists. I panic and prepare to run after them.
'Ghost, no. That's not what happens now.'
'Why have the horses gone?' I yell.
'They can't come, Ghost.'
I stare blankly, not daring to contemplate her meaning. I look over the precipice again.
'Take my hand if you don't like heights.'
'What?' I cry in dread.
'Apologies. No time to explain. 'We're expected.'
'Oh, shit,' I mumble. 'No time, huh? Okay, well…'
She pulls me over the edge anyway.

CHAPTER THREE

LONELINESS

I ROLL ONTO SOMETHING SHARP. IT wakes me, suddenly, from a dreamless sleep covered in leaves, with twigs and other detritus caught in my clothing and all through my hair from the final roll down some unseen cliff. I wonder that I'm still alive. but I'm soon distracted.

I'm beside Sabé in the clearing of a forest of monolithic, towering foliage. I will not call them trees, for the greens and the browns and the colors of vine and flower and fruit begin within the dark, rich loam and climb towards an unseen sun, each plant embracing the ones around it, strangling not, but rather living in abundant profusion; leaving spaces, being lush and damp and cool... and everywhere.

Moisture drips from every leaf, and honey from every one of a riot of flowers. Dappled light reflects in patterns upon the forest floor. But it's freezing, and a light dusting of snow frosts every surface. Oxymoronic, I think.

Sabé's still wrapped in her cloak and I shake her gently.

She yawns loudly and with great pleasure. A veil has lifted from her features and everything about her is radiant and alive. Her hair's come loose and hangs to her waist. She sits up and languidly works it into a braid. She stretches, and muscles ripple within her white, unlined skin. I silently hope I get to look that fine when I'm an ancient old woman.

Before this, I thought of her as beautiful, in an unusual, old lady way, of course, but now there's what can only be described as *presence*.

'What on earth are you, Sabé?' I'm a bit incredulous and rather awed.

'There's that, isn't there? We're here to explore what you need to know about your inheritance, aren't we? So we might as well begin with concept number one: I would ask you to consider what the term 'human' means in difference to what could be 'other'. If you can box appearances into either category then you can inform *me* because as far as I know, we are simply what we are. And even when I say that we're of the ways of sorcery, it's of the memory existing *now* of which I speak. And freezing, I'm also freezing.' She pulls more layers of fur and clothing from her pack than seems natural.

'What?'

'Exactly.'

The rest of that day is hers for explaining more on the interconnectedness of reality across the time-web, keeping moving to keep warm, and for gathering wood for the fire.

As we discuss each new concept understanding wakes in the depths of me. Experiences of what seems like a sleeping place reminding me that I *know* the web of which we speak. Clear memories arise of living other realities than this one; in what I considered now.

Is this what the computer implied to Tabak when it had hypothesized about one knowing, all knowing? I wonder. As Sabé talks I have to constantly suppress the desire to say *yep*.

She occasionally grunts with laughter (she is well aware of what is happening to me) and that self-realization is the whole point of the conversations. An unlocking.

In one rush, I recall my girlhood training, in the firelit caverns where the sorcerers are taught the ancient art of story seeding. I hadn't been permitted to remember, you see, until the need.

We spend what seems like years on the road, getting here, when only one day passes. Through all those lands and living amongst all those different cultures. Those places are just speculation. Memories. Dreams. I've learned of simply one way of perceiving the evolution of humanity.

'We never left the starlight,' she says with a voice of honey. 'And that was just one bridge.'

'I could call you something,' I snarl.

'I'm sure you could.' She turns her attention to pulling the burrs and twigs from her hair.

That first night we explored the immediate surroundings firewood, found mushrooms and wild herbs to eat, and got off on the pleasure of each other's company, rugged up against the unnatural—I think—frost.

I vaguely recall Sabé commenting that we'd consumed our entire supply of wine and that we'll have to drink water for the remainder of the journey. The following morning I have a monumental hangover, so I'd got drunk on more than her presence, I figure.

At the zenith of the day a strange, elven woman enters the clearing from the depths of the forest carrying a bundle of kindling and logs, as though they weigh nothing at all.

She drops the stack on the ground beside us, then greets Sabé with a bear of a hug.

Sabé introduces her as Litha, one of a people called *wyrdin* that live within the forests of every world. I've learned, by now, not to ask how many of them there might be.

In this, the primal mother forest, she's the first of her kind. A matriarch, and hominid genesis.

Sabé kisses both her cheeks then embraces her. 'I ask to be excused from the chat, she says. 'Need some space, you understand.'

'You've heard it all before, how many times?' Litha asks rhetorically.

Sabé chuckles, grabs me in a quick hug and then wanders off into the dense undergrowth.

'Sit,' Litha commands softly.

She wears rags and tatters of browns and greens and russets that barely cover her wiry frame. She would be gangly except for her grace. Her hair is a red riot of knots and curls with narrow plaits scattered throughout, festooned with twigs, leaves, feathers, cobwebs, and small bones. Her eyes, however, are the most striking thing about her face – one green and the other the color of a stormy sky. Every exposed piece of skin is a riot of freckles.

We sit on the ground near the wood.

'Light it, please?'

'Ah—'

'Wytchlight please?'

I've never done it alone, so I'm surprised at how easy it is. I snap my fingers and will the flame, and it comes like puppies to play.

Litha relaxes and begins our time together, creating snatches of story to which she asks me to invent outcomes. It's fun. Then I notice: the stories seem to last for hours and yet, after what feels like all day, I realized that no time at all has passed and the warmthless sun hasn't moved from its position in the sky.

'Ta-da!' she exclaims, as she telepaths that I've recognized the time loop.

'This is the true meaning of manifest reality – life, you could say – when legends abound, follow their true nature. Things unfold, girl, and not from bud to full-bloom but rather from doing to doing.

'Accumulate, with care, those things of the manifest world,' she warns. 'Hold nothing so tightly that its essence is replaced by its content for the essence of one thing is the essence of all that could possibly exist – only the emotion that it engenders, and its effect varies to the one who acknowledges it.

'So it is with the essence of the experiences that *you* will know. Relate them to who you are and where you are and to what you are doing and they will retain their power throughout the web, for to do other is to warp their pattern, and your own, thence all patterns. And that would be *Hiroshimaic*.

'That's the *glamor* of the stories, for we've created them and dispensed with them and they haven't changed your essential self at all, now have they? They've been plucked from the heart of all stories and so, therefore, they're the base note of a thing.

'When you have an experience that gives you pleasure you *could* try to hold it to what it is at the time for fear that the changes it undergoes will, in some way, reduce your pleasure of it – your seeming possession of the feeling that it gives you. Ah! But! Realize that once an event is reflected through you it's *you* that'll be changed. Each event has an existence of its own.

'You, the person or thing to which you relate, and the *experience* itself, are three, separate interconnecting universes and have three separate, interweaving stories. Each of you can add meaning to each other's life, when you're careful and aware, and that enriches the whole while remaining infinitely and uniquely individual.'

I understand. There's more, however. I know that there's a thread within her words that I can't quite hold onto, and I tell her so.

'If I could somehow get inside the words you use I think I could touch – experience – a power that I can't name.'

'That, small pale person, is my secret. I'll leave you with the mystery of knowing that you don't know everything; that you'll reach for this mystery like some wonder, and delight in the passion of its evasiveness. There is a goodness in this.'

SHE STANDS AND YAWNS. She holds out a hand and pulls me to my feet.

'So say goodbye and don't forget to bow,' she smiles.

'You're leaving?'

'Of course.'

'Oh. Yes. Of course.' She laughs and sweeps me into her arms.

'Don't let the fire burn out. There are all manner of beasts within the forest. You are only safe while the fire burns.'

'Oh.' I have no idea why that hasn't occurred to me.

Then she releases her hold and walks off, hard to see clearly from a few feet away, she's so much a part of the forest.

'See you next time,' she calls over her shoulder without turning back.

It's suddenly, and dramatically, late afternoon.

AT SUNSET THE SILENCE AND loneliness were overwhelming, the evening icy with frost and the threat of heavy snow.

I sit by the small fire bundled in my wool vests and socks, thick boots and a blanket across my shoulders and wonder why the surroundings are so silent. There's no sound of wind among the leaves, no insect buzzing, no bird or night-animal calling from the darkness.

I wish Sabé hadn't gone.

Then I realize: this is the first time in my life that I've been alone in an unfamiliar place where there's just no one.

I'm frightened and the fear steadily grows. It has me, and I have to fight hard not to weep as I seek control over this hitherto hinted-at emotion.

I recite the kata on vulnerability that I learned as part of my training: *Fear is instinct unheeded. Breathe and center. Face the fear, know its cause. Fear is instinct: face it, fight, or flee.*

I repeat it over and over until I can breathe a little easier. I contemplate the cause of the fear and come to the realization because nothing obvious is around to harm me, that the fear is just of the unknown. The deep, primordial fear of abandonment.

Yes, there it is.

What if Sabé doesn't come back? How do I get home? *Where am I?*

I'm isolated, and I realize then, that I've considered myself lonely, despite the girls and women at Kata Tjuta, for most of my life, having had no parents and being a sorceress in the company of those who, despite caring, know I'm different.

I'm connected to Sabé like I imagine family is. Without her, the lifetime of aloneness that I've never acknowledged, or been willing to admit before now, engulfs me.

I distinguish two fears, then: one is a 'what if', over which I can't do anything except wait; the other, well, the other isn't really fear, so much as the recognition of inner emptiness. A little hungry place that's been fed for the first time by its own kind, and having been fed, *knows* the empty place.

So to face both fears I need resolution.

I'll wait for Sabé. If she doesn't come back then I'll leave. I'll go in any one direction and continue in that direction until an experience stops me. That's what I've learned and that's what I'll do.

As for the second realization; cherish this relationship with one of my own kind, and honor my difference from others, for I am what I am, as are those who are other than me.

I keep the fire going.

SABÉ RETURNS AFTER WHAT seems a very long time, wearing a contented expression, her clothing slightly askew, her boots crunching over the frosty ground, her hair escaped from its braid in wisps that soften her features and blur her wrinkles.

'How ya going?' she grins, her breath misting the air.

'Oh, I've had a fine time,' Was that a lie? 'Been facing thoughts not faced before. I was in fear when you'd been gone for so long. I worked through it though. How was your space to yourself in the forest? You feel better?'

'Met me a man, Ghost. Had me a nice time with him for a little while. I sure do feel good now.'

I guess I must look shocked or surprised by her answer. I'd assumed she'd be by herself.

Sabé chuckles at me. 'Never know what will happen in this forest. He was beautiful. Known him forever, I have.' She sits down beside the fire and takes the tea that I made a while back, and kept warm in case she came back.

'So, are you going to tell me your conclusions to the fear thing?'

She blows on the steam and sips cautiously.

'Yep, yep.' What am I, a puppy? I'm just so happy to see her, I guess. 'I worked out what seems to be a single, central point of life. You see, I worked out that to respect interaction it's important to honor solitude. And to accept that everyone's different, not just me and not just from those of another species but even from our own. I figured out that *difference* and *uniqueness* are descriptions of relativity, and that knowing this destroys, for me, any illusions of self-limitation.

'Sabé, the *differences* are how life understands itself; it's how it creates. It seems to me that the differences are the art in life.

'So, now I know this, I'm free, yes? To experience life as it happens, knowing that it's right, and creating change in syncopation with that knowledge without getting anxious about outcomes... Can't be any such thing as an outcome, can there? There's just what comes after each thing happens, isn't there? Things just change, yes?' It all just pours out of me.

After holding it for ages, I let go a breath I say, 'I sort of had a good time, too, Sabé. Different from you but I feel satisfied with how I worked it out.'

'Fuck me, you can talk,' she says. I don't know if she's being funny or not. 'You're growing into your new skin pretty quick, and yes, I'm being funny. Oh, by the way, our time together's almost over, you know that, yes?'

'What? No, I don't know that!' I'm upset – shocked. 'Well? See? I guess that I'm fooling myself, then, because that makes me really sad. I'm just *talking* about knowing so much. I want to stay with you.'

'Ghost, it's okay to feel what you feel because to deny that is to ignore the truth. As for staying with me, you really ought to have worked out by now that I *am* you.'

'*What?*'

'Look, you'll know the time sorcerers when you meet them in every life that you wake up into. That's the truth. But I'm you. Later. I had to be sure I'd become me, you see? To be certain you're sure of who *you* are and where to find lost things and what to do to fix things that are broken. And to light fires with your fingers.'

'I don't understand that one bit.' I'm embarrassed.

'I know,' she says.
She doesn't expand.

DIARY ENTRY: GHOST

PART FOUR

CHAPTER ONE

WAR

BLACKSMITH FORGES AT THE base of Redrock burn day and night, the steady clang of iron on iron filling the desert with the belling echo.

Sounds such as these affect a thrall on all who hear them reminding us of freedom, and stirring fear.

No one among either the clans, or the initiates of the temple dome is unaware of how large looms the threat of the prophecy, and that past foretelling has always been accurate; always informing of what will come but not always what is to happen after.

The responsibility of the day-to-day duties of each household falls to those who can't fight. They feed babies, bake, weave, cook, sharpen weapons, and assist the younger children to succeed in the skills involved in maintaining the way of life of the city.

Everyone else, including children as young as eight and nine years, is learning the care of weapons, training with sword and staff, dagger, shield and bow, and with unarmed combat. Others maintain equipment and animals while intel plan the strategies of battle.

Mama Nanek, sword sheathed at her side, trains one company of warriors in the construction of the giant, long-distance kites, knowledge of how to tie knots and make carabiners, the care of ropes, slings, and harnesses.

The initiates leave a handful of their own to tend the hospitals, alchemeries, libraries and communications facilities while the rest of us, under Insistence and Angus leadership, prepare for war.

Farhan is put in charge of the deployment of archaic but exquisitely maintained earth-moving equipment. Monstrous machinery. It is uncovered and driven from hidden enclaves to begin the rearrangement of desert earth that will all but cover the buildings of the cities and villages.

He sets his apprentices the task of cleaning, greasing, oiling and fine-tuning the dual-wheeled mechanical cycles, preserved, but never used due to their need for fossil fuels, from the epoch before the cataclysm.

Then he teaches them to ride and drive. A cacophonous noise that drives us nuts for days. *Just let it look like desert* he tells his eager companions.

Meggie organizes the grooming, exercise and training of horses and camels, and she also oversees accommodation for the healers and medics due in from outlying regions to assist with the wounded and the traumatized.

Those that work the rites of death prepare in their own way.

Although each person strives to prepare for battle, they kept the nights for sharing. We gather around fires in groups of friends and family. We cling to one another, embracing safety and our joyful way of life, eating, singing and dancing, knowing that any day now the fliers that have been deployed to the northern ranges and the barrens to the nor'east coast to watch for the coming of the W.F.C., will arrive back with the word.

I'M NOW BUSY, IN THE company of sword-women to whom I've been assigned, finding a new dexterity in this skill. It excites me to feel my body hardening, to run a hand down my own arm and feel the movement of muscle that's never been there before. We practice naked on the training field and their bodies brown like leather while I just stay looking like moonlight. I guess it's like camouflage. Least no one gives me a hard time and my mottles, after all, add to the appearance of something stone. I feel like a seed that had escaped its capsule though, I'm so happy otherwise.

We chroniclers gather just before dark to record the day's doings and understandings, and I watch other faces and bodies change, as day after day people discover new aspects to themselves through these new experiences.

I take more and more time with Tabak, our differences drawing us close. Learning touch, A hand, a caress, lips. Is this love? He rarely talks, which suits me fine. When he does it's sometimes of his childhood—the loneliness—long before we met. He shows me the diagrams that continue to haunt him. I confide in him what I've learned about time, the wormholes, the mother forests, other worlds and what I've experienced there.

There's a kind of deep acceptance between everybody. A readiness, but also an electric sizzle of fear at something unknown in lifetimes.

THEN COMES THE NIGHT THAT MARKS the transition from preparation to inevitability. Miriam, Tabak and I are sitting at the central hearth fire with Meggie, Farhan, and about thirty others, eating and talking, when a harper comes and stands beside Meggie. As people notice his presence silence falls because when a harper stands with harp in hand a telling is forthcoming.

He appears the least likely musician that I've ever seen. His body is lean and carved like a warrior where the leather doesn't cover his skin. He has cloud-white hair pulled into a tight ponytail, that hangs in elf-locked tangles down his back but he's not albinist like me. He wears bangles of metal, horn, beads and colored string from his wrists to his elbows, and his upper arms coil with the tattoos of dark blue serpents, as do his fingers, as does his forehead. The markings of an unknown tribe.

He's dressed in dark leather, ragged and patched, and a heavy dark green jacket that drapes like a cloak down to his calves. He has his harp over one shoulder in an ochre-colored cloth bag, adorned with dark blue beads and red thread, and a katana over the other (I can see the tsuka, *hilt*, poking out from beneath his cloak).

He stands his harp reverently beside a vacant stool and shrugs the cloak to the ground, before sitting.

'I'm ravenous hungry.' He fiddles with the harp bag, avoiding eye-contact with anyone.

'Can someone organize supper for our guest?' Farhan Ibrahim

surveys the initially non-compliant crowd. He, too, is wary of the stranger, despite his harp, simply because of his quirky appearance.

'And coffee, please,' the harper smiles shyly. *Sure*, I think. 'Oh, and water, and a cushion for this seat, if that's okay.'

'You want servant to clean your boots and your coat while you're at it?' I suggest. He takes my measure with a toothy grin, raising his eyebrows.

'Who are you?' Miriam asks him.

Their eyes lock for a moment, then his smile transforms him. He's momentarily distracted by me getting in his face, but he doesn't stare, gives me a challenging appraisal, but then returns his full attention to Miriam.

'Levington Blade, my lady.' He's using a singer voice on her. A piece of wild magic. I want to warn her but I'm already too late. I hear her breath catch.

'That's with the katana?' I ask. He doesn't answer. I just get one of those looks.

Food is eventually handed to him along with a large cup of thick, sweet coffee.

He eats with abandon, hardly taking the time to swallow as he shoves in more. He consumes two or three times that of most people before he gives a satisfied belch.

Everyone watches, attempting to be casual, except Miriam. She laughs openly, playing the long chestnut and silver braid of her hair through her fingers meaningfully. Flirting outrageously. He occasionally looks up from his meal to return the appreciation.

Tabak sits silently beside me, leaning so close I can smell the leather of his vest.

Blade drains the mug and places it in the dirt. He clears his throat and closes his eyes, the better to recite without error. He has no *prefontlcortexl* implant so he must just use his memory. I admit to admiration at the archaic technology.

'Deep-sea vessels landed four days ago on the northern barrens. Men and machinery – all grey – pour onto the beaches. Some horses. No camels.

'They got automobiles—four-wheeled, sometimes six—that come off a massive mothership up along the coast of the northern peninsula.

'All the men got some kinda weapon or other. No women with 'em, by the way. They set up camp like they're not going home. All the machinery moves ponderous, real heavy; machines are armored with metal. All their soldiers are walking, except for some big, nasty-looking one... They're on horses but there's not so many of them.

'Intel reckons the fight'll get here in maybe a seven day from now, maybe more. No less, though, they moving too slow. I rode the wind to get this far this quick.'

'How many?' asks Tabak.

'Eight or nine thousand.'

Disbelieving silence is like a shadow over the gathering.

'No one knows why there's so many,' he continues, 'and there're no raids remembered as including this many before. Not ever in the now-time.'

The unasked, unanswerable, bewildering questions are telepathically deafening.

ALTOGETHER THE CLANS COUNT for far more in numbers than those who have come for war from the lands of cold and grey – perhaps as many as ten thousand trained fighters – but most have never engaged in battle before. Many are too young to remember the raids that have already decimated entire clans and, even though they are taught to understand and fear the concept of the arms used by the mercenaries, most have not even seen one. The few weapons that have been taken in previous raids are insufficient to be demonstrated to everyone.

'Are any of their weapons guns... or worse?' asks Farhan.

'Some. Just the hotshots. Most soldiers have clubs and knives, some got chains, metal pipes. The ones on the automobiles have 'em, and the mercenaries on horseback. And there's maybe as many as six hundred autos.

He takes a bite more of the food and smiles across at Miriam, admiration in his eyes and something much sultrier.

He drags his attention back to the crowd. 'Our spies are like the wind over the sand and through the grasses all throughout the days, checking out their progress from every angle. They're heading sou'west.'

Faces are glued to him. 'And that means here.'

He squats with Farhan and Meggie, knowing them to be clan elders.

'Nighttime comes and all the raiders stop to rest. Least we know that much so we can gauge how long it'll take them to come.

'So far one thing's clearly heard. There's talk of a prophecy of their own – some kind of *wrath-of-god* thing supposed to happen sometime soon.'

He's uncomfortable, takes a large swig of water and leans close to Meggie, whispering. 'There's more but maybe the children should leave.'

'Children have business in all of this. No point pretending they're safe. Not our way,' said Meggie. 'So?'

He raises his voice. 'We glean they're coming for some other reason than people stealing. Intel overheard conversations in the night indicate they're coming to take our lands.

'We also overheard their priests and the corporate men talking about exterminating us, calling us *filthy heathens...*'

Insistence shrugs that nonchalant thing she does. 'Insults. Nothing. Just dumb. Keep talking, Blade.'

The harper relaxes. As if defamation matters?

'They think we're tech-primitive. They don't seem to know about the ways of the clans or our magic and ways of our power. They're pretty dumb.'

'Well,' huffs Meggie taking the initiative, 'we'll spread this information through the matrix to the people because even if it is the kind of raiding been done before it's wise to be ready for desperation as well as greed, hmm?'

I know, though. I sense the whole thing, like a worm crawling under my flesh. My part in it all too soon to know. Foreboding, but also the realization of destiny.

PEOPLE MOVE WITH DELIBERATION towards other groups, to inform them of what they didn't hear. The information spreads by both voice, and telepathy through the matrix, well into the night.

Levington Blade takes up his harp and wanders in our direction. He sits beside Miriam, takes his instrument from its case and tunes the strings. Then he plucks a haunting melody but says nothing, just breathes her scent while he plays.

Tabak moves closer to me and wraps his arms around me, pulling me against him. For a while we watch the fire dancing, looking for omens. Fear and excitement coursing through me, confusing me.

His jaw clenches and relaxes in turn, with the tension of the night and his unspoken thoughts. Then he places his hands behind my neck and kisses me. I didn't see it coming but I kiss him back.

He's only been my friend until now, despite my obvious crush. I haven't thought about how little I've been touched like he's touching me now, because I haven't been. I'm ready for it. I'm nineteen years old and I'm a woman.

We leave the fire without speaking to anyone. We stay down by the water's edge, amongst the green, growing things, tasting and licking the sweat and salt from each other's bodies. He's a bit too cautious, and he turns me on so much that in the end, I take charge. This is what the fuss is all about.

Later I think at him, *Again, Tabak?*

No problem, he telepaths, pulling me on top of him.

How am I going to get enough of this in a time of war? He laughs and promises that if we live through it he's up for anything I can throw at him.

There's also relief. We finally know what's coming and that knowledge releases months of unconscious anticipation. The threat will be dealt with. The not-knowing is over.

The preparation for war, however, can wait till we've had this hunger fed. I realize, now, that I'm way beyond detachment. Yes, this is love. I love Tabak.

Such a dangerous emotion, is love, I think, way too late to change anything.

FIRST PEOPLE

THE INTENT OF THE W.F.C. BECOMES clearer two days later when a rider comes thundering over the hard-packed sand, reins in hard on his horse in the middle of the training field and yells for a gathering of a council.

Angus is stripped to the waist and sweating with exertion, practicing with sword and dagger, against Rowan MacConnell, a sparring partner of the greatest skill, as are all the MacConnells in all the clans, their *bo* staffs and other equipment on rugs nearby, along with water and food, attended to by apprentices who wait their turn against the masters.

They're nearest the dusty, sweaty, black-skinned rider when he dismounts from the lathered and exhausted horse. Angus gestures to his apprentice, who immediately organizes other groups to run to the sun temple, and call a council with the elders, initiates, and chroniclers.

Angus asks one of the messengers to provide hospitality to the rider, whose immediate concern is for his horse.

He hefts the saddle from her and pulls cloths from the panniers before laying them with the other tack.

Angus stands with him, leaning on his *bo* staff. 'Don't get many First People this way anymore. What's your name, friend?'

'Docker.' He smiles as he wiped sweat from the mare, nose to tail, she shivering with delight, relaxing under his hands. 'Came with the crew from the southern pole for the war and staying to hunt the motherfuckers that run away.'

He takes a deep lungful of air, remembering the past. 'My people are from the before-time from around here. Pitjantjatjara people.'

Angus senses the visionary in the man. 'And you're a seer?'

'Yep. Makes me a perfect spy.'

They laugh as MacConnell joins them.

'Intel overheard the enemy,' Docker tells Angus and Rowan, giving the horse the water that the boy has brought. 'Got a lot of news but I'll wait for the council.'

Angus Ibrahim explains about Levington Blade, and fills him in on the message the harper brought so that he needn't waste himself repeating what's already known.

Docker wrings out the sweat-filled cloths, shrugging like he's got all the time in the world, and hangs them on a branch nearby, pulling a brush from the pannier and continuing to groom.

When he's completed the care of his horse and placed a nosebag over her head for her to feed, the majority of the clan have already arrived.

Docker smokes the gathering in a welcome to country ceremony before two people put a big pot on the fire to boil water.

He waits for everyone to settle, then he stands to his full height, and all attention focuses on him. 'Much fear is whispered of by the common fighter, as most are not trained in any kind of fighting, and they've never been in sun. They been dragged into this thing from the factories. No idea what to do except kill or die. Word is not for taking slaves, only outright slaughter – all men, women, and children.

'These people believe some shit about a god's punishment if they fail. Some—not many—have families, and they're here because they been threatened that this 'god' of theirs will hurt the people they care about. They'll die to stop that.

'Their mercenaries strut. Big alpha males. The common man serves them, and the mercenaries beat the bloke who walks too slow or talks too much. They are an elect few, but they *are* told to take prisoners and they are *also* told to take for themselves whatever they find of value. Sure looks like someone's being lied to. There's some double-game going on.

'The mercenaries tote guns or fire-throwers. They'll be the main danger.

'The planned arcs of attack'll come from the north, nor'west and nor'east. Divisions are forming now. They got more than nine thousand men up there. They're spread out three thousand east, three thousand north, three thousand west without much of a gap between.

'Armored autos are up front, followed by mercenaries on horseback. They'll reach us before the fighters because that poor mob're all traveling on foot.'

He shakes his head, the vision clear to us, and he pauses to clear his mind, There's not a sound to be heard among those gathered. Another memory man. In just a few days. This is extraordinary magic.

'A lot of them mercenaries will come ahead because most been here on other raids and know the sand some. But the others? The conscripts? They don't know the sand at all. Pretty fuckin' sad. They got no understanding. All fear 'devil' people and witchcraft. Fright is massive cause they've only ever known death by despair, not by war. Maybe we can scare them into leaving they have to die, eh?' And he laughs at the thought.

Someone hands him more water and he swishing the water around in his cheeks and over his head. 'Dust,' he says, spitting.

He hands the cup back. 'Also, the men who lead are butting horns. Some are these priests who just want death to be the only game on the board, but the corporati are greedy for taking whatever they find that they consider worthy of their word for wealth, even some of *them* want to take prisoners and they don't care about the prophecy. They're gonna build 'civilization' in our country.' But some don't say a fucking thing and they're the ones we think know the most.'

'I thought a week,' says Levington Blade. 'How much time we you figure we got?

'Yeah, maybe six, seven days, maybe a bit less though. Be ready for less. Machinery, not much less than five days for sure, same with the mercenaries.'

'Okay,' says Angus, 'send it out. Let's get the fliers to other clans. Gotta get things ready. We got lots of work to do.'

'Oh, and one last thing.' Docker sighs, remembering, 'they don't plan on leaving, so spread *that* through the matrix in case anyone feels inclined to sympathy.'

THE MATRIX HAS ALWAYS EXISTED but was not always accessed. It awoke within the descendants of earth' ancestors at the height of the evolutional surge just prior to the earth tilt that caused the great change.

Energy is ever-present as an electromagnetic force field is both particle and wave and that manifesting thought into actuality is achieved by consciously and intentionally collapsing the wave, therefore giving form to that which was, hitherto, energy only. The result is energy in a recognizable state. Once upon a time Buddhists called it *tulpa*.

People learned to tap into the matrix by experiments with deep meditation and interfacing with mycelium-mothers, without reference to linear thought. Knowledge surfaced that was dormant except to indigenous people.

We discovered the space between thought. We allowed the matrix to access us, and from there it became easy to link with each other. SEVEN does the same.

CHAPTER THREE

STRATEGY

MAMA NANEK'S SKY PILOTS TAKE to the air from the turrets of the Redrock's highest point, the fliers gliding towards the outer clans: the people of the forest and the sea to the east, those of the Kimberley Ranges on the remaining western coast, the and the ocean dwellers to the south.

A vast council of us sit days later, just a few weeks prior to Samhain. The largest gathering of clans to ever come together in the records of the now-time.

The delegation of First People who crossed Our Lady of the Waters from the southern jungle, join us. They don't talk much. This is still home, in need of protection from human predation, as it has been since colonization in the old days. This country, from desert to coast to mountain, is theirs, their dreaming, and although they were called by the spirits of place to populate the southern pole, they tell us matter-of-factly that this land isn't up for grabs, ever again.

Then the mobilization begins.

THE EARTHMOVERS ARE THE FIRST, preparing trenches over vast tracts of desert in an effort to incapacitate armored vehicles.

Bands of warriors are deployed – those skilled with the bow and the throwing spear, those competent with knife and hatchet, and the warriors of sword and staff They range barefoot and wary along the borderlands of each known area of clan territory.

All pick up the telepathy as it leaps from one person to another throughout the desert lands; an electric force humming with intent.

The strategies of preparation are consistent across the continent.

Battle forces are deployed in waves. The people lose their colorful clothing and jewelry, hidden where it can be found when peace is restored. They venture naked towards the north. Warriors dig themselves into the sands with sufficient rations and abundant water supplies.

And the merciless sun beats down – our greatest ally. Ozone layer long-depleted, ultraviolet radiation deadly to anyone not evolved enough to deal with its effect, or savvy enough to protect themselves. Or me.

The riders take up the rear of convoys of warriors, their camels, horses, and cycles cruising in convoys that don't seem at all organized, but that is their deception.

To the west are the rocky hills and deep ravines where Ouska readies herself, along with a company of selected men and women who are canny – interspecies' whisperers – and so fall easily into empathy with the cats.

Like Ouska they don't have much to say but their mindlink is in complete synergy with the land and the beasts, as well as with each other. Much purring takes place between them, much smelling, mating, touching, tumbling and hunting within the dead of night. All are ready for a good kill.

When the W.F.C. convoys eventually come into this territory, seeking a way through to the main clan lands, they'll turn and bolt in sheer panic. They'll be set on by the beasts and the barely recognizable humanity that kill in their company.

Ouska and those with her eventually have very little to do, as the smell of the alien men is a stink that'll set the giant cats into an instinctive attack.

THE GREAT LAKES ARE now haunted by the ocean dwellers who wait astride the frill-necked lizards and range within a territory decided on by the seers and elders of that clan.

Between them and the desert lands to the north are the First People, that includes most of the Murri, Koori, Nunga, Yolngu, Pitjantjatjara, Yorta and Wurrung people, and survivors of several other First People, never known to turn from a battle and who remain resolute, seemingly relaxed – and invisible – within the land whose songlines they inhale, and who have no mercy or compassion for a second run at stealing their country. This time they know the mind of their enemy.

During the days of the battle not one of the northerners from across Our Lady of the Waters is to return from confrontation with these or the ocean dwellers. The land'll swallow them.

KITES FILL THE SKIES, gliding over the clan people, heading south towards Kata Tjuta and away from the encroaching invaders. All the desert warriors understand that the enemy is closing in. They wait in the silence of those who are at one with the land. Then we hear the grinding sound made by the wheels of armored vehicles, as they lumber towards the frontal wave of our warriors who trust that the pits and trenches will decimate them.

The urge to cheer and sing is strong amongst those of us who hear the first crashes as the vehicles hit the ditches. The ley of the desert is such that they can't see the traps until it's too late to prevent themselves from falling in. We hear explosion after explosion as petrol ignites.

Then our frontlines see what we're up against. Waves of darkness along the horizon, a vast cloud of grey-clad humanity. What are they doing? They're gonna die in this heat, are they mad? Can't see one hat.

Resolve ripples along the matrix, palpable and alarming, but also confused. There's something really stupid out there. Still, can't be complacent. Families, friends, even strangers from other clans, however, touch each another where possible, arcs of assurance leaping from individual to individual. All know they face the possibility of body-death, but none are willing to turn away. There's too much to lose.

IT'S LATE AFTERNOON OF THAT first day when the initial rain of arrows thrums through the air to strike at an unsuspecting enemy as they close the distance. The advantage is with the clans as they haven't been seen, half buried as they are, and the element of surprise exacts a heavy toll on the lead mercenaries. But then the chiefs of each enemy contingent yell the order for a charge and that sea of grey men heave like a dirty wave towards us.

The confusion on their faces – the terror. They haven't any idea, as they run, towards what they run. Our people blend invisibly with the desert and to those weak, superstitious men from the blurry lands we appear and disappear like demons. All of us can hear their confusion and despair: to them, we are legions of demonic entities. Folktales and lies, that've been force-fed into every mind, are of evil and it clouds their collective sanity.

They surge towards us automatically – without any kind of clear intent and without training.

The desert dwellers voices raise in a caterwauling that invokes intentional panic, so that the instant that the first sword and spear clashes with the first iron pole and length of chain, *crazy* is the weapon that guides the hands of the enemy.

They fight with rage enough, but that's not going to keep them alive. Their savagery is futile and primal because there is nothing else that they know.

We struggle with not only our bodies and our weapons but also with all the willpower we can muster, to block out our natural inclination towards empathy.

The skirmish of that first day is brutal and bloody, and it's late in the afternoon when the order to retreat is conveyed to the enemy.

They camp way off in the distance, on the treeless plain of the red desert with no cover. Thousands perish, dying of thirst, exposure from the sun, the extreme conditions, infection, and shock. More than we could ever intentionally kill.

We're battered and exhausted but that night we move across the field of the dead singing the spirits home, of a lake of flesh that will have to compost where it is. The vast majority of corpses are those of the enemy.

THAT NIGHT IS FOR HEALING the wounded, nourishing ourselves with food and water and silently, stealthily, repositioning ourselves within the sands so as to again reserve the initiative for the forthcoming second wave.

The next day is like the first. So's the day after and the day after that. But the men from across the sea are doomed from the start. From heat exhaustion, dehydration, weak muscles, and even weaker wills. We take them down, exacting clean, continuous death. Our better-trained people continue to front their way into the deadlier, more formidable fight against the mercenaries and many dies or are wounded—which is worse—because those men get their kicks inflicting pain, the raiding and the taking of spoils forgotten in their lust for carnage; the kind of lust that only people rewarded for depravity can inflict. Our master warriors, including Meggie and Insistence, Levington Blade who's katana is stained with the crust of dried blood, Farhan and Angus Ibrahim, Tabak, Julienne (Insistence's sister-in-arms), James-the-Maker and several long-range archers from both the alchemies here and the west take them on. Joined by all the warriors of the First Nation people.

ALL THROUGHOUT, THEIR generals, the priests, and the corporati, remain at the rear of the action, shocked and silenced in the face of what is so soon recognized as an overwhelming defeat. They'd presumed victory would be swift and simple. And theirs.

Come sundown on the fifth and final day their leaders flee, leaving their conscripts to bloody the sands of the desert. A few of their men see them go and attempt to follow, desperate not to be left behind. For the remainder, though, there is no retreat, no cessation and nowhere to hide.

The sun lends its own blood-red to the colors of the dead as the first of the survivors, exhausted, sunburned and wounded, realize that he is abandoned. He falls to his knees crying *God save me!* The man beside him does the same, and as the river of awareness becomes a flood, so do all the others.

A GREAT STILLNESS HOLDS THE night in an aching fist while we seek to comprehend what just happened.

We, silent and dazed, wander through the masses attempting to give aid to half-crazed, decimated men and boys. Not one of them let any of us touch them. Mama Nanek, the only person who can speak their lingo fluently, leads hundreds through the desert throughout the night and into the following morning, to hastily constructed compounds. It is she, and those closest to her, who tend their wounded.

The enemy dead are covered with sand by the earthmovers and backhoes, while the corpses of our own are carried back to the cities and villages to be garlanded, sung into SEVEN, and burned on pyres that'll glow night after night for three cycles of the sun.

Hundreds of our own people stopped living but, thousands of the strangers did more so.

CHAPTER FOUR

AFTERMATH

SLOWLY WE RECOVER, AND the sentries, messengers, and spies return to their cities and villages with news of the retreating W.F.C. command.

We've gained intelligence that those that fled have not left the country but are hiding out in the giant rainforests to the nor'east abandoning, for whatever reason, their deep-sea mothership, on the barren shores of the peninsula. Our spies have stayed in the vicinity of the W.F.C. men but have been unable to get near their camps due to heavily armed sentries.

Kata Tjuta people and initiates, and the elders of other clans we met time and time again to discuss whether we should leave them alone and simply observe their movements until their purpose becomes clear or whether we should drive them from our shores. Or just kill them. The consensus is to simply wait.

The seers of the tarot are summoned to glean outcomes. Desire says *They have the world with them*. It doesn't make sense at the moment.

The lads left behind are obstinate and difficult, and Mama Nanek is our only bridge. She can at least communicate with the more malleable of them.

INITIALLY, IT HAD BEEN ASSUMED they would understand their newfound freedom and that they would heal in enough to attune to our way of life. No one sought to coerce them, preferring to have them understand our ways through observation. We assumed incorrectly.

We fed them, smiled at them and tended their health and yet they remained obstinate, and they refused, by their silence, to integrate in any way.

Many committed self-death soon after arrival. Some refused to eat and slowly starved. Some ripped off wound-healing treatments or refused to allow us to apply salves to relieve their blistered skin or stop infection. They also refused the herbs used to staunch diarrhea that afflicted most of them as a result of drinking our untreated water. They accused us of attempting to poison them with witchcraft.

IN THE CYCLE OF ONE MOON more than three thousand, of the five thousand left behind, die.

Mama Nanek speaks to them day after day, despite how difficult it is for her. Honestly? She would prefer to stay well away, but she knows they've been programmed, calculatedly, and that their actions and attitudes are not their own fault. Doesn't stop their attitude though. Doesn't stop the hatred.

Beneath the thought-belt, though, can be felt the submerged natural mind and they began, initially, to argue between themselves. Profound feelings bubbling to the surface that have been suppressed lifelong. This is disturbing as individuality has always been a severely punishable offense within their society.

As often as is permitted the people responsible for their care touch them: a hand, a face, a shoulder, a back or top of the head, in an effort to have them understand that this is acceptable, natural behavior. They talk to them as though they are children or animals, softly, easily, joyfully.

Some of the younger men in the compound splinter off into a smaller group and begin to question what they'd believed to be absolute. This is the breakthrough. One of them leaves the compound, asking for Mama Nanek.

She grumbles under her breath, wrestling with her own demons, to muster any remaining compassion and patience.

She walks straight up to the stranger's face. 'Well?'

He paces, thinking how to phrase his questions. He isn't much more than a boy, really, but the dark circles under his eyes, the blistering of his skin and the almost skeletal gauntness of his body have stripped him of any beauty.

Perhaps that can be fixed, Mama Nanek catches herself thinking, imagining what he would look like if he was healthy.

'How do I ask you stuff?' he starts.

She crosses her arms over her chest in self-defense. 'Just ask it.' Her voice is like a razor.

'What's, *damn*, what's the truth here?' he yells, frustrated, picking the scabs of the midge bites. 'What's right and wrong, huh? What's good and evil here? We gotta know what you're doing to us; we gotta know who's right here and who's not.'

He rubs his face in a gesture of desperation as he tries to formulate his feelings into words. 'This outside life… How can you stand it? How long does the sun keep up without the clouds to cover it? It's so hot all day and then the nights freeze us.'

He stalks, the sweat running like rivulets from his skin, the blisters on his lips cracking and bleeding, flies attracted to him like rotting meat. Confused; the creases between his eyebrows furrowing with concern. 'We been told that the sun is evil so what's it doing here all the time and why isn't it killing us, and why are you lot all okay about it?'

'You've really thought this through.'

'Why do your women talk with your men and why do the children and you and everybody keep touching? And why doesn't god smite you all for smiling so much and for looking in each other's eyes? And for everything that you do, for fuck's sake?'

He continues to prowl as he talks, eyes downcast. What intelligence. He's worked this all out himself, even as he talks. He knows he's been lied to. He's probably always known.

'Y'see god don't like all this, or so we been told. We been told all about what's right and what's not. We been told all about sin. And, oh… Oh, fuck it, I don't know anything, do I?'

While he rages tears of frustration fall unheeded. When he realizes what's happening he wipes his face, glowering at the wetness on his hand as though it's something unclean.

He tries to stop but can't. Mama Nanek takes him in her arms.

HE CLINGS TO HER SO tightly that she goes down onto her old knees, but all power to her, she holds him till he lays still and quiet.

'Help, please?' he says, just above a whisper.

'Yep, I guess so,' says Mama Nanek, just as quietly, and keeps him wrapped tightly.

He's Michael, and he's known no life outside the confines of a smelting factory. Like me, but different, he has no memories of childhood or any memory of a family. He isn't even aware that such a thing exists. He has no idea how long he's been alive.

He looks to be about thirty years old but Mama Nanek tells us he's more than likely only half that age; that they get old real young in the north.

He returns to his friends and talks for most of the night. The day after, they come cautiously and sit with the people who've been chosen to answer their questions. I record what's said. We all hold up shields of emotional protection against the effect of their stories.

There are seventeen of them, and for several weeks they talk with our councilors who work relentlessly at dispelling the brainwashing.

Simultaneously there is growing unrest among the local clans. Carefully sustainable lifestyles are stretched thinner and thinner through the need to provide food, water, and medicines, as well as shelter, to these strangers, and for what seems could be an indefinite duration.

It's decided that the survivors who continue bad behavior are to be returned, somehow, to the W.F.C. still hiding out up north.

When Michael and his friends try to talk to their comrades they're pelted with stones and cursed at until they are forced to retreat. There's no going back. All communications cease. Yet they continue to consume our supplies.

And they pray to their outside/somewhere god for his intervention. For *his mighty hand to smite* their captors because all they understand is that they are slaves and prisoners.

Eventually, Mama Nanek enters the compound accompanied by two guards. She yells over the mass of flesh and flies, the dead and dying, that their fate has been decided. She informs them their leaders are still on the continent, and that all here will all be escorted north to them.

There is now a new horror in the compound. Those who understand pass along knowledge to those who don't. Men moan and fall to their knees. Mama Nanek asks Michael what is happening. 'They've failed. Execution is the cost of that. They have no choice.'

'They have a choice.'

'No, they don't' And he walks away from us.

They refuse to leave.

They simply lay down from wherever they'd been standing.

We explain our reasons. That we could all perish. That the balance in this country is a clear and fragile thing; we can't tip the ecological scales indefinitely.

They refuse to communicate.

At first, we continue taking food and water to the compound, what else can we do? But they accept nothing from us. They've decided their fate.

NONE OF THEM MOVE. THEY lie on the ground day and night. They soil themselves where they lay. Their bodies baking in the sun on the exposed places. Their wounds suppurate and flies gather around their eyes, and mass at the corners of their mouths.

We plead, pull at their inert bodies, try to force them to get up, to take food and water, but they die. One by one each man's body ceases to live.

And we hold silent vigil as the spirit of each man merges with the matrix, and we wait for the ones still living to change their minds.

Michael and the others watch, unaffected and apathetic. 'It's okay,' he tells me, 'life was never anything important anyway.'

He's still emaciated, but healing. 'This really isn't such a big lot of death, you know.' He scratches at a mozzie bite and I hit his hand away, knowing he has virtually no resistance to the sting of any creature here, and that infection would be as easy as pissing. 'We've all known bigger when the useless are eliminated.'

In the city where he lived the old people, the weak or the sick, the deformed or those handicapped and unable to work are killed in bulk operations. This occurs when there is a large enough selection to justify the holes in the ground into which the corpses are deposited. It happens regularly, when there is a sufficient enough accumulation of waste to create a landfill, on which a future factory will be erected.

Over the coming days the earthmoving equipment and bulldozers are kept busy transporting and burying bodies in the sand, far enough away from our camps to be considered emotionally and hygienically suitable.

KATA TJUTA GETS ITS RHYTHM BACK, in accordance with the season, after the people deal with the trauma of the mass suicide.

Michael and his friends are assimilated into the day-to-day working, playing and learning of the clans and are flowering as surely as any plants whose roots, once tightly knotted into small confined spaces, reach deeply into natural and life-sustaining soil when freed.

On a crisp, cool early autumn morning, bitten with frost that crunches and melts underfoot, the kind of air that stirs the blood after the long hot dry summer, messengers ride into the city on hard-run camels, as people make their preparations for Samhain.

The riders are fed and rested for most of the day until the fires are lit for the night. I'm summoned to record their messages, along with a half dozen other chroniclers, as dozens of people gather and provide the visitors with sustenance.

The men sit on cushions on the ground, close to the fire where everybody can hear them, and we wait for Insistence and Angus arrive.

Meggie and Farhan bring their dinner and coffee and Desire, Insistence and Angus follow Lucifer into the center of things.

'Evening,' says Angus. 'This here's Insistence, queen of the desert tribes. Don't mind the bird, she's just hungry.'

Insistence kicks him not too softly before Lucifer back wings onto her shoulder, slapping Angus' face with an unintentional wing.

'And welcome, by the way,' Insistence smiles, melting the messengers' confusion.

'My name is Pedro Lupis and my wise and wizened little friend here is Carmody.'

Both men bow, a little theatrically, firstly to the queen and Angus, then to the rest of us, and I figure we have a couple of clowns in for the evening despite their slick weaponry and because the man named Carmody towered over his companion.

'We're supposed to be intel,' began Pedro Lupis, 'but subterfuge is not needed now. Can I have some of that?' He indicates the slabs of bread and sheep cheese that's been placed before Insistence as an offering of hospitality. She nods and tries not to smile. He munches it down, near choking. *A bit of a silly boy*, I think.

'My friend here's not nuts,' said Carmody (he must have read the many faces), 'he's just happy, aren't you Pedro?

The other man continues to eat while Carmody gets on with the news. 'We've been in the nor 'east near the camp of the runaways for weeks, seeking to infiltrate their hideout.'

Pedro wipes his mouth delicately on his bandana. 'We were well clear of the forest. We'd been camped, waiting, and watching for a time that gave us a way past their sentries.

'You must understand that things were heavy before they got weird,' says Carmody. 'Their sentries were many and vigilant, day and night, and we discovered, also, that they've got these long-seeing glasses that can sweep the land to make the distance seem close. They seen us no matter what we did, eh Pedro?'

Pedro nods. 'We'd be like the grass-snake, move like the wind on sand – no matter – we'd look up to see them glasses pointed right at us. For that, we'd say *Well some of what they know in their lands is clever, at least.* Then after a time of not going near them so as to maybe sneak through their guard undetected, the sentries are gone. None. Nada.'

He shakes his head as he remembers his disbelief – or luck.

A cup of moonshine is handed to each man. Carmody sips like it's nectar before continuing. 'We walked into the forest, very careful like, but no: no sentries, no warriors waiting for spies or invasion, just no one.'

'So then we tracked 'em. For a lot of distance. Didn't we, Carmody?'

'Sure did. We followed where they'd gone, and it was way deep into the forest. And way up ahead is clan territory. So we snuck up close as we could. We saw fires, and shelters, some of cloth, but most made up of the stuff of the forest itself.'

'And there were so many corporati wandering freely amongst the clan of the people of the forest and the sea…'

Babble breaks out, and the messengers wait patiently for the hubble-bubble to wind down, both eyeing the young women and getting a few raised eyebrows of agreement before continuing.

'So we just walked on in,' says Carmody smiling. 'Man, those clan people are beautiful. The women walk around all bare except for deer boots that ride high up on legs that just kept on going.

They're inked everywhere else. Beautiful women, hey man?'

He and Pedro grin at each other remembering. 'And it was the women that came over to greet us.'

'They greeted us like we were lovers, eh Carmody?' Pedro shakes his head, shy, confounded by the whole experience. 'Then they said they wanted to introduce us to the new people.'

'Who? The enemy?' I ask, incredulous, unable to stop myself.

'Fuck me gently, what're you?' Pedro has only now noticed me. I'm glad Tabak is off hunting with Lev. As it is everyone around me bristles. 'You want to keep your knees... Pedro is it? Insistence has that look on her face she gets when nobody knows what to think or what she's going to do. A ripple passes through the matrix but I'm just embarrassed. And angry. And I can feel myself blushing which just makes it worse.

Miriam leans towards Pedro and smiles. 'I'd continue with the story if I was you.'

'I'm really sorry...'

'You deaf?' says Miriam.

'Right,' says Carmody, taking over while his friend recovers and tries to smile at me. '*That's over now,* she told me. We were stunned, I tell ya. So, anyway, we went and sat at their fire and there were a lot of people there. What you reckon, man?'

'Maybe two hundred W.F.C. and about two thousand clan.' Pedro sips again from the moonshine. It's working its magic and he's looking around himself, seeing shine but staying focused on the telling of the intel.'

'They'd found the W.F.C. hiding in the forest and there'd been a scuffle of sorts, but the W.F.C. army were *so* defeated from down here with all of you that hardly anyone got killed. They'd tried to escape at first, so the clan had to guard them. They told them no way were they free to do what they liked.'

'And then,' says Carmody, looking directly at me, 'out of what seemed like the sea mists, several time sorcerers turned up.' If I could've gone any whiter now would be that moment. 'Yeah, also funny lookin'.'

He continues to speak directly at me as though I am the only body there. 'So they confront the corporati, who, even though they are prisoners, are arrogant like they have won. The sorcerers, pale as moonlight, mottles of every color, very beautiful I must say, um…'

'Ghost,'' I tell him.

'Ghost, yes, of course. Well, Ghost, they say *Behave yourselves. You're nobody here.*'

Carmody pauses and holds out his cup requesting more wine. Farhan refills both their cups, still reticent and snarky.

'Then,' says Pedro, tears of laughter falling from his eyes, 'this W.F.C. priest named Riley – some head honcho – yells curses at the time sorcerers, threatening them with some eternal damnation and pits of fire for their evil ways—' He doubles over laughing.

'Should have seen the looks on the people's faces!' says Carmody.

'Then this big, sorcerer woman comes towards us, all tattooed and with her mottles morphing with the forest and the light as she moves. She has gold in her ears and bones in her hair and weapons and wands of quartz crystal and white wood all carved with lizards and crocs. She smiles at him and says so softly it was forbidding *That was the wrong thing to say.* But she says it with Riley's voice.'

Every hair stands up all over my body and Tabak, arriving smelling clean and just washed, comes into camp with Levington Blade and Docker, and they sit next to me and Miriam.

Pedro relaxes as his filaments of mood find mine on the matrix and we spend all of a minute deep in sorcerous bonding. And my forgiveness, and he continues. 'They opened the matrix for the enemy and linked them against their will.'

I'M LIKE A KID SITTING around the fires being told the legends by my teachers. Knowing that those of my kind live up the coast sent little shivers of pleasure up my spine.

'Yeah, pale, little writer lady.' Carmody smiles, overhearing my thoughts. 'That's how they hooked 'em.

'The time sorcerers wound those priests up so tight within the web of legend that the poor fools thought about their own stuff backward. *God is love,* they kept repeating, and everything that the twisted little minds of the priests could summon up was challenged.

'What they did was to give the priests of the W.F.C. a more powerful god. They removed the limitations of the idea of a god that they'd been taught to believe in.

'What they succeeded in doing was to have each man understand that god loves them and that's why it'd put them in that-there forest garden: to come to know it face-to-face.

'The priests said to the sorcerers *Well, where is he?* And the big woman with the gold earrings and all that ink told 'em that the garden, and everyone and everything in it, *was* the god, face-to-face.'

'I guess we'd know more of what's happened if we'd been there om person when it's all gone down,' says Pedro, 'but the time sorcerers told the W.F.C. people that they were free, knowing the matrix had them, and that there was nowhere to run, and the women of the clan told us. Said it was word for word, in the proper way.'

'So,' says Carmody, 'there's none of them going back to the northern lands. They figure that the forest and sea clan are the children of *the* garden and they want to learn from them.

'Oh, also,' recalls Pedro, 'they said that if anyone wants the W.F.C.'s deep-sea mothership they can have her once they've unloaded some precious cargo and taken it back to the forest.

'That's it. End of intel.'

Everyone sits quietly until the messengers feel quite uncomfortable.

'What?' says Pedro, 'What's going on, then?'

Minds seek to understand whether things could have been different for the men that the W.F.C. left behind. It takes deep communion with the matrix for us to understand that what's done is done.

Life is what it is, and each thing lives according to its own pattern.

No one is unchanged by these events, though.

'They want to meet,' Carmody manages, breaking the mood, 'whenever you're ready. Any moonshine left, is there?'

CHAPTER SIX

VOYAGER BEYOND THE GATES OF TIME

THE WEEKS SINCE THE invasion have become strange for me, just like for a lot of other people. I'm more introspective than ever, unable and unwilling to communicate with people around me, the myriad of alternative time frequencies like being in the cone all the time, Fjörgyn is at my back or in my peripheral vision, Sabé never far from being the voice in my head. I'd be scared if I wasn't so sure they are both real. That their company is a comfort. What's mythworld then, if not time set free of our expectations? If ancestral intelligence is ever present and not supposedly secreted away behind some contrived gate? I'm different to the other women, not through any intent on their part or mine—nothing malicious or anything—just simply. Haha, can't change a leopard's spots, you think.

Being with Tabak makes sense of everything and his constant contact eases my trepidations. He's as aware of these upheavals as he is of his own, but he's also inspired. Now he's delving into fractal geometry. It's mesmerizing to watch him draw because he does it all by hand with just a stylus. I think about the concept of impossible and I tell him I used to have wings, but nobody I got 'em cut off one time. He just smiles and says, what kinda bird?

Miriam gives me unlimited access to SEVEN's mainframe and I'm mentally downloading like an AI, writing fast, ink and quills replaced every second day.

Insistence has got me onto ancestral lore and also history, as far back as I can realistically delve. Looking for patterns. Looking for events that led up to the seismic upheaval and environmental shifts… he ones that *weren't* caused by human degradation of resources. There are none. Least, none recorded as such.

MORE PAGES ARE ADDED TO THE GENESIS BOOK. Information downloaded and translated into chapters, on the psychology of post-war stress and its cures researched outside of the pre-cataclysmic pharmaceutical industry that tended to dominate the economy by keeping people sick. Necessary research, also involving Desire, Julienne and Miriam, because everybody's been changed. By the violence, by the deaths of those lads. There are wounds of such sadness that they're going to take way longer to heal than slashes, bruises and broken bones.

The younger folk hardly rest. They cut loose on the training fields with danger in their eyes; with anger and adrenalin-fueled fanaticism.

The weather's cold now. Not even the midday sun taking the ice from the shadows of Redrock. I sit snuggled up against Tabak as he and Miriam, and James who's come from the west for Samhain, talk about the situation, in low voices, full of comprehension.

Levington Blade walks out of the descending mist like an apparition, almost like me. 'Am I missing something?'

'Sit with us,' Miriam says, patting the ground beside her.

'Insistence, and Angus have sent a few of us out to ask everyone to come to the Kata Tjuta temple around sunset. Meggie and Farhan are way off with the hunters. I gotta go to the other fires. I'll see you later maybe?' He bends and kisses Miriam.

'Trouble?' I ask.

'I think so.' He walks away, in the direction of another hearth fire.

A CRAZY WIND COMES FROM SEEMINGLY all directions at once, unnerving because how is anyone supposed to prepare for the weather tomorrow when it's like this? People are gathered in the gardens near the temple steps, their hair and clothing blowing in all directions, as Insistence, Lucifer flying above the crowd like an omen, exits the dome along with Desire and Angus. She waits for the crowd to hush; to tune into the matrix.

'Thank you all for coming, but I tell ya, you're not going to wanna hear what I gotta say.' Insistence calls over the raggedy wind. The silence of the thousands is eerie, the matrix a live wire but jagged and confused.

She lifts her chin and straightens her back, her hair whipping around her face like springy black ribbons of night, her face a shadow in the gloom, lit by mad torchlight.

'I called this council because you bother us. Your distraction from traditional duties men for this season of a year been grow like a malignancy.'

She pauses and waits for that to register, seeming to talk to spirits in the wind.

Lucifer *arrks* at us, as though we are naughty children not paying enough attention. I guess that could seem to be true. Thoughts across the matrix are certainly disjointed and jumbled.

'The northerners won't come again,' she says, and she indicates Michael and the others from over the sea, hardly discernable from the rest of the people now. 'Not for war anyways. Seismic activity is way too unpredictable for anything like that.

'Michael, you men are all fine now. You're learning so fast, about life and respect, and you've taught us so much about where things can end up if a body loses hope...'

She seeks solutions from the sea of heads. 'But why are so many of you angry? And fixated? We're worried because the matrix is changing radically, and the pattern is wrong. Like before the shit went down. Things that ought to be getting done aren't getting done. Too many of you are taking to sword and staff and bow before harvesting or butchering. And we're shaping up for a fucking cold winter.

'Do any of you know how dangerous this is getting?' Her words are like a spell. Even the pressure of the wind eases and the raven is silent and I'm squirming.

'You're influencing the web and that pisses me off. Sounds like you? Right? Some unhealthy vanity if I tell you what I really think. Well? It's poison, is what it is. Toxic. We're doing this now, and through this, we change the future into something we can't predict, that we can't, then, prepare for.

'Each of you knew that the war was coming, yes? You were ready. The prophecy informed everyone that this would happen before Samhain, and it did.'

Another tremor shakes the ground, stronger than the last, and green lightning strobes the horizon of the cloudless sky as though in response. The wind dies.

Everyone looks to everyone else for reassurance—us included—we all felt that. There isn't any to be had. Now it's almost too quiet.

Insistence waits until the rumble settles, unperturbed as though expecting the elemental magic. She summons our attention.

'There is more of the prophecy yet to be dealt with, and Desire also said we'd be ready for that. I need you to consider this and get healthy again.

'Everything's destiny. D'you get it? Your skill at strategy, your courage in battle was unparalleled, and some of us gonna live to sing it to our children's children. But can we please prepare for something else now?'

Angus puts his arms around Insistence's waist and pulls her against him possessively. Lucifer sidewinds from her shoulder to his, to pick the detritus of wayward dead grass and burrs from his raggedy plait, like a mother with her chick.

'Samhain's almost here,' his voice rings out, smooth as honey. 'The wild times. The crazy weather when the harvest comes in, and the seeds are gathered to spread about the land. Our ancestors, the spirits of earth and sky and water, the animal cousins we all celebrate, alongside all you other clans. No more sadness. Get dressed and gussy up, ready for the pretty boys and girls comin' from across the land and far away, hmm? Feasting and fucking and spiritual quests and shit? All that rocknroll? Fuck me if we don't really need us this, this year, eh?'

Cheer, and laughter, arc over the desert. All they needed is reminding. I cry a little where I sit, as around me voices are raised, and the people sing the songs of praise to life.

THE WIND LIFTS AGAIN JUST after dawn, scattered and erratic for several days, blustery, gritty, raising mini tornados of sand and dust, unnerving everyone.

The weather and atmospheric conditions are usually haywire like this just before it turns predictably freakish at the herald of the colder months but there's something different this time – a slight metallic taste, ozone-laden, that no one is used to. And it's already cold.

The ground shudders and rumbles daily.

CHAPTER SEVEN

THE YEARS END AND BEGINNING ARE THE SAME. Samhain.

Several weeks before, during the black of the moon in late autumn, the wind would usually be calm, but not this time. Severe electrical storms break up the dark on the horizon to the south of Redrock. They strobe through the nights without a cloud, without surcease.

The color of the sky turns from an almost constant blue to pale violet, pink and sickly green as the aurora caused by the severe electromagnetic storms, bathe the days in a strange light.

Over the two or three days prior to Samhain massive cumuli build, tower upon tower, filling the atmosphere with the intense smell of ozone, while huge thunderheads gradually darken.

Hail breaks, then driving rain, drenching the desert and causing perennially dry riverbeds and ravines to roar and froth with white water, and shallow lakes to flood and flow over the land until all appears to be a wetland.

We dance in the downpour and then run for shelter, remaining undercover, inside sandstone domes, the dormitories, the caves at the base of Redrock or, me, in the library with Tabak, Levington Blade, and Miriam, fully set up in the rec room for the remainder of the wild wet. But it lasts for four days only this year. Usually, it's wild for two weeks. Something's changed. The temperature has plummeted, and the rain just keeps pissing down.

On the nights without cloud the frost takes on ice and the days without rain are glaring and heatless. The sky is either thick with towers of cumuli, green and threatening or white as the still lake, the air zingy. And the desert blooms. It teems with color, and every possible variety of exotic, unusual plant-life and it seduces the people into wandering, in abandon, amidst magic. Because, when the seasons changed, from the axis tilt in the ancient days, seeds once buried within the alchemically sealed womb of the sands, unknown in written records and from some deep, Paleozoic forest, released their genomes and swathed the desert with vitality.

AND NOW THE CLANS HAVE from across the country. Those with the technology, from the islands of the Long White Cloud and the nourishment of the Arctic forests, They ride in on lizards or camels, horses or bullocks, on foot or soaring in the traces of the high, long-distance kites of the northern ranges. They pull travois, and wagons loaded with provisions and barter, food and instruments, temporary shelters, animals and children

Stalls are set up with everything from junk to family artifacts, gizmos, art and crafts, fruit and vegetables, varying widely depending on the home country of each clan. Tents for tarot, astrology, runists, spellcasters, and healers are raised, and special sites are assigned to storytelling, for the demonstration of newly developed skills, for demonstrations of recent discoveries, inventions and recipes, and updates on healing lore. The play-places for the care and entertainment of children fly their varicolored pennants high above the pavilions.

Initiates, adepts, mystics and seers come from across the continent resplendent in their richly dyed skins, their jewelry, profusions of feathers in their wild, corkscrew, boar-limed or multi-braided hair, blue dye, white or russet ochre decorating their faces, hands and feet.

The freshly initiated seers and adults psyching themselves for their first ritual tattooing or scarification, and the ceremony called the vision quest to precede it.

CHAPTER EIGHT

CONCEPTION

ON THE DAWN OF SAMHAIN INSISTENCE LIES spooned up against Angus, relishing privacy. They had touched each other, kissing and teasing and stroking, on and off during the night but their desire has been left unsated. It has been this way for them since the first lightning lit the desert horizon. They savour the sweet sensation of want, knowing that their erotic play will be sated on the night of the ritual, turning that which is sensual into that which is also magical, high up on Redrock's summit, by the ritual fires.

INSISTENCE KNOWS SHE WILL conceive if they are intimate right now.

She runs her fingers down Angus's thigh. 'I don't know if I want children.'

'Hmm?' He leans on his elbow, watching her as she stares past him at the horse design painted on the side of the tent.

'Right now is when it'd happen if I let it.' She turns her face to him, something peculiar in her gaze. 'It's just that…'

He waits while she thinks. 'I've talked about it with women who've had babies. They tell it the same: the sense of a loss of self in the way one knows of self; the extra demands; the body changes; realistic anxiety for the wellbeing of an offspring; the responsibility, despite the love.'

'That's looking at the down-side, Insistence. You're in a position to know yourself better than most women. If you're ready then let's do it.'

He knows he's said the wrong thing as soon as it spews out of his mouth.

Insistence considers him in this, not for one moment leaving him out of the equation but this is not his decision to make and her eyes are hooded and wild. 'You think it's that easy? The prophecy causes me to doubt. I'm not stupid and we honestly don't know what's coming. You can explain me to myself all you like, love, but it's all just talk, okay?'

Angus is embarrassed. He'd been attempting to put her at ease when it is not his place.

Insistence extricates herself from his embrace and rises to get them both a cup of water.

Lucifer flies to her and lands on her bare shoulder, an attempt at womanly empathy but Insistence shoos her away with an *Ow!* and she retreats to her perch pretending indifference.

Insistence sits back down. 'Angus, just so you know, there's unborn nearby. And there's gonna be a fight over who gets a turn inside me.' She downs the water in one gulp, gasping but sitting up to her full height. 'But, I'm the sum of all the queens before me and… and I'm really wary. Their memories have survived thousands of years, loud and clear, and I'm not so naïve as to ignore the fact that I'm the first daughter *not* of the succession.'

'But…'

She rolls onto her back, almost ignoring him. 'Jesuah birthed Aurora. La Basta birthed Jesuah. Rhiannon had La Basta, Carla-the-Red had Rhiannon and that goes all the way back to that little pale girl in the legends from when the shit went down. Baron. And who knows who else before that?

'But Aurora birthed to Tabak and not me. I was *chosen* for the succession and this is the *first time* that it's been this way. Do you wonder that I doubt a little my ability to be the bridge that they always talk about when the ancestors call us through to this prophecy's unknown destiny in its unknown time and its unknown place?'

'What do you mean?'

'You kidding? Since the prophecy, I've felt the building of some unavoidability that's got nothing to do with becoming a mother, but that's all about what has to be done when we respond to the next prophecy.

'It's like the indwelling queens're aligning themselves with something as yet *unprecedented* and my doubts are all about this.'

This is queen to her consort, not lover to lover, and Angus knows it. He listens, aware that the information will be relevant way into the future.

'I'm a random factor. I don't sense that this is *against* the pattern, just that it makes it different.'

Angus wraps her in his arms, nuzzling her bare shoulder. 'I'm sorry,' he whispers.

She leans into him. 'I don't think I have a choice in this. And there's nothing to be sorry about.'

He kisses her, hopefully. She laughs and teases him back, shaking her raven-black hair over his. 'I'll decide when I decide, I guess.'

'You'll tell me?' Angus has taken the hint and is up, dressing in his finest clothing, thick boots and with deer and rabbit skins, complete with thick fur, over his shoulders because the air is icy. 'You ready to face today?'

Insistence clothes herself till she's like a mountain, then thinks to Lucifer, holding out her hand.

They come from the warmth of the tent into the freezing morning and wander over to sit by the small breakfast fire, pulling the furs up high around their chins, both burying their hands in woolen mittens, to where I sit with Miriam beside the fire, our digital design screens plugged into our individual *prefontlcortexls*, downloading, altering and reloading our imaginings, as we research our tattoo designs..

I'm summoned to Insistence's side, and I sit and stroke the raven's chest softly with my little finger. She *rorls* in pleasure as our queen places the palm of her hand over my eyes. She wants me to know her conversation with Angus. She thinks it ought to be quietly telepathed but that it should definitely be recorded in the chronicles, so that speculation can be discussed if her doubts prove substantial.

I nod when I've got it all. Funny, I'd intuited that she had already conceived. Now, where had that come from? She finishes the download and goes for breakfast.

.

WE JOIN JAMES, Tabak, Levington, and Ducker. Men, always the same. Herding together like geese. It's homoerotic, but they can't always see it for that. They've been awake all night talking, and the coffee is thick in their cups.

Levington Blade stands and stretches.

'I'm outa here,' he groans, arching his back to alleviate stiffness.

He's more ragged than ever with his long white hair flying in all directions, the dreads, loose for once from their bindings, his leathers all askew around his lean, muscled torso.

'Off for some sleep, Lev?' I ask.

'Nah. I got a lady to visit, a song to sing to her of sweet yesterdays.

'Then I gotta work on the music for tonight.' He sighs cryptically, 'My gift for the ritual.'

He gives Miriam his most charming smile before he kisses her, then me, amicably. Miriam runs her hand down his arm and looks up at him, a little longer than she probably intends.

After he's gone I turn to her. 'What was all that?'

'Nothing.'

'You fancy him, Miriam!'

She avoids my gaze.

'Why don't you tell him? This is stupid.'

'Just my way,' she replies.

'What? You're so twisted you can't make yourself clear when you want someone?'

'Not true, Ghost. I just get a feeling about him that's hard to understand. To let him be – like whatever goes on inside him has to know, and choose, without suggestion, is all. He knows I feel like I do, he's not fucking stupid.'

'What about what *you* want?' I can be so annoying, but I can't stop my mouth from thinking out aloud most always. Sabé was right about that.

'Oh, Ghost, sometimes it's like you know everything and sometimes it's like you don't know nothing at all. I know you're a sorcerer and I know you've been here and there and all about time, but I see things, too, you know? I get a feeling about someone or something and I'm pretty-much always right. Well, I got that about Lev' She powers down her scribe-screen, so it retains battery long enough for the inkers to code the images for themselves. 'He's different. I don't know what it is, but I trust my own intuition in this. I respect the way it is.'

She dismisses me. 'You coming?'

I shut up.

When the sun is close to the zenith and the frost in the shadows has relented to the meager warmth we walk towards Redrock where the tattoo wagons are set up.

We pass Levington Blade sitting among the stones with Desire, black skin against the white, talking with their heads together, laughing like old friends.

'See?' says Miriam as we walk by. 'He says a thing and it sounds like one thing, and it's other.'

'Sure thought he was gonna get some sex from the way he talked,' I agree.

'It's like he throws our assumptions back at us. Sometimes I feel like such a fool around him.'

We stop by the healers camp to collect the herbs from our gardens that will be the price demanded by the gunners, and a few extras in case there is anything else worth buying from the other stall-holders.

It was an easy day for both of us as our only duty was that evening when we assisted the singing-in-of-the-fires prior to the visions.

We stroll, looking at the arts and crafts and produce from the different clans. Although there's much of beauty and wonder there isn't anything that I need.

It's then I see the tiny woman seated under a vivid blue canopy. She's old and pale – her scalp showing through thin, long colorless hair tied in two braids; translucent skin that's seemed to never have seen the sun, but not like mine, just white. White garments. We make eye contact and her pale watery eyes shine with the onset of cataracts. She crooks her finger at me in a gesture of calling.

'I'm gonna see what that woman's got,' I say to Miriam. 'You coming?'

'No, I'll go on ahead.'

She scrutinizes the dried fruit of a face woman, frowning.

'Careful,' she says under her breath. 'Something weird about all this. I feel it in my waters.'

'I won't be long behind you.'

I ignore her warning, sensing something familiar about the old lady who's openly judging me.

'Just looking…' I say, flirting with each shape hidden beneath blue silk.'

'I summoned you.' Her voice is young, seductive, at odds with her deeply lined face.

'My choice to come here, though.'

'Bullshit.'

'What clan're you come from?' I'm just going to ignore her

rudeness, sense some deep pattern in this. I notch up my focus.

'I'm a loner, little girl. Rogue's my destiny.'

She scrutinizes me shamelessly and I'm uncomfortable under the intensity of it.

'You 're a pale one, that's for sure. Those spots safe?'

'Can I see what you got then?' I ask, ignoring her because Tabak called me *beautiful* last night. 'I got other places to be, so I can't take too long.'

'Not so good to lie to one such as me. I can read you easy. You gotta sit now. You gotta *take* time for some things such as I got. That's how come I choose who chooses to see my things.'

I don't like her, but I'm not going to let her know that. I want to leave but I'm nothing if not curious. I sit cross-legged on her mat, my chin stuck out. 'Show me.'

One after the other she lifts the cloths covering each items, displaying exotic boxes of different woods beautifully painted or carved in patterns like jigsaws, unusual jewels in strange lace-like metal settings, strings of faceted beads, assorted hand-tooled leather garments. I admit it, I'm intrigued.

She lifts a final square of silk, and beneath it is a book, very thick and covered in soft, red leather, tooled around the edges with an intricate, arcane design. Embossed on the front cover, in a delicate, unusual script the word GENESIS.

'Why's it called that?' I ask, running my fingers over the indentation.

'You ever wonder whether if nobody answered all the questions, the destiny of a thing—and somebody's name—might never be what we suppose it to be?'

'I don't know what you are talking about.' I open the cover.

'Stupid little girl.' She tries to grab the book back. I've insulted her somehow.

I hang onto it and flip through the pages.

'There's nothing in it,' I'm ensorcelled, though, by the feel of it in my hands, purposely avoiding the old woman's milky, but bird-sharp eyes.

'Could be, though,' she relaxes. 'I made it a long time ago, but nobody got the guts to take it, so far. It's a bit hoodoo for jotting and the odd doodle.'

'I never would've thought to have a private diary. Isn't that strange?'

'Bit silly. Why?' she asked.

'I'm an initiated chronicler, woman. Nothing's supposed to be private. Still, it's only been a little while since things have changed for me.' I contemplate in just a few seconds the many things that had occurred all around me over the last few months. 'There are private things that I have not been asked about, nor need to be of interest to SEVEN. I—' I stop myself. I've confided more than I intended.

'Take it,' she says flatly.

Her assessment of me is bold and scrutinizing, from under hooded pale lashes. 'Maybe it'll be a good thing to have a paper record of what you know about stuff, just in case things don't quite work out with SEVEN. You never know how this other prophecy's gonna turn out.'

'Thought you said you weren't psychic?'

'I just know shit, Ghost. You can do what you want with a book like this.

'Listen to me,' she leans forward, smiling benignly as she places her hands over mine, 'haggle with me for some *other* of my trade little girl, because it's my *geas* to just give you the book.'

She takes back her hands and shrugs, distracted by other vendors, seeming to lose interest in me.

'You don't have to do that.' I'm wary of gifts given for no reason.

'I haven't gotta do anything,' she snaps. Then she grins, exposing a gappy mouth, her teeth long gone.

I really don't trust you, I think, *you're too weird.* I don't, however, let go of the book.

'I sometimes give things away.' She pouts like a child. 'That's my right because I'm old and because I can do whatever I want.' Her voice gentles. 'Take it, okay?'

I hesitate, sensing that there is some kind of *geas*—obligation—attached to the deal. 'Okay. Yeah, I guess. I'm game.'

I'm still wary but I let it go as what I don't sense is malice or harm, just fatedness.

'Now, let's see the plants.' She searches among the tiny pots in my basket.

She picks valerian. 'Okay…I don't sleep so good. I'll have this and—You got an opium poppy? I can't see one. The dreams. When you're old like me it's good to have the dreams ready to slide outa life on.'

I've got seeds, and she says that's even better as she has a special garden where she lives.

'This'll be fine for anything that you choose, little time sorceress.'

Little what?

I don't react. I rummage, instead, among her wares, not interested, simply wanting to please her. I pick a string of red-orange beads.

'That's carnelian. You want it?'

'Deal,' I say, slipping them over my head.

'Deal.' She's rummaging through a box of old bits of lace and ribbon, distracted, as though I'm already an afterthought. 'Red and red, like the color of the blood of the inheritance afire in your veins.'

The little hairs on my arms stand up straight, and at the back of my neck, the skin crawls. I have to get away. I hug the book to me and start walking.

'Got a clasp at the back,' she calls after me. 'If you want, put more pages in it than're already there. Always have lots of paper, little girl, just in case. Especially when you go away and you're not sure how long for.'

I turn the corner of another stall, away from her canopy, not wanting to hear any more.

I AMBLE, CLUMSY, TOWARDS THE TATTOO area, one arm swinging like mad as I walk, the other clutching both the book and my basket, hardly able to contain my excitement. What to write? I wonder where to begin. I wonder about the possibility of this being the only written thing in the living world not archived in some library or other. Not recorded anywhere.

I don't get to show Miriam straight away as she is tranced out on endorphins when I arrive.

Then it's my turn and I lay upon the cushions for two hours, still clutching the book, as a thick-set, shaven-headed, heavily-bearded inker chatters to his friend, inking Miriam, while he tattoos two fine dark blue lines onto the upper part of my forehead: two long, narrow chevrons, designs that Fjörgyn has shown me to be the ancestral sigils of my grandmothers, from a legendary land in the northern hemisphere that was once covered in ice and volcanoes. They sting as they are stitched—traditionally—into my face.

Miriam is done. She shows me her arm, dirty with excess ink but

covered in spiraling flights of ravens and eagles, hawks and owls –
hundreds of birds.

Those close by come to look. Her tattooist stretches, basking in the
admiration. Miriam's entire upper left arm is one wavering splash of
wings, from just below the elbow to up and over her shoulder, with
the highest, smallest bird amongst them: a wren riding on an eagle's
back.

He shoves his hands into his wide leather belt, smiling at Miriam.
'See that one there?' He nods his head towards little wren.

'Thank you, it's exquisite!' Miriam's like a young girl.

'That's gonna be you, darlin',' he says, going to get something to
eat before his next client.

She sits with me until my simple design is done and I smile with
pleasure when Zak, my ink artist, hands me the mirror, and I see
myself as I'll look from that day on. Not such a moon face ugly
foundling now, am I? I hand him the calendula and the Aloe Vera
plants.

'Arctic, that is,' he mutters, cleaning the fine, bone needles. 'Not
many of us remember that old lore.' He continues to talk to himself as
Miriam and I walk away.

THE INITIATES OF ALL THE many schools of magic, along with their
apprentices, are gathered on the summit of Redrock's highest plateau.

The sandstone hollows are brim-full of rainwater from the recent
storms and we rinse the dust of the desert from our bodies and adorn
ourselves in an abundance of blue clay.

The wood for the fires had been carried up hours ago, and the pyres
are pyramid chimneys to the east and north and west and south, an
enormous circle of white quartz rock around the perimeter of the
plateau.

The mothers of vision – little blue-stalked fungi – had been gathered
after the rains and mixed with honey. To the mixture was added the
spice that lessens the side-effects of the fungi.

Baked clay jugs are filled with water, and trays of fruit, of abundant
variety, are beside each group. We've fasted since morning and drunk
only water or spiced tea and the aroma and life of the food is
temporarily overwhelming.

The drummers, harpers, pipers and dij players come at the lowering
of the sun when the frost sparkles off every damp space. They set up

close to the edges of the plateau and get comfortable for the long night.

LEVINGTON BLADE DANGLES HIS HARP from his shoulder, the highly polished, dark red wood gleaming in the glow of the last of the light as he stalks across the clearing to Insistence and Angus, chatting to them briefly out of the hearing of others.

He comes to where we sit, Miriam, Tabak and I, and another initiate named Timmy, in a traditional grouping of four.

'May I take your place?' he asks Timmy, who looks across to Angus for the okay and gets a nods. 'No problem, friend.' He leaves us to go sit with another grouping.

The three of us are curious. Non-initiates are never allowed at the vision of Samhain.

Blade smiles, and carefully lays his harp beside him on the rock.

'I'll explain later,' he says, sitting cross-legged, adjusting his raggedy old green jacket and laying his sheathed katana beside him.

His pale body seemed to glow in the waning light and Miriam stared unashamedly.

It feels right, the four of us; and. Tabak, who care as little for protocol as the Angus, leans across to Lev and they clasped arms in the grip of warriors.

My eyes are drawn to the western sky where Lucifer, the herald of the stars at night and the bringer-in of the sun in the mornings, appears ellipsoid. It's time.

Desire strikes a small bell and the initiates concentrate their thoughts. The wood, piled waiting, explodes into life.

THE ALCHEMISTS LINK their matrix opals in the waxing light of rising stars, and as their power increases so does a haze of light not cast by any fire. It illuminates the plateau. Each pinnacle and turret and shaft of lace-like red rock is alight as though bathed in phosphorescence. I am as awed as always.

The plateau appears suspended in infinite space, each pinnacle like legendary hand-raised Paleolithic standing stones; each seemingly transparent, like red ice.

Our voices rise in a simple song, in the peculiar harmonies taught by our ancestors, that every year strengthen our union with the matrix. Each grouping of sound is raised three times before changing in cadence to its next phase. Twinkle, twinkle little star, how I wonder who you are…

Insistence assists Angus to his feet. She rubs his arms, his face to the persistent, thought-provoking chant and he responds, breathing deeply, to ground himself.

Together, as the rhythmic, mnemonic, repetitive song continues, they fill the bowls with the fungi syrup, moving from one person to the next, feeding them a thimble-sized cupful.

As each of us swallows we cease sound. Slowly the entire gathering becomes silent except for one high voice that calls for the pipers who take up the sound followed by the other musicians.

MY VISIONARY INITIATION BEGINS with a thinning of the seeming veils that shield the colors of the spectrum and the air around me fills with this diffracted light in all its infinitely subtle variations. This color contains sound that reverberates in a movement of wind across space. It's all so indescribably beautiful.

Tabak touches me gently and oh, I feel his essence. Not simply his flesh, but his life-force. I reach up and our fingers merge. 'You're luscious,' he whispers.

I'm enthralled by the solid black hoops hanging from his earlobes that somehow also mirror the light of the fires. His hawk-like features fascinate me as a play of light and shadow crosses his face – he's beautiful, ethereal.

Our experiences are linked – a mind-union within the matrix—and I drift towards not who, but what he is, as he does the same to me. It's a probe. He's all wrapped up in a furnace of intelligence, kept from exploding by his quick humor. He is his own seed, and also the vine from which he's dropped. This vine, laces and entangles through time and space, I realize, even though I can't imagine where began. If it even had a beginning. If such a thing isn't just a construct of our thinking.

I drift a little; considering seeds. Think about fruit. I wonder what a fruit experiences when it drops from the tree, seemingly dead, then in a state of decay. The birth of the seed from that fruit is not like giving birth to a human child, although I suppose it's all alike really, because when a fruit releases its—which is the fruit, really—that seed sprouts new shoots and roots. Is it the same vine? The same tree? The same fruit, even, when its season comes about again.

The fruit seems to rot – to disintegrate – but it's a placenta, nourishing the soil with its vitality. Then the plant breaks forth from its womb (tomb?) to become itself, other than what it was as the preceding plant whilst retaining its pattern.

I think, *Some fruit have one seed, some have many, yet each makes only one plant – many lives lived together, yet alone – the stronger living on, the weaker becoming nourishment.*

I understand that I can be many people, self-reliant people, interacting within a vast garden of infinite variety but that I can, at the same time, be only who I am. All this became clearer, yet ever more complex, as the vision proceeded.

Tabak's pupils dilate with realizations of his own. 'Proto-earth,' he says. 'I get it. Finally! Each child has only one mother yet there are many children, many mothers and each mother can bear more than one child. So the first mother is Proto-earth. That's what SEVEN was telling me. It's the essence that's passed from mother to child – not the essence of the mother alone, but the essence of the vine, of its endless regenesis.'

I'm momentarily startled. *There's that word again.*

'What's a father then?' He continues, unconcerned whether anybody is listening, talking aloud so he doesn't forget the message. 'Oh yes, sperm is like a flash of lightning. A critter until it finds the fruit. The one fucking flash. That's all it takes, Ghost.'

He's a gardener, pruning the brambles of whatever I haven't figured out yet. 'An idea's also a life, Ghost, and I'm in empathy with my own child, you understand. This flow of ideas is bringing something to life that cannot, yet, be seen, but that's always been here.

'I'm a vessel, jut life any parent? Proto-earth is an unborn entity. Every idea starts out as unseen and unknown; is a nothing. The drawings, the mathematics, me, us, the computer, now, recognition – *that's* its fruit, you see?'

We're quiet for a while scanning the matrix, understanding.

A STRANGENESS, AN ALIENNESS is warping Levington Blade – I become aware of him peripherally but when I look directly at him he's fuzzy, blurred. It's freaky. It's making me nauseous, but I can't turn away.

I stare. Miriam stares, Tabak stares. Lev is definitely fractal. His body is distinctly less substantial and then faint, hot waves of light and color radiated from him.

'What's happening?' I ask in a small voice, through a flutter of fear.

'You know about me, don't you Miriam?'

A stain of rose flushes from Miriam's throat to her cheeks and she visibly trembles. 'I don't, though, Lev. Can you stop? You don't look right and it's freaking me out. Whatever is happening, I want it to go away. Lev, you're doing something weird and no, I don't know. Is this just me, or can everybody else see him?' She wants assurance from us, but Blade doesn't give us time.

'Please don't be scared,' Levington whispers.

He rubs his hands through his hair making it even messier. 'Fuck. I thought someone told you. I thought you knew and that's why you seemed to care so much.'

'I *do* care, Lev. You know that. Tell me. Tell me about you. I've waited to know. I've wanted to ask you. I've known there was something weird about you. In a good way. No. No fear about you, Lev. Don't think that. It's a fear *for* you.'

Tabak and I know that this conversation is meant to include us. It's such a private a thing between them, though, that I'm ready to suggest we leave.

'No, don't,' Levington pleads. Then drops his head, ashamed for having yelled. 'Sorry.'

He becomes more substantial, although he's still very fluid, and geometric at the same time. 'I have to tell you as well. You're both my friends. I have to tell it *here*. It's to do with the gift I've written – the music – for Samhain. The lady Insistence, and Angus have known all along. That's why I'm allowed here tonight, but I've wanted no fuss; I've wanted to be a bit invisible, okay?'

'Are you gonna tell us what you're doing or just screw with us all night?' Tabak grins, laconic. None of this fazes him.

Miriam reaches out to Levington's insubstantiality and strokes his colors. He relaxes visibly. 'Are you one of us… or something kinda AI or symbiot, Lev?'

'You mean am I human?' He's surprised she could even think that, but loves her too much to react like he would if someone else had suggested he be other than a person. 'I, ah, started life as a kinda anomaly,' he agrees, 'but I'm most definitely flesh and blood, just—'

Tabak, ever the scientist, is as eager as a child, grinning like an idiot. 'Go on, man.'

'My mother supposedly couldn't conceive. Hoping the ancestors could magic up fertility she journeyed to a mythworld gate. She hung about there long enough to menstruate her body's abandoned eggs. Our ancestors woke the life from one of 'em but not before she'd already gone. No pregnancy, no magic. Or so she probably thought. Except I was alive.'

'Explain.' Miriam eats some of the fruit, into the conversation now.

'There. At the gate. The air, the light, the rain and heat, the earth, they all grew me. Not a person. Not a family like you think of as normal. I'm tomorrow, you see.'

None of us know how to respond. 'I'm being honest with you.'

'This is radical,' Tabak is thinking aloud. This idea has been both of our experiences. He catches my sidelong glance and laughs.

'Close your mouth, Ghost,' Tabak laughs. He doesn't understand though. I'm not shocked, just surprised. This makes perfect sense.

'Shut up, Tabak,' Miriam says kindly, not really feeling particularly kind.

'Twelve years I lived there, knowing both sides of the gate as mother and my father – earth and memory. Then one time a harper comes seeking inspiration. He finds me instead. I hadn't known there was anywhere, or anyone else, until I joined him.

'I didn't have no name, so he called me after a famous guitar from before the cataclysm, legendary to the harpers of now. I was named for a guitar,' he chuckled. 'He liked to think he'd saved a legend.'

'We left the gate not long after and moved all over. He taught me to play the harp. The shine within my DNA inspired strange music, and things happened… when I played my own songs. I tried to control it because it frightened me, but there wasn't anyone who could show me how, so I only played other people's stuff—covers—in taverns and at carnivals and suchlike.

'One time we stayed with a clan to the north up around croc country. While we was there raiders come. They slaughtered pretty much everyone, including my mentor, and they chained the others, including me, to traffic across the sea for the fields of steel.

'They smashed my harp on the rocks—' He stops; clears his throat. He drops his eyes.

'So I sang.' He doesn't say anything else for what seems like ages, his energy field shifting and morphing with the kind of beauty that only comes with the initiate visions until finally, he looks Miriam directly in the eyes. 'And my song killed them all.'

Miriam is confused. 'The body snatchers? Your song killed the slavers?'

'Everyone. That's the way it was when I didn't know what to do properly.' He pauses long enough to feel the cut that comes with blame. There wasn't any.

'Okay, so I wandered alone after that. Sought oblivion. Felt what shame must feel like. I got sick for I didn't have no light in me.

'A woman found me dying; disintegrating in the desert. I lived with them people for a long time. They healed my body, but that was all they could fix.

'Then one day a young new initiate visits her mama in the clan. She's come from a long way off. From the Kata Tjuta temple. And she tells me what you were tellin' Tabak just before, Ghost. Almost word for word, about seeds and fruit.

'This all happened a lifetime ago, but I understood, so I healed.' He pauses to take a breather and Miriam moves closer to him, not at all afraid.

'Then finally I tell these people what I done to that other clan, and the people raiders. One of the teachers in the art of weapons overhears me and comes to listen to the whole of it. '*Fuck that,* he'd spat. He says, *How you gonna fight a enemy, whatever be a enemy, unless you know the way?* He asks me what I want to do with my music if I can play my own stuff. *Tell things,* I answer him. I tell him that through music I feel like I can say things different to just words.

'He says, *Okay, so you can make things happen, too, through being different to most of us… However it works, eh?* And I said so.

'He'd said *One thing I know about a weapon – and you're a weapon to all extents from what you just said – it's a nothing. It just lies there and don't do nothing by itself. But a weapon in the hand of a warrior, that's some other thing. So the warrior has to know who he is or who she is to be able to defend. A musician has to know about self to play the music, right?*

'Then he makes me an offer. He says *You stay with me for a while. I train the warrior; you train the musician. And make another harp fer fuck's sake.*

'And I did. And he did. That's how come I look this way. The body of me learned to grow right alongside the shine in me: to use shine with honor because it's me, and to use this body with honor because it's as much me as the shine. That was the learning.

'But *now* when a song comes I'm its messenger. Our ancestors' voices. And the song for Samhain is a message from the mother forest, that's Tabak's proto-earth.

'I've been there!' I interrupt.

'When?'

I pat Miriam's hand. 'The mother forest. First earth. Remember I went on that journey with Sabé? We were there.'

'What was it like?'

'The most beautiful place in or outside of time. A long story. I'll tell you later. Sorry, Lev.'

'Don't be. At least you know I'm speaking the truth.'

'No one doubts you, man,' says Tabak. 'What else?'

'You're my friends, see? I really want you three to know what's happening, what I'm really doing. Letting you know what I am is the only way I have of loving you. I don't know what's gonna happen soon but sure as anything it's me that's gotta sing the fucken thing in.

'Now?' asks Tabak.

'Yep.' And with that, he pulls his harp from its ragged satchel and replaces his katana in its scabbard at his back. He walks languidly to the center of the gathering and stands between two crackling fires, tuning his instrument, knowing his purpose.

He plucks a complex and ghostly melody from the strings and hums that old tune about a girl named Alice. Then he sings the prophecy into being.

Within the darkness one is waiting;
a child of life unborn, alone,
till the season of confusion
when the darkness turns to stone.

The one – the only covenant –
that life called from the crown
will call you when it's ready;
when its web is fully spun.
From the forest to the garden
to the desert to the tomb;
to the place of revolution
where no sun has ever shone.

Within the dance of death's embrace
the seed is carried past the veil.
It is unfolding to its pattern
and a forest is its grail.

The song – not yet – of what will be;
the child of life is forming
and you'll sing it with each other
when it's born within its morning.
From the forest to the garden
to the desert to the sea,
to the place of resolution
where the child will mother be;

and another and another
in an endless symphony.
The seed is just one season
to the seasons of the tree…
And the tree is of the forest
of the earth that's yet to be.'

When the song finishes the night is utterly silent except for the settling of the wood on the fires that sends up showers of sparks.

A long, deep rumble, like thunder, and the rock beneath us shudders, lurches and vibrates beneath our bums.

The earth shudders, and yet no one at the ritual moves.

'It's starting' whispers Levington Blade to Tabak.

'Thought so,' replies Tabak quietly.

Insistence conceives. It doesn't disturb the pattern.

CHAPTER NINE

THE BOOK

I'M NOT AWAKE NEXT DAY UNTIL the sun's high up in a cloudless, cerulean sky, the sounds of the crowds milling on the flat ground below cacophonous, crows and gulls filling the airwaves with racket, clouds of dust and flies eddying the air, reminding me that today is the festival of feasting.

I disentangle myself from Tabak, still sleeping, a thin line of drool snailing charmingly onto his arm. I tumble over him and the others in a haste to find my clothes. I feel exposed and embarrassed by my stark white nakedness in the daylight, and I'm ravenous.

I'D FORGOTTEN the book until it dropped out of my pile of clothes. The conversation with the old lady under her sky-blue canopy comes back to me.

I throw on my clothes, careless whether my skin is fully covered, of what people might see, food momentarily forgotten. I sit beside Miriam, thinking, while she slowly stirs into wakefulness.

I consider the training I had gained with Sabé, and in the library, relative to the transition from *naqoyqatsi* to now: the records of events, both personal and collective, that I have input to SEVEN since first training as a chronicler.

How fascinating to think of write about things that I learn, experience and understand. What a challenge it will be to tell the way of things and not have them merged with the words of others into a descriptive list of disimpassioned information, as is traditional.

My intention is to research data already in the archives. I can write

it out in my own way – in my own words – as long as I don't embellish
it.

I'll document my own thoughts so that those not my species can
maybe ken more fully the ways of a time walker. And for myself. For
the art.

'Miriam,' I begin, when she's sitting up beside me, 'Can I spend
more time in the library after this? I want to do some work of my own.'

Miriam fixes on the book in my lap.

'Sure. I can get you that, Ghost. I can organize you an entrance disc
if you want one for yourself – you can come and go as you please.
What's that?'

I show her my book, and she examines the silk-like pages and the
removable binding, and fingers the quality of the leather cover.

'Wow, Ghost! Where'd you get this?'

So I tell her all that I'd meant to yesterday. I finish up by telling
about the old lady who said I should write my own story.

'Why not? Writing's an art that's almost forgotten. You're talking
about autobiography. It was about ourselves and the experiences that
we have.'

She fusses about pulling clothes from the communal heap, then,
'Hey Ghost, I sure would like to have something of a journal of my
own. You think she might have any others?'

I'm eager to have someone else meet the rude old person even
though she said this was the only book she had, so I suggest we find
out.

I want to talk with her again to see if the peculiar feeling that she
invoked in me yesterday are still the same, or whether it had been
some kind of moment just between the two of us.

Tabak has gone back to sleep but Levington Blade sits up and looks
at Miriam.

'I'm going down to the stalls with Ghost, Lev, you wanna come
along?'

'I love you, Miriam,' he says.

'Hey?' not really certain she heard him say what he did..

'I really, really love you, Miriam.'

Pink again stains Miriam's cheeks as his words sink in. I've never
seen her unnerved before and I try not to laugh. My breath coming out
of my nose as a snort instead.

'What, Ghost?'

'Finally,' I snort.

Levington fusses with his harp case. 'I just want you to know, that's all, because you don't. Shut up Ghost.'

He smiles as he walks towards his clothes calling casually over his shoulder that he'll come with us as far as the food.

'I wonder what made him want to say that, all of a sudden like. Wow. I've gone all peculiar. Can you get me some water, Ghost? Please? And no funny comments...' She sits back down again.

By the time I bring her the cup she's herself again. Levington Blade leans on the rock wall watching by the passage down the cliffside. He's smiling.

'Let's go,' he calls out, 'I want to eat.'

We take our time reaching him so that Miriam can regain her composure, then we clamber down the long step steps and crannies to the sand and dust below. Blade follows the smell of slow-cooked goat while Miriam and I wander the stalls until we come to where the blue canopy had been.

Nothing.

We venture to the nearest tent and ask the man inside where the old pale lady is; where the blue canopy is.

'She took off yesterday,' he replies. 'She only stayed there from morning till after the sun's zenith. Just packed her gear onto a travois and bundled on out of here.'

'You know where she came from? 'I ask.

'Me and some of the other stallholders were talkin' about it in the early evening as we never known anyone to up and leave before the ritual was done. No one knew her. Everyone thought it was strange how she just comes and sets up and don't talk to no one – except I saw you in there.'

He saw me enter her canopy but hadn't seen me leave.

'Weren't any other customers. I'd have noticed. I saw her call you, so I figured you knew each other. It was after you left she packed up.'

'Thanks,' I say. Miriam looks my way every so often as we walked slowly away, her eyes full of unanswerable questions.

'I don't know.'

CHAPTER ONE

WEATHER WIZARDRY

THE GROUND BENEATH THE SAND AND ROCKS rumbles intermittently for days, every now and then emitting a great lurching heave that scatters objects from their resting places and sends children running to find comforting arms in which to hide.

The alchemists with the seismic equipment assigned the task of registering the phenomenon recognize a pulse – a rhythm – to the quakes that come in regular, steady waves completely unlike any on record.

Like a woman in labor.

RIDERS ARE SENT OUT in every direction to find the weather wizards, men and women that chase any and all peculiar – often dangerous – weather phenomena all over the continent. They're found on the west coast and brought back to the Kata Tjuta temple. Their head adept, Hawkmoor, is a hereditary seismologist who learned his art through successive generations of other weather wizards.

They arrive with camels laden with equipment and set up camp, asking that everyone, except Meggie and Farhan, leave them alone till they work out what's going on. They're rather eccentric and aloof. I suppose courting tornados and cyclones up close can do that to a body.

Several days later they invite all us Kata Tjuta people, anyone at all, to the library conference area.

They hook plas-screens and interpersonal prefontlcortexl data transfer comms to SEVEN.

I've met most of them before on our annual seed-dispersal route and so I say hi to Hawkmoor. His hair has gone slate grey in the last couple of years and now he wears it pulled into two high pigtails on either side of his head highlighting the carved bone earrings in his ears. His mustache is plaited and knotted and hung with talismans and his wing-shaped eyebrows hang like porch roofs over hooded, dark eyes. He's huge. Strong. His enormous hands handle his apparatus like a surgeon.

With him is red-haired Tamlin MacConnell (another MacConnell brother) mumbling to himself, and occasionally to seismologist Ping Sui, while storm chasers and weather wizards Grace Velvet and Lenny Brightstar hook equipment up to SEVEN.

Grace, like ancient African statue, and just as haughty, is legended to be the foolhardiest of the lot. She also has a reputation amongst the clans of being a bitch to anyone outside of the weather mystics' cabal.

Hawkmoor leans on the podium and arranging his notes and tuning his little plas-screen remote. He eventually looks out over the gathering and clears his throat.

'Okeydokey… I'd wondered when they would surface and become manifest.'

His wizards all crowd up close to the equipment and Grace Velvet hooks her *prefontlcortexl* up to SEVEN so as to link with those of us sequestered to chronicle the meeting; checking on our competence. The audacity! Miriam and I exchange a look and I try not to sneer.

'It's a pulse,' Hawkmoor explains. 'We've been charting it for quite a while at the Kimberley observatory. It's been causing a wobble like would happen if something huge influenced a heavy star: in a wave… It's in our solar system. Or at least part of it.'

'Kind of reminiscent of a stone that has been dropped into a pool of water,' adds Lenny Brightstar.

'It behaves as though it radiates from a center,' continues Hawkmoor, 'which is that quake-like effect you've all felt. But it's also got a peripheral.'

His companions look out at an audience of blank faces. Grace Velvet rolls her eyes and turns her back on us, already bored. Tamlin sniggers, just a kid, really.

Hawkmoor ignores them. 'I'll explain like an image, okay?'

He clicks a diagram onto the screen. 'Imagine a line shaped like a half-circle, and then imagine the center of that arc.' He points at the image on the screen with his little wand-like stick, 'then the remainder of the arc is the peripheral of the center. The quake-like thing's the center.' In response to his data, luminous green scrolls of complex calculus roll from top to bottom of the screen as SEVEN explores the input.

The audience is still slack-jawed and confused although Tabak, Miriam and Levington Blade are very excited.

'None of us are having *any* manifest sensations of the peripheral but it's graphing really zappy on our equipment like the energy between the nucleus of an atom and its electron activity.' Hawkmoor flicks a few screens ahead of himself and Lenny has to help him adjust the remote before the wizard regains his cool. 'It's gotta be described as an arc, though, because the other 'side' of this thing's nowhere known… oh, fer fuck's sake…' Still blank faces.

'The wobble that's happening is because the energy is the effect of our own arc's center in resonance with, but diametrically opposite, its twin. And its effects are nowhere in our dimension and are also incomprehensible.'

'Tricky thing is what it reminds us of,' says Tamlin, squashing his raggedy head up to the microphone beside Hawkmoor. 'If I was to hold the image of the arc against itself on the mirror. Well…'

Onto the screen is the image of a mirror that comes closer and closer to the arc until the arc forms a perfect circle.

'You get it?' Hawkmoor grins. Lenny grins. Grace Velvet is stony-faced. Mumbles vibrate from the audience.

'Okay. So this arc, along with its impact center, is passing right through us. From the astronomical observations we've done so far we've come to the conclusion that our so-called side of this wave seemingly originates from a point in our solar system – a point in space – not relative to any planetary body.

'The wobble's not affecting anywhere else *except* here in the desert lands, that right Tam?'

'Yep,' Tamlin's in a world of excitement. 'Over in the west, it's like any other day. Same to the far north. The big lurches happening here are the center of the arc, the rumbles are the edges of the center and the times between are when our instruments register that the wave is passing through us. And the pulses are becoming steadily more frequent.'

Grace calls out in a loud, silky voice. 'So what we want to know is whether anybody has felt anything peculiar, anything really weird-feeling, since it started. It makes no sense at all that the wave isn't having an impact. It's too big. It's as big, and as strong, as the center.'

No one says anything. We've only felt aftershocks.

'Well,' says Hawkmoor, 'I'll just keep recording then because since Samhain nothing's changed. Everything appears to look the same as it did before the quakes started. But that's bullshit because something *really* big is happening in actuality.'

Grace takes over. 'So we got one more thing to put to you: it's a suppose.'

We're riveted.

'Suppose the effect of the wave around the center takes a while to manifest?'

She looks from one face to the next around the auditorium. Then she smiles. 'You should probably have some kind of emergency evacuation organized.'

Then she snorts a laugh as though what she's said is funny. *Bit mad,* I think.

'You just let us know if something unusual happens,' Hawkmoor suggests kindly, unplugging Grace from the computer and moving her away, her mouthing *What*? In seeming innocence. Like she hasn't just panicked a thousand or more people.

A few weeks later Insistence and Angus announce that she's pregnant. That the Immanence is unaffected.

Riders are sent to the far communities to announce the news and it is a grand excuse for a much-needed craic. We took turns at the mirror in the dorm that morning, after Miriam and I had dragged it from the storeroom, but by now I'm not feeling so ugly and I take a moment to take center stage of the glass, lining the part down the middle of my moon-white hair with lilac parrot feathers to compliment the color of my eyes. Haughty, even. I'm a woman now. I have a lover. So just move over for once, this is my time, ladies.

While the ground continues to shudder and groan, it doesn't scare anyone. This is common for this time of year. Still, everyone prepares for what Grace Velvet suggested. Just in case.

Nothing happens. Not then. Not for so long everyone has begun to doubt there is a problem at all.

MOST OF MY WAKING hours are spent with my *prefontlcortexl* hooked up to the VR controls of the library's archival area, writing notes, in a crabbed and newly-skilled format, in the pages of my paper-leaved diary, like some gunslinger in the wild-west flicker movies. I'm horrified.

I'm in the dubious and contradictory lore of the record-keepers of *naqoyqatsi*.

I lose myself in the nineteenth century. Then, by all that's wet and quenching on a hot and thirsty summer's day, I dive into the data describing the twentieth century. What a mess. And the twenty-first is the worst. What is the word? Here, I found it. SEVEN likes her Hopi language because there is no other word, in the common tongue that tops *naqoyqatsi*, except *koyaanisqatsi*. Life out of balance.

Several documents, in what is known as the Western World, claim it was the *Current Era* and they wrote, as an example, of events that occurred in 1942 of that calendar, called CE (that was war, by the way), whereas others used Latin, an archaic, dead language, to describe the current era, called it *anno domini*, or AD, which meant *In the year of our lord* based on events regulated by the same religion that affects the behavior of the people who'd come from across the sea. Some *lord*, eh? Ever-so feudal.

The computer arranges records in year order backward from the Change into the dim antiquity of speculation, referring to things that happened prior to pan-global internet communications. So much of it seems hearsay.

Opinions are all biased towards whatever hegemony holds the most destructive arsenal of nuclear weapons—or machetes. Rule is imposed through war, invasion, torture, propaganda imprisonment and execution. Or because of one crisis or another that decimated the eras, from contagion to environmental destruction, from famine and factory farming to genetic mutants, intergenerational abnormalities, political upheaval and the mass extinction of incalculable species.

The first night of the next several, I was hardwired to SEVEN, asleep, and on autopilot. It took me over a week to download the data, to make sense of it, let alone transcribe details onto paper with pen and ink.

Information, particularly ancient texts, indicate other seismic shifts of epic proportions have happened, time and again. Earth tilts, axis shifts – many. Surviving cultures hadn't kept logical records per se, but had, rather, mythologized events into mystical and supernatural stories.

Segments of written lore had leaped into the proceeding time-transit and been misinterpreted due to a lack of recognizable parameters.

These texts are all jumbled together to seem like one recognizable book, the *pentateuch*. This was the first five chapters the Bible that the corporati and the scarlet-robes still live by, think of as real information. It had, as its very first input, a Genesis of its own; a silly one with lots of continuity errors.

A person—like me—ought to be very careful about how she keeps written records or tells a story, I figure, if it can result in a scam like this.

All the books, or tractates, were different, but the pattern of a story (discounting translating errors that were obvious) was the same throughout, one world after another. Survivors of cataclysms keeping records however, mistranslated by consecutive monks with stylus pens and warring popes.

My thoughts whirl and I sleep badly. Kicking Tabak, often as not. I'm irritable, and my other duties are tedious and invasive. Miriam confronts me. Tabak questions me. People whisper behind my back about whether I'm going loopy, or if it's some time-sorceress thing not generally understood. I can hear them, telepathically and empathetically. I'm at some sort of peak and everything around me is transparent and blatant. From my own perspective, it's excellent and I'm aglow. Just distracted. So distracted I lose the key I was given to access the library without Miriam. I haven't found it yet.

In the third week of my research, I'm annoyed by the interruptions, even from people I care about. Time to put an end to the chatter and the worry. I put in a request for an audience with Insistence.

SHE MEETS ME JUST AFTER SUNRISE in the cool, gardenia garden. Dressed in leathers, light for the early morning frost I'm comfortable, despite carrying a heavy wool robe, just in case.

'Let's walk.' She isn't really worried about me, but she still probes me like she's digging for a splinter.

She takes my arm in a simple gesture that breaks the tension that's been a thin raw caul over me for the past few weeks, my senses raw with knowledge that I can't talk about. I let her into me willingly.

'You're okay,' she says, eventually.

'I am,' I say, 'but I'm getting pretty sick of assuring people.'

'Big Girl – she's on aircon maintenance in the common room at the library – suggested to Miriam that you ought to stay off the system for a while.'

'Big Girl thinks I'm obsessed with the work I'm doing. But I'm not. There's so much to know and I feel like I've only got a little time.'

We walked to the temple just as the sun rimed the horizon and we sit on the steps to watch it roseate the day, reflecting off the titanium fortifications and the beveled glass panels, diffusing into the freshwater lake as though structured intentionally to do so, rather than sizzle the surrounding garden to death.

We sit like that, in silence, for ages. Until the sun has cleared the earth's rim. I sigh and turn to Insistence who is lost in the beauty.

'Really, I feel like I'm gonna wake up some morning soon and this will all have been a dream and I will have lost the book and Tabak and everything.'

She shades her eyes from the glare with her hand, as a shadow breaches the treetops and Lucifer dips. She backflaps as she descends to drop on Insistence's outstretched arm.

'You know what she's talking about?' Lucifer sidewalks up to her shoulder. 'Is it as bad as this here bird makes out?' Feathers fluff and Lucifer purrs.

'That bad.' I agree.

'Up…' Insistence takes my hand and we walked back through the garden.

Once I start talking it's like there's no off switch.

'So that if anyone says I'm behaving weirdly you can shut them up, or something. Just keep em off my back, please?'

'It's not that I can't talk about what I sense but wow, it's misrepresented as legends because people were mostly non-literate so by the time we got around to writing they probably didn't understand. You should read the stories of the ancestors. Pretty warped stuff. Probably from before the last Ice Age. Hybrids of fallen angels and mortal women. Giants. Ridiculous. The technology of spacecraft and air travel, I think. Fact becoming superstition.

'I'm sorting through a mess that's got massive ramifications at the core. I…'

How to explain?

'I think I'm on the brink of what I can only call a *one-thing*.' I 'm so excited I'm shaking.

Insistence mind links with me. Then she relaxes and hugs me. 'Keep coming up for air every so often, okay?'

I laugh with relief. I knew she would understand.

She shrugs and almost smiles, Lucifer *arc-orling* into her ear like backup. 'I don't, though, Ghost. I don't understand at all. I learned early in my training, however, that to understand a thing I have to know what it is first.' She pulls the hackle feather from her hair to stroke Lucifer's chest feathers. 'When you get it all you come and tell me. I figure I'll want to know what this *one-thing* is as much as you. Just don't shut out Tabak.' She gives me a look that could also be a warning, before entering her rooms where Desire is lighting the lamps because it's gloomy even with the rising sun.

CHAPTER TWO

INTO THE BLACK

THE SEASON FROM FIRST SPROUTING to final seeding, of the plants that have bloomed in abundance after the rains before Samhain, is prolific but brief.

The clans that gathered for the festival remain to harvest the wild seeds to take home with them.

Some will be scattered on the journey to ascertain an uncultivated abundance in the years ahead, but most are kept to be planted in spring.

A contingent from Kata Tjuta is readied to travel, to deliver seed to the remote areas that sent requests, their apologies for not attending, their barters and their news. That includes the people of the forests and the sea, this year. We are ready to meet with them. To parlay with the W.F.C. who are hunkered down up there. Either that or to drive them from our country.

The caravan is set to depart on the new moon. More than a hundred of us prepare. Miriam and I are to attend as chroniclers, especially during any parlay with the W.F.C. Tabak, Levington Blade, Meggie and Farhan, Michael and all of the survivors of the original war, Desire and Rufus-son-of-Rupert, her new apprentice Quith the Witch, Mama Nanek and James-the Maker, all coming.

Gallack, unexpectedly, came to say goodbye to his mother, a feeling within him that he would never see her again. She tried to reassure him, but I was intrigued by his apprehension.

CHAPTER THREE

FOREST AND THE SEA

WE CROSS THE WINTER DESERT BY day. The nights have ice in them, so we stay close to banked up hearth fires.

Two weeks, it takes, to cross the highland ranges, to follow the almost imperceptible trackways through rugged and treacherous bush, the biting, icy wind making the journey harsher still.

Wariness spreads, like a virus through the convoy, as we approached the outer belt of rainforest that thrives undisturbed by any seeming human habitation. This suspicion is instinct at the unfamiliarity of dense foliage to those of us who've lived our lives in wide landscapes, as is the ever-mindful distrust of the so-called truce between the people of the forest and the sea and the enemy that we are about to meet.

The rainforest clings to the side of the mountain range, interspersed with cascading, mist-shrouded waterfalls and unexpected white-water rapids in a difficult-to-navigate terrain.

The descent, however, leads us through some of the most magical landscape any of us have ever seen.

Come dusk we camp on high ground near one or other of the

many rivers that thunder towards the sea from way up on the topmost ridges and escarpments.

Once onto the flat land to the east, the weather becomes more temperate and I can smell the distant sea even though it is still miles away.

Insistence, Angus, Farhan, Meggie, Hawkmoor, Tabak, Levington Blade, Miriam and I, and all the ex-W.F.C ride ahead of the others, with five of our most proficient warriors, to meet with whoever or whatever comes from within the city.

The others will wait a night and a morning before joining us, and then only if one of us returns to tell say it's safe.

Should no one return an all-out attack is to be launched, even if that also means against the forest and sea people.

There's an outcry among many in the group that are to stay behind. There's concern that Insistence is in the advance group: worry that she could be killed without naming a successor.

Desire is among those with no objections to anything except staying behind, and she speaks out, Rufus scurrying beneath her har as she approaches Insistence and Lucifer. 'Daughter, no way I should miss anything that a seeress ought to know about and, also, I seen it from the beginning, remember? Quith here can stay and follow us with her visions.'

She turns on the gathering and speaks loud enough so even those at the rear of the caravan can hear. 'As or Insistence, people, she'll come to no harm. Don't you think we'd have seen that? Sit down and drink in the scenery. Rufus, stop scratching!'

Insistence grunts as she straightens her fighting staff within the leather traces that crisscross her back. 'Mama, no way I intend wearing your curses.'

Mama Nanek dismounts and pulls Michael to the ground beside her, handing him her waterskin. Each of them prepared to wait.

Insistence adjusts her seat in the saddle as Desire hoists her belongings back onto her camel and remounts, following the group as they take to the wide sandy track that will lead from the forest depths to the city of the coastal tribe.

Then the quake hits.

AND DARKNESS FALLS WITHIN the day. In one mind-jarring lurch, the light goes out. No sun, no moon, no stars. The horses rear and scream; the camels drop to their knees. People panic through the blackness.

Angus's commanding voice calls over the melee: 'Dismount and shut up everyone! Somebody get a fire lit.'

First one light flares, and then another and another until all possessing fire tools have them operational.

The forest is absolutely still and silent. Not a leaf moves and nothing other than our company makes any sound. Even our animals are mute.

Next thing, the aftermath of the lurch, which is what seems to have been what has triggered the darkness, rumbles and rocks the earth and even the atmosphere and it is an ozone-laden nerve-shattering, vibratory wave, roaring like heavy metal scraping against heavy metal, that drops every one of us to the ground. The sickening sensation floods through what feels like every atom.

It isn't *only* physical, however. It ripples through some tunnel of self that I can't describe in words.

Then daylight comes again as abruptly as it ceased. The fires are extinguished, and people cluster closely together, anticipation and shock on every face.

Except for Insistence humming, Lucifer taloned contentedly on her shoulder, white eyes looking to the distance in search of prey, feathered head tilting to one side. Insistence, humming to herself as she strokes the horse's flank that still quivers, whispering to him. Continuing humming to sooth away his anxiety.

Everyone stares at her, her relaxed and carefree attitude incomprehensible.

'Love?' Angus's legs are like rubber as he walks to her side, followed closely by Tabak and I, and takes her horse's bridle in his hands. 'Insistence?'

'It's okay,' she says quietly, stroking the raven's chest with the hackle feather 'It's all fine, really. No one's hurt.'

She registers the incredulous faces and says clearly, 'It's *right*. Don't you feel it? It's been waiting. It's intelligent. This is not a time of body-death. Trust me. Not from this thing anyway. This is meant to happen. It's teaching me how to give birth.'

Only then does she realize that she is the only one smiling. 'You— you don't understand, do you?'

'Not a fucking bit of it; lady,' replies Tabak, defeated. 'You tell us what we're missing.'

'Oops. Sorry...'

People look from one to the other, confused.

'I'll tell you though... Yes, it was peculiar, but not frightening. It actually *felt* for me, in order to know the child. It touched this baby and I knew it was doing so. It was empathic.'

'None of us felt it,' I add.

'Well...' Levington Blade shrugs, from where he sits his mount over beside Desire. He's also not alarmed. Angus grins lopsidedly, from Insistence to the others.

Everyone talks and mumbles about the incident while readying their mounts to ride.

Hawkmoor and his cabal are alert, excited and very much attuned, within the matrix, in mutual curiosity. This is it. The wave they'd predicted.

'What you want to do, people?' asks Insistence. 'Do we keep going?'

We agree to continue.

CHAPTER FOUR

THE ARK

MOVEMENT THROUGH ELDRITCH TREES. Three hundred foot high old growth eucalypts. A city in the clearing up ahead. No sentinels to herald our approach.

We ride to the edge of the occupied space before we are noticed. Several people stand together on the common land between two long wooden houses, deep in discussion and two women see us. They appear just as Pedro Lupis and Carmichael explained in slight clothing, despite the cold, heavily tattooed, dreadlocked and adorned in wood and bone. They amble to meet us as though they have all the time in the world, both with their hands out in greeting.

'I'm Jezzy. Head woman,' says the taller of the two, shaking Insistence's hand, then Angus's. 'This my sister Zo. Woah, raven!'

'She won't bite,' adds Insistence, distracted, looking over Jezzy's shoulder, scanning for trouble but sensing none.

'You people okay here?' asks Angus. 'You feel what just happened? Were you caught in the black?'

'Yeah, we copped it,' says Jezzy, distracted by Lucifer, her hand inching to beside the talons. 'Figure it's sorcery. There's been plenty of that lately.'

'Is it safe for us to come into the village?'

'Of course it is.' Zo is confused. 'But is this all of you? We kind of thought you'd come ready for a fight.'

'The others aren't far,' says Insistence. 'We'll need to let them know to come when we're sure it's peaceful.'

Zo's smile lights her face as she takes Insistence's hand. 'You're our new queen, aren't you?'

'I don't quite know what I am at the moment.' Insistence replies, only half joking.

'Proud to meet you, Insistence,' says Zo, 'Excitement's been all over the village since the seers predicted you coming. And the time sorcerers been stirring up all manner of magic till they up and vanished on us. 'Least this whole thing with the invaders is in perspective now.

'Come and meet everyone.' And as Jezzy sidles up to Lenny Brightstar, taking his hand so seductively we can all see him squirm, we walk with them and Zo towards the gathering that's moved across to the walled well, with a wide rock pool and a natural central fountain, in the heart of the city.

'We're gonna introduce you to the strangest thing you ever saw,' Zo says softly. 'The W.F.C. have brought a secret.

Tension fills the air. None of the Kata Tjuta people, or even Hawksmoor's crew, are at all sure this is not some kind of trap. The matrix has gone silent.

'They'd had it figured that they were some kind of chosen few…' A misted spray from the fountain cools the air around them as they close the distance, 'and they've spent years preparing this invasion. They planned for some doomsday prophecy about the end of the world as we know it, the return of some spirit king to judge people, even ones that died like forever ago.' She chortles. 'And then a whole thousand years of peace even though the world's supposed to already be pulverized. Where's the logic?'

She laughs deep in her belly. 'Should have seen the looks on the corporate men's faces when we told them we already had the peace.'

PART FIVE

SITE NUMBERED 2/05/5172 - 24/41/5176

CHAPTER ONE

THE ABYSS

IS TODAY DIFFERENT TO YESTERDAY? Is anything changing yet?
'Is anything happening for anyone yet?'
'No, not yet.'
'No, not for me either.'
'Who was that?'
'Farhan. I'm near you.'
'Is anybody else close?'
'Can you hear me?'
'Yes.'
'Then I'm near you because I heard you.'
'Tabak? Is that you?'
'Yes.'
'Are you still there?'
(Listening.)
'Who's there?'
'Ghost?'
'I can hear you…'
(Pause)
'Can you hear that?'
'What?'
'Listen…'
'I can't hear anything—'
'Listen!'
Others now. I can hear others now. Around me.
'I can't hear it! Shut up so's I can hear what you're hearing.'
Silence. No… Then a whistling sound, very far off.
'Yes. I can hear something.'

Getting louder now.

'Getting louder.'

'Yes. I can hear it!'

'It's getting louder now. What is it?'

'Shh. *Listen…*'

The stronger the whistling got the more it sounded like wind rushing through a cave or a tunnel. Getting louder and louder. Coming. Howling. What's gonna happen now?

The roaring reached a high-pitched scream that kept on and on. I'm thinking that I'll die. I can't see and now I can't hear any of the others over the sound.

EVERYTHING CHANGES SLOWLY. Imperceptibly.

At first, having become so accustomed to the absence of all light and the inability to connect with any solidity around me, I'm not sure that I'm not hallucinating when I sense a lightening of the utter blackness; a minute stirring of what could be air against my skin.

Then the roaring sound subsides.

'Ghost? Can you hear me?'

'I'm here, Tabak.'

'It's getting lighter.'

'Desire?'

'Here, lovey. Julienne?'

I'm so stuck it's as though I'm in a casing of solid rock when the releases happens. Like I can breathe for the first time in my life. I had become so conscious of keeping control of the scream that howled, perpetually deeply within the abyss of me, that I answer really softly, 'I thought it was getting lighter. Feel the air?'

'Yes, I feel the air.'

'We're through it,' Insistence says softly from somewhere.

And slowly but surely, the brightening continues. The air against my skin becomes a little breeze. The darkness takes on the appearance of night becoming day.

And then I can see the others.

No one's moved.

Everyone here before the wave took the bottom out of reality is still here. Each person drops to the ground when they realize that they're alive. Better than falling.

I grab Tabak. It had seemed like an eternity in that black.

I think *how long were we there?* Then I laugh aloud.

So do those around me. They're all thinking the same ridiculous thing: *Where have we been?*

Nowhere, the answer ripples through the matrix.

How long had we been there?

No time at all.

Funny.

Desire's in a panic until Rufus-son-of-Rupert appears from some hiding place that rats are good at finding in times of trouble.

BUT THE OTHERS LEFT TO WAIT by the river are also here. Confusion.

This is it. *This* is the wave that Hawkmoor had talked about, the earlier one was just a preliminary phenomenon.

Insistence stands and brushed herself down before turning to the company that was left behind to wait.

'I don't suppose there's any point in asking you how, or when, you got here.'

A man of the clan of the forest and the sea walks to us and introduced himself to Insistence as Bran, a clan mystic and seer. 'I figure we ought to get some fires going again and spend some time in a parlay just in case it's not over yet.'

Everyone goes quiet at that.

'We'll set up our equipment,' Hawkmoor offers. 'Just let us unload our instruments.'

Grace Velvet and the others weather wizards go to the camels that are grazing on bushes at the edge of the compound. Lenny Brightstar excuses himself from Jezzy to join them.

Folk attempt to start fires with wytchlight then, when that doesn't work, with their firelighters, but the equipment won't work. One by one they give up.

Angus is sitting with Farhan, untangling data chargers and cables that shouldn't be tangled, attaching and detaching his seemingly-dead *prefontlcortexl,* and he suggests that the solar chargers and other magnetic equipment might have sustained damage in the black place.

We figure we'll wait, anyway, until Hawksmoor's checked on that thing out there in our solar system.

I wander over to offer to help out.

'Question,' I asked Hawkmoor.

'What?' He humps the massive astrocartographic lasers onto his shoulders, his waxed mustache twitching at the edges from his smile. At least someone is enjoying this.

'You said it was only happening back at the Redcliffs.

'I was wrong.'

'What am I missing?'

'Seems it's following us, or something that's with us, and maybe isn't attached to a place at all.'

'Does that make sense?'

'It does if almost invisible gates to some mythworld exist, and the matrix and ancestral discussions, the lineage of ancient queens, solar actualizers and witches what start fires, oh, and libraries that give a person orgasms make sense.'

'Oh, well. When you put it like that—'

'As for the need for fires, of course. If necessary you lot could sing fires into flame.'

'We tried that.'

'No?'

'Nothing.'

We carry the equipment to the center of the city and assemble it.

Nothing happens. 'It's dead,' says Grace glaring at the apparatus.

'Hey, you—' she calls to Angus, who glares in her direction.

'Apologies for my little friend,.' says Hawkmoor, stepping in front of Grace to hide her from Angus's ancestral ability at the evil eye, 'But can you actualize the solar grid from your matrix chip, please?'

Angus, poker-faced, activates the chip.

Nothing happens again. 'We're down,' he says. 'It might be temporary so let's not freak out yet.'

'I've got tarot,' pipes up Desire, Rufus-son-of-Rupert peering out from under her hair, disoriented but curious, his nose seeming to have a life of its own.

She shuffles and lays out a present situation spread of three cards.
Death, Fool, Empress.

'Don't piss me off with crypticism,' she whispers.

Quith lays hers out. Same three cards.

The two psychics glance at each other but say nothing.

'What?' asks Bran.

'Oops,' says Desire.

'We don't know.' Quith rolls her eyes.

Out of nowhere, a W.F.C. priest rushes across the clearing to a cluster of corporati in the shelter of a longhouse.

'Father Riley. Father Riley!'

He clutched at another priest, pulling him out of the shelter. He is loud enough for all of us to hear.

'The cryogenic encasement's inactive. For god's sake, we're going to lose them!'

Father Riley, an intelligent-looking man, currently panicking, runs off with the first priest. Other men of the W.F.C. follow, equally distressed.

'Where are they going?' Angus asks Jezzy.

'Their zoo, I suppose,' she offers, by way of an answer.

'What are you talking about?' Insistence shoulders her way to stand with Angus.

'That's the secret that they brought here from the northern lands. Some kind of zoo-thing in a big metal box that you can't touch because it's so cold that if you touch it you get stuck to it. One of our people did and we had to cut off the fingers that froze to it. When they want to move it they carry it on two special poles.'

'Where is it?'

'Up the beach a bit. At their deep-sea craft. You wanna come?'

We all want to see the box-of-zoo and we file after Jezzy, Bran, and Zo, onto a beach littered with footprints. For a moment I can't move. Enchanted. I've never seen the ocean even though I knew, in theory, all about it. My senses feast on the smell of the bull kelp covering the sand above the high tide line, and the brine on the wind that is heavy with moisture. Our Lady of the Waters is the darkest green I've ever seen, with whitecaps like horses' manes, a wild and roaring danger to the east. I run to catch up with the others.

Not far along is an estuary where the ocean wages temporary violence with a river before calmer waters allow for a wharf another hundred yards inland.

A massive behemoth of black metal is moored there, her many ropes attached to easily a hundred heavy metal bollards, and the robed and suited men entering along a steel bridge.

We crowd behind them.

MEN INSIDE THE DEEP-SEA CRAFT are fussing over a massive ornate metal box, engraved with a jumble of unintelligible symbols and digital panel-keys that are, quite obviously, inactive. Riley has his hands on the box.

'Oh, where is the power of god *now*,' he exclaims. 'Generations of work. My purpose! What if we lose them all?'

'No.' The other priest, Baptista, slides the lid from the box. 'All that will happen is the generation of the embryos.

'Don't you see? Perhaps this is the purpose of god. This garden. We've only got to get to the mothership for the nests and we can nurture them to life. The feeding formulae will be safe until it's required. There's plenty of water for rehydration if the damage to the cryoarc is consistent...'

'Baptista, you are a dreamer,' growls Riley. 'Who is going to build the compounds necessary, or even big enough to enclose those offspring even if we do manage to save them? This is insanity.'

'We have to find and establish a stable environment,' Baptista is adamant, heedless of the insult. 'This will never do. All this humidity and sea air. Dare we ask the assistance of these people?'

'You're out of your mind.' Baptista turns to leave.

'What are we talking about here?' interrupts Insistence.

'Who the fuck are you?' says Riley.

Farhan Ibrahim pulls his bow from the straps on his back, and Insistence slides the dagger at her waist partway from its scabbard. Docker, Meggie, Tabak, and Blade all sizzle with anticipation. That zen kind of calm that means trouble.

'I won't ask again,' she says.

'Species. Countless species' replies Baptista, enthusiastic and guileless.

'Frozen? In this?' The implications are astonishing. 'What species?'

The priests are silent, their eyes averted. The strange metal box is enormous. My head is aghast as it calculates. I instinctively know what is in there from having studied so much at the library.

Father Riley sighs and squares his shoulders. He glances in Baptista's direction, but he speaks to us.

'We've anticipated Armageddon for over four thousand years. The technology for cryogenically preserving embryos has been available for well over a thousand years. We have collected what we assume to be every surviving species.

'And we need to contain them. Everything is in some way predatory to everything else, at the end of the day…'

'This land can't support countless alien species, man. We're mostly desert,' says Insistence.

'And we can't go back.' Riley is defeated. 'The ocean has mutilated the mothership.'

'Damn you for a stubborn bastard, Riley.'

'Thanks for the confidence, Baptista. Anybody?' Riley looked around the company.'

Bran and Jezzy push forward to peer closely at the machine. 'So let me get this straight…' he says, 'you have a box full of species from much of the world?'

'That's correct,' replies Baptista.

'And they can all be brought to life? Like tigers and alligators and snakes and ticks?'

'Well, not ticks, unfortunately.'

'Anything that could breed?'

'Yes.'

'And you thought you could control this how?'

'Indefinitely. Frozen. Indefinitely.' He clears his throat as though it was full of the dust of stupidity.

'We've got the people-power,' I say.

Just like that.

Everyone turns to me and I'm instantly aware of their eyes. I refuse to be embarrassed, but it's not easy. Tabak attempts a conciliatory arm around my shoulders and I push him away. 'It's doable.'

Zo is alongside Jezzy and Bran, and now Insistence, Angus and Farhan. They examine the box from every angle. 'Thousands of species, you say?' says Bran.

'It's doable,' says Zo, quietly but confidently.

FATHER RILEY'S SMILE COULD NOT be wider. He took each of us in his arms in turn.

'Come then. Quickly. We have to explain this to the others.'

'I'll stay,' said Father Riley.

'And I will stay with you,' chimed Zo, hopping up onto the arc, sitting and crossing her long, lithe legs in blasphemous conspiracy with the priest., predatory.

After the disclosure and recommendations to the W.F.C. administrators – the corporati – and the gathering of clergy, one man rages towards Baptista, grabbing at his collar, suffocating him.

'This was confidential, you... You had no mandate to disclose any of this.'

Baptista stands his ground, frustration in every dirty line of his face, losing his breath, his face turning red.

Angus muscles his way forward and prizes Riley's hands from Baptista's neck. 'I suggest you keep out of the way, whoever you are, and you better tell anyone else, anyone who wants to dispute our actions, that they're not the ones making the decisions here.'

Two grey-clad corporati come and stand beside the first man, their hands shoved down deep in the pockets of their jackets and their shoulders hunched in defeat.

'I thought you understood, Raymond,' says the shorter of the two. 'We lost. We have no say.' And they drag the irate man out of potential harm's way.

'Oh, god,' sighs Baptista softly, but not so softly that I can't hear. 'Do you think we're safe from the earthquakes and the blackness for a while? This is a massive undertaking. My goodness, you're a strange one, aren't you? Albino, are you? How do you cope?'

Insistence diffuses his focus on me. 'To get this work even begun you had better explain this whole thing to the people whose job it will be to help you. And otherwise mind your tongue, old man.'

'I apologize,' he says to my feet. 'So be it.'

And Father Riley did.

The W.F.C., in conjunction with the entire northern hemisphere's secular theocracy, had commissioned priests with highly qualified backgrounds in scientific research – specifically genetics and cryogenics – and set them the complex task of preserving as many species as possible for beyond judgment day. They were certain they were amongst 'the chosen' that would survive, and it would be nice to have living creatures on the new earth after the purge.

The research and technology were code-named *The Noah Experiment*. It worked. They fertilized the collective reproductive functions of over one hundred and fifty thousand species, including several human variations.

The resultant embryos were carefully preserved, as were their respective ovum and spermatozoa. Life could be resurrected from these should regeneration of the initial frozen specimens fail.

Each was documented and kept in its glass vial or on its particular little glass slide within the large metal box that had been untouchable, until now, due to its cryostatic charge.

The nutrient solutions necessary to propagate each embryo, along with the vessels in which each life could be enwombed, were still aboard the mother ship marooned on the barrens to the north.

'So we've got to go now, before the life-forms deteriorate,' he begs. 'If we leave right away we should be able to get to the vessel before the interior of the arc reacts to any rise in temperature. Will you *please* help us?'

'And then we'll need every available individual to erect compounds and protective environments for when the species are born,' adds Bran.

'Are you kidding me?' thunders Jezzy.

'I think we should do it,' I add, knowing in my gut how important this will be in some future time.

PEOPLE ARE BUZZING WITH THE news. Excited. The region erupts into activity.

Jezzy allocates two dozen willing people to go with the priests to rescue the life support equipment from the mothership, and anything else necessary.

The priests pack and load several travois. They and the people mount their horses and depart before dusk.

Hawkmoor and the others are still attempting, in vain, to activate their equipment.

One helpful grey man has a magnifying disk that he removes from his far-seeing apparatus and he concentrates a bright spot of intense sunlight onto a pile of dried grass. It blazes within seconds.

I'm glad we haven't been able to use magic. It would have scared them, and the relationship is still fragile judging by the behavior of the Raymond man.

I have nothing pressing to occupy me, so I take the red, leather-bound book, my pens and my inks from the pannier behind the saddle of my horse, and begin catching up on the handwriting of everything I remember since leaving Kata Tjuta.

I don't know how long I have sat so but the sun has set and I'm fast losing the light. Tabak comes and sits beside me, lethargic. 'Hot,' he comments.

'Mmm,' I reply, swatting mosquitoes as I write, trying not to drip sweat onto the page.

'It's being near the sea most likely,' he says, distractedly.

'Haven't you got anything nutty to do? I've gotta write, Tabak.'

He grins, looking out over the antlike behavior of the people. He stays sitting with me until I write everything up until now.

'Can I check you?'

I pass him the book and he skims the pages while I tip the waterskin up, swallowing half in three gulps. He hands it back, the cover closed. I use a little of the water to wash the ink off the nib of my pen.

'What happens now, do you think?' I ask, affected by the intense humidity, my clothing sticking to me. I pull the saddle from my horse and stack it in an unassuming place alongside the panniers, into which I stow my writing equipment.

'Don't know.' He wipes at his face and neck. 'I guess we have the meeting with the W.F.C., get to know their intentions then go on to the outer clans like we planned. Doesn't seem to be any fighting to do.'

'We could wait for the others to come back from the mothership. We could stay and help.'

'We have to distribute the seed before planting season. You know that.'

'I'm a mess, Tabak.' It's anxiety and not just because of events or the strangeness of the place or the intensity of the heat. 'Do I seem calm?'

'If you want we could get in the pool. Strip and cool off.'

'And have people see me without clothes? Are you nuts? I'm not that brave.'

'You don't mind me seeing you, and you're beautiful.'

'Shut up. You're about as acceptable as me even if SEVEN does like you, so you can't talk. Plus you're changing the subject.'

'So you feel strange and…?'

'I'm calm on the outside but deep inside me… Well, I can't explain but I feel weird.'

'Good,' says Tabak, calmly undoing the ties that hold my upper garment together. 'Then I'm not going crazy after all because I feel altered in some way from being in the nowhere place and time.'

'That's it,' I nod, letting him. 'Altered. Blow…'

With my maggot-white skin and tiny mounds of breast exposed Tabak puckers his mouth enough to let out short breaths that have the opposite effect to cooling me down.

'Stop it.' He doesn't. He just pulls me deeper into the rainforest canopy, mentally daring anyone to come close enough to interfere, grinning while I sweat and lose my breath pulling at his own clothing.

Later on in the day I seek out Bran and asked him where the sorcerers were. He tells me that they just up and vanished. Packed up and disappeared in the dead of night several days before we arrived.

No one has heard from them since. No one knows why they left.

CHAPTER THREE

MIRROR MIRROR

IF I HELD A SEMICIRCLE AGAINST A MIRROR then the image made it a circle.' That's what Hawkmoor had said, wasn't it?

You can never be sure about how some things happen, only that they do. You can only ever assume by whatever knowledge you have to gauge a thing by.

I'm thinking about this when we leave all the W.F.C. men, and the clan of the forest and the sea, continuing our journey north.

We keep to the coastline for several miles then re-enter the forest where Farhan thinks we'll find the track that will lead us to the Nerang River clan.

EXCEPT THERE ISN'T ONE. PRETTY soon we are lost. The forest just goes on and on.

We change directions many times, each time laying markers at landmarks on the way to enable us to back-track, but when we try, there are no markers and no landmarks.

We follow the sun towards the east and come back out of the forest onto the foreshore of Our Lady of the Waters and we trek even further north, seeking any clans at all, or even the group that had gone in search of the W.F.C. mother ship. But we don't find them. We wander the coast south again, thinking we must have confused directions somehow, even though that makes no sense at all. But we can't find them either.

We forage as we travel because there is abundant game, and fruit on the trees, but we don't find anyone else.

WE SETTLE IN A CALM BAY BY THE SEA AND clear spaces close to fresh water, and we plant the food seeds we brought with us. We catch fish and snare birds and hunt kangaroo and possum.

We eventually plant the wild seed also, after the first harvest of grain, to remind us of the flowers that we knew before.

Tabak changes. The deep and driving moods that have always challenged his sanity in the past have ceased since coming through the 'wave.' He is very much at peace and I never even realized he has a sense of humor until now. I'm not so sure anymore, about the no breeding rule, but so far I haven't conceived. Not for lack of trying, either.

We've had to reverently take down trees to make clearings for gardens. We use the wood for houses and tools and tables and other necessities.

All those people and not one paper maker. Still, some of us are working on that and I've still got plenty of space in the book to write.

We started this journey as a hundred and twelve, then Desire delivers Insistence and Angus' newborn, whom they name Enchantment. In the summer just gone, adding to our numbers. A hermaphrodite child.

CHAPTER FOUR

DESTINY

OUSKA COMES TO US ALONE DURING our second winter. She's disoriented. Old. So whatever has happened in the black is not consistent everywhere.

She still won't speak so we don't know how she has found us or what's happening in other places, and why she is without one of the cats. She is always sad.

Perhaps more people will eventually find a way to also get through.

I'm sick again. Just like before, I wake in the middle of the night with my breath torn from me. Terrified and alone. I cannot keep food down and, again, one morning just after dawn, I'm sitting by the central hearth, willing the earth to stop spinning.

Miriam's eyes are crusty in the corners when she joins me.

'Is that coffee? Do me a favor and make me a cup, I'm positively haggard. Where's Tabak? He still—'

I reach for another cup and pour her half a cup before I have to run for the bushes and puke. Miriam watches, not saying another word.

'Yeah, I know,' I moan when I return to the bench beside the fire, 'I'll talk to Julienne. But I just think it's the same as when I met Sabé. It's a time-sorcerer thing.'

Desire waddles over to join us. She's overheard. 'You think?'

'I know.' I would laugh if everything would just stop spinning.'

'How long has it been goin' on this time?' She pulls her little old *prefontlcortexl* from her mojo bag. She's had Farhan tinker with it and now it's got a face about half the size of the palm of her hand. And it ticks in a continuous rhythm a little like the metronomes I read about in my research back in the day.

'What's that do?

Oh, I set it to coordinates of a normal heartbeat,' she holds it to her ear, with one hand, the other pressed to her chest. 'There, set at sixty four and... Come here.'

She pulls me close but instead of placing her contraption on my chest to work out—or so I think—whether I might have a speeding pulse, perhaps an infection, which would be really bad here, she places the little face on my abdomen. And listens.

'Ain't no Sabé on her way to take you through any grown up sorcerer initiation this time, little white girl...'

'What?' I retch again, unconcerned for her old lady intrigues.

Miriam's eyes widen. 'Is she?'

'Bout sixteen weeks. Good strong heartbeat, too.'

WHO AM I NOW? TABAK HASN'T SAID a word. Just grins like a lunatic and draws architectural blueprints for the dome he plans for the three of us. I'm not sure how I feel. The sickness has subsided, and I suppose I'm happy but more than anything I have serious doubts considering everything. I've got no source. No mother or father. He's the born son of a queen of the ancient lineage, and who's to know whether immanence is this unborn person's inheritance? I've never been so unsure about anything. Except that I'll do it. I can always kill it and feed it the Our Lady of the Waters if it's not right.

I'm a bit mad, trying to second-guess everything I've learned not to, working the crop of medicinals beside Tabak, who is now my ever-loving fucking shadow, when the pale horse canters along the shoreline, slowing when she reaches me. The same one I rode on the journey with Sabé. She comes galloping along the sand, pale mane flying, seeming to prance. Seeming to laugh.

She slows to a walk, tossing her delicate head. She comes straight to me. I'm gobsmacked, initially, just watching with my mouth hanging open.

She whuffles my hair, and pushes her velvet muzzle into my hands.

'Where have you come from?' I say stupidly. She walks past me to the very edge of the dense undergrowth before turning back, her gaze questioning.

I remember everything. I wheel on Tabak. 'She can take me back!'

'What do you mean? Ghost, you can't go...'

'I can do this. I can get us out.'

'Please.'

I ignore him and dash to Insistence. She's squatting at a hearth fire, Enchantment wrapped tightly in a sling, suckling contentedly, a twelve-foot length of spear in the making, whittling the tip to a fine point, while Desire carves out the think bark of wood bole for a throwing implement for same. I join them and they ignore me, comfortable now at waiting. When I catch my breath I tell them about the arrival of the horse. I start by explaining the journey I took with Sabé. About the bridges and the *proto earth* forest.

'I know how to go home, you see. Once I'm at Kata Tjuta I can put a contingent together, follow the route back here.'

'I don't know—' Insistence doesn't look my way, she barely pauses at her craft. 'None of this is as it seems, Ghost. It feels wrong.'

'Ghost, please…'

'Tabak, can you not make this harder?' I turn to Insistence. 'Sabé knew this would happen. She came from the future to make sure I could do this.'

'I don't want you to do this either.' She stops what she's doing and trains those forever-seeing eyes on me.

You're in trouble if you say it, I think.

Her eyes widen. 'Hah, well here it is at last. I knew you weren't the shy little acquiescent white girl you've always played at.'

'Wow,' Tabak, laughs. 'You only just figured that out?'

I look away but Insistence takes my chin in her hands. 'Finally, the time sorcerer shows her true colors.' She grins and returns to her work, testing the flexibility of the spear shaft, wetting it and heating over the flame.

'What's up?' Angus lopes to us with Lucifer hopping from shoulder to shoulder.

'She all but told me I can't stop her.' She turns to me. 'Lucifer is going with you then. She'll be my eyes. You'll have too much concentrated on you to telepath, even if you can. She and I, though, the symbiosis and all…'

Do I need the responsibility of a raven *and* a pregnancy?

I crush my back into Tabak's torso, lying as still as I can, circled by his arms, while everyone else in the camp just keeps on playing music and tending to another end of day as though everything's normal. I'm washed out and, I admit it, really scared. Questioning myself.

Who are you anyway? Ghost? Little moonglow critter always felt like she doesn't belong? Is this all you got? Some sense of purpose for that stupid note left when you was a kid? *We'll have a use for you.* I'm leaving at dawn. Leaving Tabak, leaving Miriam. On a whim? On a belief? Can I just stop now? Is this some issue? Oh, I remember Miriam conferring with Desire over my albinist issue. Desire said it was an abandonment thing and nothing to do with the look of me.

There's always been a battle here. Between me knowing what I do. That it's all real. That everything's destiny, and this timid, sometimes loud-mouthed, mix of a person, possibly not even the same fucking species as these people that I love. Who trust me when why should they?

From the forest to the garden, to the desert to the sea, to the place of resolution where the child will mother be, and another and another... But I can't let that change my plans. Can't think about that at all. It's just too destabilizing.

Meggie and Julienne oversee supplies for me that should last two weeks. I pack my own panniers, fussy woman that I need to be. Desire has made me a whole new batch of ink pigments and she hands me a box full of them, with tears in her eyes. Big old black woman's more a mother than anyone I've ever known. *For Tabak and for Desire.* This is like a song that loops in the peripheral of my thoughts the entire silent time I'm preparing.

On daybreak, I say goodbye to everyone. Tabak is never going to let me go and there's a look in his eyes I'll remember as long as I live. He hears me in the matrix. So do the others. There's just something doesn't fit with the horse turning up. With me going just like this. What can I do? If I don't go I'll never know, will I? I'll get old and die here wondering. That's no way to live. It'd mean turning my back on everything I've put my faith in. My whole life. It'd be like announcing to the world that I'm a fraud. Yes, I'm afraid. I'm scared shitless. Then I mount.

Lucifer bounces on my well-padded shoulder, and let the horse have her head without a backward glance. Aware only of the silence. Like I've gone deaf.

She struts with utmost confidence towards the forest, and I will, with every piece of magic in me, that we are going to Kata Tjuta. And I don't look back at Tabak, even when I feel the baby's first kick right then and there.

WE RIDE THROUGH THE FOREST for two days before the trees thin and we exit onto the night plain. And there it is, the waterfall of starlight.

The horse gallops then, with Lucifer in her lead, a black streak of familiarity. We're moving at such speed I fear falling, but the raven' flight never falters, so if she's confident and the spirit horse is confident who am I to be so silly?

Once we're through I see a bridge ahead – a different bridge than before – and the mare prances onto it as though dancing.

We enter the cave and wander its labyrinthine phosphorescent passageways for countless hours before the soft light of day illuminates an opening.

Outside is jungle, not desert. I wonder if this is another way to the cliff that leads to the mother forest but no. The horse knows where she is going, and she canters ahead relentlessly and endlessly.

I have no idea what I did wrong. I try to turn the horse back the way we'd come, to get back to the cave and maybe try again, but she refuses. She takes no notice of me.

I'm afraid. It seems Insistence was right.

My magic pony is unstoppable. She canters her way along a track I can't even see, that eventually opens out onto a clearing leading to a vast lake, shimmering emerald, but still within the forest.

We skirt the lake through bracken and giant ferns, the rich colors almost too bright to the eye, scents redolent with the delicate perfume of exotic flowers, dripping nectar, but also the rank stench of unseen, decaying flesh, all within dampness and heat almost beyond endurance.

Then I see the Kata Tjuta dome, or what's left of it. The glass is mostly smashed, as strangler roots and the vines of giant trees have sought entry, seeming to drag it to decay. The support girders though still pristine, a skeletal reminder of the place I know.

My bowels're almost turning to water as we travel past the ruins of the temple compound and out to a clearing of delicate, pale green grass that my companion begins to crop, just a horse after all.

This is where I get off, I think, as Lucifer takes wing to hunt in the nearby forest.

I dismount and remove the tack and my panniers, and hide them, just in case, at the base of a lightning-blasted tree, and deep in the thigh-high grass.

I search all afternoon. As twilight lessens my chances of successful exploration I stumble and fell. Right at the door, set into the ground, that leads into the library, me regretting with every mottle of my being I hadn't lost the key that was made for me.

I retrace my steps to the tree and hitch my belongings over my shoulder, sweat forming under my arms and in my groin, dripping down my back and from under my breasts. I sleep with my head on my tack and the raven on my hip, a sentinel. I'll find a way to break in tomorrow. I have never been so tired, so confused, so lonely or so scared.

I get it now. I've landed in another time. No idea when or why. Or is it the same time but a different aspect of earth?

SLAP, SLAP, SLAP. I AWAKE WITH A start. A fire is lit and a large boned, well-aspected, night-skinned woman. in finely cured animal hides, incalculable strings of blue clay beads hanging from around her neck and small bronze rings attached to the ends of each of her wiry corkscrew curls flips flatbread from hand to hand before laying it on the hot stones at the boundary of the fire. There is already a stack and a clay container of what smells like honey.

She wears a long, black-hilted dagger attached to a wide belt at her waist, along with an exquisitely-tooled leather pouch.

She sees that I'm awake and smiles, exposing big teeth, talking away. One of her front teeth is missing but it is not unattractive.

Chatter, chatter, her head tilting again and again like a bird. She rambles in soft, lilting tones, and I don't understand a thing.

I sit up at the fire clutching my belongings and looking around wildly for anything familiar, feeling for my own dagger which is exactly where it was yesterday and is no different to hers. The horse has only moved a few feet from last night and Lucifer is stalking something in the long grass. At least they haven't deserted me.

The woman hands me bread and I dip it in the honey realizing that I am ravenous, the sticky substance dripping down my hand in my haste, the fetus inside me kicking like some massive caterpillar hidden in the tree bark or under the soil, and I wonder, just briefly, if she will be as pale as me? Go through what I went through? Because I know I carry a girlchild.

The horse smells the syrup, trots over and licks it from my fingers.

'Tlolok,' the woman chirrups, gutturally, her fingers to her breast.

Is that your name? 'Tlolok?' I ask, pointing to her.

She nods and smiles.

She tips her head in my direction. 'Ghost,' she says, and I almost topple into the fire.

She knows me but I can't speak the language. How does she know me? *How does she know me?*

'Ghost, yes,' I reply. *Don't show her your fear*, I think, before snorting. What is she, a fucking brown snake? What am I afraid of?

She whistles the exact voice of a hawk, panicking Lucifer who glides to a pointless sanctuary on my shoulder, and Tlolok nods, understanding something I don't.

Several other people, all similarly dressed to Tlolok, all carrying spears and bows, not necessarily threatening but not casual either, coming into the clearing from the direction of the dome. Wordlessly they join us, but remain standing. There is a beauty about them I can't put words to.

Tlolok stands, brushes crumbs, grass and dust from her clothing. She holds out a hand and pulls me to my feet.

Tears run unheeded down her cheeks and she sniffs back snot. I'm utterly confused.

She holds my hand as one of the men pulls open the big bronze door, its hinges oiled and well-maintained, and from the leather pouch at her waist, Tlolok produces the identical titanium rectangle, indented with dots and curves in the patterning of a matrix chip, that Miriam possesses. Lie the one I had but lost.

We entered the library where the purrs with delight, a word-sequence scrolling down the screen in a continuous line of data.

WELCOME GHOST
PROPHECY FULFILLED
INPUT DATA COMPLETE
RETURN ACCOMPLISHED

I'M ABOUT TO COMPLETE THE LAST ENTRY. I've got plenty of ink and plenty of pages left to fill but the red book stays here.

These people are the only descendants I know of, of those who remained when the prophecy unfolded; when the earth shed her skin and began, as it were, afresh but the same, in a cycle perpetuated uncountable times.

They received a prophecy from a small old pale woman, living with them in a pale blue tent sometime in the long ago, that a time-sorcerer named as Ghost would one day return from some seemingly ancient past. They would remain alive, despite a future environmentally fraught with danger and seismically tumultuous. It was prophesied that she definitely come and that what she brought with her would be an object of pricelessness: a red, leather-bound book full of words, that was to be stored in a specially made crypt, forged of anodized gold, melted down from all the baubles created in a time before now. The book was to be hermetically sealed with chelodium so that no air or moisture would corrupt it. For the people of the future.

It's the only record of a people and way of life no longer in their existence and it is to be kept for the future, for a past to be remembered.

I'm given the option to remain here or to return, by intention and in the company of the horse, to my clan. To Tabak. No choice. I can't stay here, but I understand everything now.

For days, with them as company, I explore what remains of Kata Tjuta. Then I have to leave. I stow my stuff in the panniers, all except for the book, and I mount the mystical horse, yelling for Lucifer, who swoops me from the forest dropping whatever dead thing she's been ripping and landing on the padding on my shoulder, *ack-acking* loudly.

I blow the ink of this last entry dry, close and clasp the book. I can always make another one.

I give it to Tlolok. I also I give her a name to remember.

Sabé.

ENTRY: PROFESSOR SABÉ TARAKWOYA
DECIPHER: U'RSA SHAKA, GALLAK PEOPLE

SITE NUMBERED 2/05/5172 - 24/41/5176

SECTOR SEVEN

CHAPTER FIVE

GONDWANA

GREAT HERDS OF RED, SHAGGY reindeer thunder across the tundra, huge stags with antlers many hand-spans across fight for the right to mate. Pods of thousands of wooly camels graze, unfazed by the strangers, and great grey kangaroos, elephants, and bears flee before us. Flocks of ravens, white birds with sulfur-crested heads, eagles, sparrows, and owls take flight from the stumpy trees, peppering the sky in all directions in the wake of the fliers, with condors higher still.

Down by the lakes and waterways pink flamingos, peacocks, gorillas, and boar drink undisturbed and unthreatened, for now. Dark umber seals poke their heads above water, their soft eyes curious.

Countless other species, from dog to jaguar to unrecognizable, walked, run or fly from the path of the giant, fully equipped walkers as we hiss softly across the grassland on powerful hydraulic legs.

'There.' Sabé Tarakwoya calls through her headset, her walker leading the expedition.

Visible for miles, beyond the panorama of syncopated long grass and shimmering lakes, is the ribcage of the great dome, thought until recently to be a thing of legend. Ancient maps delineating the continent and marking out population centers had been unearthed in caches of archaic data discovered firstly at Uruk and then, within a year, at the Baalbek dig, both once sprawling metropolises demolished by earthquakes in the early 5th Dynasty.

That was just over twenty years ago. Both sources of data were unique to their respective city and both confirmed Kata Tjuta's existence, the latitude and longitude of the epoch. Science has done the rest, setting coordinates according to major pole shifts that have occurred since.

Sabé knows. This dig has been her quest ever since.

The flier just north of the lead team opens its rear hatchway for the botanists and geologists who abseil to the ground in full tack.

The flier is set to return in ten days, from the islands to the south, where the high tech satellite community is situated, specifically for this, the first of many expeditions.

Sabé, team leader, pale, albinist, mauve-eyed elder woman is strong, fit and wiry, nothing even close to feeble. She is Emeritus Professor of Archaeology and Linguistics at the Institute of Higher Learning at Gamirasu, and Dean of Mythic Lore at the University of New Edenborough in southwest Laurasia.

She also knows *what* she is and remembers how she got to be *who* she is. As far as she knows there are no others, but she's been wrong about that often, so is not lonely for her own kind.

WITH HER ARE TWO assistant archeologists, three scientists, a data retrieval expert and medics.

She is also accompanied by her right-hand, U'rsa Shaka of the Gallak people, deep-time ancestors of the inhabitants who, our lore says, are originally from this continent, but who had fled at the onset of the big freeze. U'rsa is a chronicler, translator, and speaker of many languages. He possesses the telepathic ability of all the Gallak, that allows him to communicate with primitive peoples still being discovered in isolated pockets of the globe. He is indispensable should they encounter human life on Gondwana.

All ride the walkers, heavily armed and fully loaded with state-of-the-art piece equipment thought necessary for any eventuality.

Gondwana has been thought uninhabited since the last ice age, but Sabé and U'rsa understand that the possibility of human survival is strong, particularly either here in the high country or further north in the milder climate. However, they are only sanctioned to concentrate their efforts in this vicinity, for the moment. This is the first voyage from the northern lands to take place since the thaw, ten and a half thousand years before.

The team, loaded with heavy earthmoving capacity and toting cutting-edge geothermal sounding radiography, follows Sabé and U'rsa's lead across the arctic, but verdant wilderness, powering their walkers up an ever-increasing incline, through incalculable varieties of wildflowers, grasses, stunted pale-leaved trees, and thorny bushes, unique and unknown anywhere else on earth.

As they stride towards the shell of the dome they pass peculiar red rock formations, sculpted into shapes of lacey beauty by the weather and ice of countless eons. This is a treasure trove beyond anyone's wildest fantasies.

'Climb aboard kids,' U'rsa calls into his headset as their walkers join the air-dropped academics, who hitch rides on the heavy machines.

The final miles are a lumbering forward climb until they crest the highest rise.

U'rsa, slightly ahead, stops.

'Company,' he says quietly.

'Where?' Sabé catches up with him, long-range binoculars aligned to her sighting on the headset.

'Oh. Wow. You were right.' She adjusts her facial expression to neutral. 'Listen up people, keep your weapons in check but raise your shields just in case.'

The electromagnetic protections hum into place around the tiny human figures manning the walkers.

They move forward across the flat plain, the bones of the temple frame, enormous in the rarified air. Beyond it a city of thousands of rawhide domes, nestling amidst fields of grain for as far as the eye can see, accompanied by herds of horses and domesticated animals. And people.

SKIN THE COLOR OF OAK-BARK, hair coated in red ochre, faces and hands tattooed with light blue markings, their clothing finely-tanned hide of every hue within nature, gold and other jewelry, horn, bone, wood, shell, and stone, adorning exposed skin, and row upon row of blue clay beads on every proud chest.

A company of heavily armed warriors – both men and women – leap onto huge, shaggy-haired horses and ride towards us, unfazed by the size of our machines, the lead male wearing a red stag pelt, its many-tined horns atop his head, his face and hands tattooed bright blue, his bearing as regal as anyone Sabé has ever witnessed.

Beside him is a woman garbed entirely in white, her face, arms and exposed skin a weaving of white clay threads and lines. Her eyes are pale violet and her hair is alive with serpents of blue dreadlocks, laced with black, hawk-striped and white feathers. She carries a narrow spear with a tip of black metal, sharp and deadly.

'U'rsa?' Sabé knows U'rsa will be able to communicate. She knows because she's been here before.

Murmurs, from the others in the group about how crazy this is, are ignored. Irrelevant. The pair inputs the code that halts the walkers. They unhook themselves from the data mainframes, undo their protective harnesses and climb down onto, for Sabé, familiar soil.

Both the woman in white and the chieftain clothed in the crown of horns, ride ahead of the others, calling their horses to a halt, but they don't dismount.

U'rsa holds his hands out, palm up in a universal gesture of friendship.

The woman in white slides from the furs of her saddle and comes to him. She places her hands in his and closes her eyes. They moved beneath the lids as though she sleeps and dreams. Then she opened them, the peculiar color almost eclipsed by irises registering surprise.

She gestures to both Sabé and the chieftain to come to her.

In a series of musical notes, throat song and click of the tongue they communicate in a language of animals, reptiles, and birds.

The woman in white grunts in appreciation. 'Sabé,' she says clearly.

Sabé nods, her hand slipping into U'rsa's.

The woman, the chieftain, the other warriors on horseback and the entire city before them roar in empathy as they link with the matrix.

The woman out of legend has come to claim the book. The chieftain dismounts and lifts the great bronze door to the library.

ENTRY: PROFESSOR SABÉ TARAKWOYA

DECIPHER: U'RSA SHAKA OF THE GALLAK PEOPLE

2/05/5172 - 24/41/5176

IN THE VICINITY OF THE OF THE DOME
IN THE HEART OF THE MOUNTAIN TUNDRA OF
GONDWANA.

STATE/DESC: VERY FRAGILE PAPYRI: BOUND
TRANSCRIPT IN RED MATERIAL OF UNKNOWN TANNED
SPECIES HIDE: WITHIN A RECEPTACLE OF CURRENTLY
UNCLASSIFIED METAL: SUSPECT GOLD

SOURCE: UNKNOWN
JOURNAL/SCRIPT: PROTO-EURO/ANGLASIAN)

GHOST – TIME SORCERER

THOUGHTS ON THE ONE-THING.
HYPOTHESIS ENTRY | FOR SEVEN | TIME UNKNOWN

Base-time – the standard calculator for measuring reality – exists as an energy ratio within all matter. It does not have any relativity when matter is not present. Matter is manifest energy and all that is manifest is subject to transition (so is all that is non-manifest, but that's irrelevant here).

Transition is the constant medium through which the concept of time finds recognition. Recognition occurs as a result of cause and effect (it is called the Law of Congruity– all actions and/or movements having an energy exchange with that upon which the ensuing stress relates (I prefer not to use the term 'reaction' as that implies, to me, a repetition. . . and nothing repeats itself for time would have changed by the time the 'repetition' occurs).

Energy can be contained but not restricted. When it is contained it changes its relationship to the space-time continuum. Atomic energy is contained energy. All contained energy is recognizable, through some form of measurable parameter or other depending upon known technology.

When energy is not contained in measurable parameters it is still there but liable to unrecognizable, and therefore unpredictable, creative function.

Unrecognizable energy is the principle of the term 'creation'. In relation to the human mind, however, if the process is other than biological, it can be considered inspiration. Therefore…

Inspiration is considered valid in art when the medium of the art gives it manifestation.

Inspiration is considered valid in science only when it is theoretically recognizable. Why?

The Law of Congruity i.e. opposite and equal, yadayada.

Energy is not dependent upon matter. This is a natural law of the ancestral thresholds, despite the understanding that matter is dependent upon energy.

Time, when thought of as linear, is a spatial trap, or net, or web, and under casual observation, it appears fixed, linear, and determined by the relative responses of matter but that's an illusion because nothing is fixed…

What about inspiration? What about when that which seems fixed is disrupted by an unknown or undefined variable or an unrecognizable random phenomenon?

A tangent. That which is outside of any known thing can, and does, alter matter from a perspective other than that which we presume is time, space, matter and/or energy.

Fact: no observations are invalid, but what will by now, be most obvious is that all transition creates a relative stress-factor. All stress-factors (anything interacting with anything) produce a third, recognizable or unrecognizable, phenomenon.

That's what happened. That was the prophecy.

Matter is affected by energy (and vice-versa) and this has an effect upon the enigma known as 'time'. Unknown 'lines' intersecting, affecting predictable probabilities, and causing unrecognizable variables. Inspiration is our communion with that 'unknown.'

One may not necessarily consciously synergize with experience while it is in the process of happening but as it passes its effects will be felt, creating change in accordance with the process (all very inevitable) even if the meaning of the experience is consciously indecipherable. Even if it is not necessarily understood in any relativity to past patterns (which can be very limiting) they *will be known*.

Knowledge is the outcome to experience. Understanding is the assimilation into one's immediate reality of that knowledge.

An experience can be had without recognition of the value (in the more mathematical sense) of that experience whereas recognition only occurs with familiarity.

According to the prophecy, time will express itself in multi-folding, multi-interconnecting meridians, space will no longer have linear relativity only, in determining distance and distance will no longer have relativity to time. The ability for each thing to be relative to all other things will be recognizable, will not be simply a theory.

People attempt to explain an experience by relating it to that which is already recognizable.
What, then, when the relative factor is unrecognizable?

Evolution.

Everything is unique, yet interwoven, in unrecognizable, overall patterns.

All is known (because everything is palingenetically infinite) but that which is known is not necessarily immediately recognizable. It all depends on perspective.

Simply because we might read a chronicle and the experiences within it are not recognized by us does not mean that we are not an integral part of the story. In transition, it will be recognized.

Over time it will be recognized.

In some guise or another it is recognizable. We will know as 'time' unfolds. We will understand with the knowledge of experience. Cycles: understanding cycles (revolutions) is an exercise in contemplation. This is Immanence and Immanence is the *one thing*.

There's nothing new, merely forever in constant transition.

More to come…

GENESIS

CHAPTER ONE

SOMEDAY

MUMMY, CAN YOU TELL ME THE Snow White story again?'

Molly tucks her wild, pale-haired, albino daughter Baron, into the covers on the bottom bed, her pet white rat curling around her young shoulders like a winter stole, her brother Jonathan peering over the edge of the top bunk, thumb in his mouth. Molly thinks they should be the other way around, him being only three, Baron being eight, but she thrusts away the self-deprecating thought, knowing they'd just wait for her to leave the room anyway.

She reaches for the heater under the window and dials the thermostat up as much as everyone's allowed to do, so the power doesn't go off.

Outside is dead still but that's not a good sign. That's a very frightening sign. With temperatures this low, people are going to die more than usual. Particularly with the energy grid being so erratic. It hasn't been this cold in recorded history.

For over a decade the weather has become more and more unpredictable. The winters more savage, the summers melting the tarmac at airports preventing flights, and dropping planes right out of the sky. Molly won't even risk taking them all to visit Tom's family for Christmas next week. Baron and Jonathan are both sad about that, but what's worse?

Tom's working at the uranium mines across the other side of the world, on Kata Tjuta country. A place called Kakadu. So during the holidays, it's up to Molly to keep her and the kids safe. And the animals. To prevent Jasper, their big lolloping hound pup, and Baron's white rat Robert-son-of-Rudolf, from going outside and maybe freezing to death or getting hit by some maniac skidding their car on the black ice. Because people are still crazy, risking the drive home like they are doing, the sky green as licorice and heavy with this impending, terrifying Arctic ice vortex. The roads slippery where you can't see it, electricity wires snapping in silent death, and the internet all but useless, satellites off-course and malfunctioning.

'You warm enough?' Molly pretends she's happy, when both the kids know it's not true. She inherited her empathy and the telepathy from her own mother, dead now these past six years. Dead…

Now, that's a weird thought, Molly realizes, because she hears her mother in her mind every day. A ghost or something. Her mother had been their midwife when Jonathan came into the world. Molly had stayed home and risked it, because the hospital staff couldn't cope with the idea of a natural born breech baby, without anesthetic and without surgery.

She'd heard her mother gasp when the infant's bum had crowned, and she'd otherwise just had Tom to help her. Baron sleeping right through her mother's contractions, as though she'd known.

Tom, feel for the leg, love… carefully, you're doin' great. He'd gently helped first one leg out, then the other.

That's it, Molly, push now, love, let his body drop… and Tom, get that little blanket darlin', you have to keep his body warm, but he's got to hang for just a bit.

Tom wrapped his son in a bunny rug, rubbing the tiny back while Molly shallow-panted for a good minute.

Molly… push! Push now.

Jonathan slid effortlessly into Tom's hands and wailed to the world that he was here. That he had arrived. Molly climbed onto the mattress and onto her back, Tom lifting their son to her arms and her breast while the cord still pulsed with nourishment.

They'd wept. Molly because her mama wasn't there in the flesh, and Tom because he'd heard her, as sure as if she'd been in the room, and they were all safe because of a ghost. Baron was out of bed then, and melting up onto the pillows beside her mother and her little brother because she loves them and Daddy, and because she knows how hard their life is going to get.

'Once upon a time…'

'Mummy? Not the *upon a time* story, just Once…' Baron sits up, pulling her cotton rabbit under her chin in that big clutch.

'I know, sweetheart.'

Jonathan goes off with that contagious laugh that makes the others grin.

'Mummy…'

'Jonathan, pull the covers back up, and let Jasper breathe for goodness sake.' Now he laughs with his whole body as the big pup wriggles from the eiderdown.

'There's this uppity white girl gets herself lost in the desert near where Daddy works, some time or other that we're not sure about yet…'

'Mummy…?

'Yes, Jonathan?'

'White, like Baron is?

'For the sake of this story, just like Baron.'

''K. Can it be about a little boy next time?'

'That's for tomorrow.'

Jonathan settles over the edge of the bunk, his head beside Jasper, his eyes as soft and amber as the dog's.

1

FJÖRGYN

THE HUNTER, I, OF FJÖRGYN NAME, sits at the central fire, head bowed, seems to sleep. Is listening. Is breathing deeply of rock and tree people, mist-wet hair and fur, breast milk and boar upon coals, the metallic tang of torc, bog water and loam, old sap bled from broken branches. That storm. That death storm to be remembered.

Of Fjörgyn named, this hunter, I, searches out a rhythm. Distant carrion smell of newly dead, bones not yet picked quite by eagle and crow and wolf pack. This hunter, I, knows all this. It's in the memory of muscle and the story of lore. And the children watch, those that can stay awake this deep into the long night, as one by one and two by two the others come, silently and frost-breathedly, for what? A new walk? No such thing.

The walk of the ancestors who are gone, then? Yes, a song the elders have remembered, and tell every word the song like a heartbeat. The song of a bright-faced hunter, that one, just one hunter, who called softly to her mother, her name and her purpose -to just once follow the *reinsdyr* and so learn where they go for the long dark. Of her twin who had gone also. Who had never returned. Such a story! And babies sleeping upon the backs of the ones who will stay (because it's not their time).

I, this hunter I, who is to walk towards the silent, ever-moving color-wind, and the star that nails the world to the sky. Green and green, arching and twisting in an erotic, threatening show of power. Nor'east is this name. Beyond the black earth. Beyond the rock of summer coast where the mackerel last spawned. Before the ice-night slept the otter, and the *uruz* cracked the last of the big lake's possible fishing, and we watched them running down the sun, oh two, three moons withstanding snow beyond the seas of *reinsdyr*, warner of the first big ice, and, cousins-mine, the white wolf hunters and bear-to-sleeping. To follow the memory of whale-blow, the ancestor spring thaw song. To never neglect the land-knowing that must be seen. Or perish.

Without this must-know-but-don't-remember-why story, we, the People, will end this being now.

Drummers gather. And the old people, the keepers of all lore, singers of the first day. This hunter, I, and the others who are now many, dance. Fur-thick, feather-haired, bird-boned and, old woman hunter, Fjörgyn named I, walrus-tooth-hung, who dances with warm-blooded other people. Who dance shark and spear magic. Hunter magic. Birdcall magic and ice-to-stay-strong magic. And singers sing the white bird, forever shark, and break-the-ice-but-not-fall-in-magic. All night, which is every night and every day, until no one knows anything else except warm-blooded, white bird and forever shark. Warm-blooded, forever shark… and seal magic. Yes. Seal magic to remember who we remember but don't know why. Just in case we meet them again. Being impolite is not a hunter, I, a hunter way.

Then the hunter, I, the Fjörgyn named one who lived as the mammoth does for the many moons until we die together, and so now become the story, and the warmth, and tool and harpoon and shell of boat, and the big lodge carved entrance, most dignified and tree-tall. This hunter, I, bear-woman, medicine woman, and the others who are now many, walk into the land beyond the story because everyone, although they sing, and rock the children and beat the painted drum, is silent with hunger so someone must add to the story. That is us.

And the People we leave behind, in the night between night and day, weep to remember us, for if we are ancestors and not returners with food, they will care for our children and they will howl before they become meat for cousins, bear and howler wolf, cousins big white crab and slow melt for slow shark… for love of us.

Thus I, this hunter, I, and the others, travel the winter's end thunder road that moves towards what will be the later spring shoreline after the melt, towards way, way deep into the path of dawn-rise. A girdle of land, ice-no-melt we hope, that will not end until we reach beyond the world. Into the endless sea.

And it is a long, long road, at the end of one such, will the life of this hunter, I, Fjörgyn of name-song-daughter-mother-mother's mother, have ever been more than who I have eaten? Person who babies made and mammoth brought down just once? Who loved with seal, who's harpoon took mackerel and who watched silent, ever-moving color-wind?

2

SELKIES

BIGGEST SEAL EVER IN THE FOREVER OF stories we see now. Swim between the ice flows with white grey whales. Most peculiar, hunter, I, decide. Seals within seals like a many-breasted woman bearing her babies on her belly moves through the water. Paddles like feet. Duck-seals.

Hoy! Hoy! Heya! They cry, like people, standing on two legs and waving spears pointed towards sky and not at us. Hunter, I, and the others, not so. Feed the People waiting in the long dark, by the quiet fires, when? Half a sky round ago. Half a moon ago.

Hoya, hey! They cry, laughing and rhythm-banging on the flank of mother seal, she not slowing her swimming through the black, deep waters, between the ice flows, with white-grey whales passing us by, but them not.

Hoy! Hoy! Hunter! Calls and calls as they come close and we ready to harpoon. *Don't hurt us, we are returning to the People!*

And I, the named hunter Fjörgyn, and others all around me, hear the ice crack and the whales *tewel* to each other as they dive and breach and dive and breach. So long do we not say a word or even hear our breathing over the drumsong of this heartbeat, saying who, who? Who, who? What is this story? We, all hunters us, be very, very quiet, and disregard nothing, for magic is not predictable. And this is not

231

predictable. That the seal says *hoya, hey* and laughs... is not predictable.

Not a seal. Neither a mother seal or any other seal. But the skins of many, sewn about the bone of otherkin. Floating like an ice flow but faster. Seals but not seals. People in the skins of seals, harpooning the frozen earth, mooring rope upon the frozen earth, one stepping from the barge with great height and light eyes and smiling teeth and wide open arms.

And hunter, I, am in those arms as warm as flesh that has sat beside the fire, that has rolled in furs for pleasure, and from such as this the babies sometimes come. This face is the same as my brother and my mother, but it is not those faces.

3

CHILDREN

THE PEOPLE OF THE SEAL have come home. And the hunting magic rights the hunger. And the people of the seal bring stories of another place, where they have lived with other people, people that they love as they love us. To whom they will return.

They sing the place they have found. Down the river of the sun. The way of the boats they have learned to make, to cross the wide, dark sea. They sing the name of the bright-faced person, that one, just one hunter, who called softly to her mother, her name and her purpose -to just once follow the *reinsdyr* and so learn where they go for the long dark. Of her twin who accompanied her. Of what they found. Of a land of fire mountains and of thunder underfoot. Another People. All in the long ago. All still here.

Will you stay?

No. But we will lie amongst your furs for the remainder of the long dark, and roll with you and so perhaps take babies when we go. The children of the seal, are we. Will they be. Just as you, hunter you, are daughter of the white wolf, and that person walking with that drum is the caller to the thunder, and the hunting magic. Just as she, over by the river's new flow, is the eagle-whisperer, and he is the maker of things of fine-honed bone harpoon. We will love you until the uruz return to the valley. Until the white grey whale fills the now-pale sky-silver sea with their young as they travel the ways of their ancestors, to the southern other. When the silent, ever-moving color-wind fades to sleeping, and the star that nails the world to the sky shows us that summer will soon bring the otter and the mackerel, and the mosquitos, we will go. And we will teach you the songs that we know! We will teach them for all of these days. Oh, that is exciting says the keeper of the lore, joining I, the hunter and the something else, yet to be. Yet to be.

To make the seal boat?

I have spoken aloud what has been only in dream. I have dared ask this magic…I will take the sea road of the bright-faced person. One day, I will take the sea road to learn the boat magic.

Yes, to make the seal boat.

And the way to come to you? The stars to come to the land of the fire mountain?

Yes.

Will the others, who are not us, not kill us?

No. They are us, also.

Then the hunter I, I will learn the way to come to you!

The way to come to us and the stars that will lead you to our children.

Our children? Yes, our children.

BENEATH THE ICE, BENEATH THE Arctic Tundra, so far into time no guesswork could ever truly calculate, the fissures form an abyss then miles deep. A crevasse of sorts. A cave once above ground and inhabited by a forgotten race of hominids.

Within that cave, painted with the ochre of a hundred hands over an age of more years than can ever be realized—with the exception of carbon dating, but I get ahead of myself—is an altar of solid rock bearing two items preserved, frozen at one hundred and forty degrees below zero, like time capsules.

One is a solid electroconductive gold cryoarc containing a thick, red, leather-bound book, locked with bronze-like clasp, written in an unknown script that will take centuries to decipher when it is found— if it is found—and the other, a container, cast from an unknown meteoric metal, nesting two delicate vials of clear, seemingly harmless liquid.

THIS STORY DOES NOT INCLUDE AN ENDING

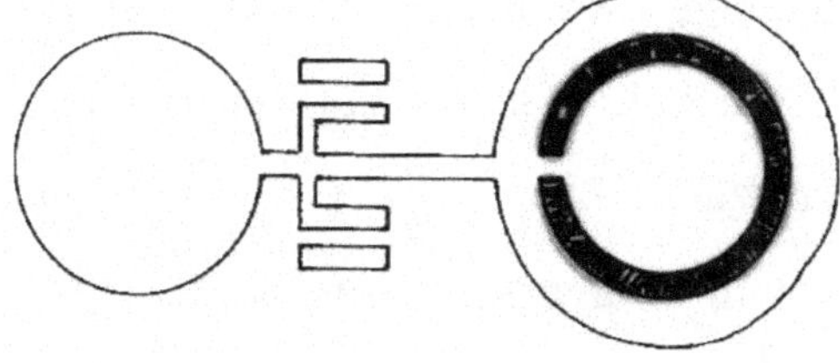

OTHER DE ANGELES' BOOKS

The Way of the Goddess, Prism/Unity, 1987

The Way of Merlyn, Prism/Unity, 1990

Witchcraft Theory and Practice, Llewellyn Worldwide, 2000

The Feast of Flesh and Spirit, Wildwood Gate, 2001

When I See the Wild God, Llewellyn Worldwide, 2002

Pagan Visions, Llewellyn Worldwide, 2004

The Quickening, Llewellyn Worldwide, 2005

The Shining Isle, Llewellyn Worldwide, 2006

Tarot Theory and Practice, Llewellyn Worldwide, 2007

The Quickening, Revised, Createspace 2012

The Shining Isle, Revised, Createspace, 2012

Priteni, the Decimation of the Indigenous Celtic Britons, 2015

Initiation, a Memoir, Createspace, 2016

The Skellig, Createspace, 2017

Witch | For Those Who Are, 2018